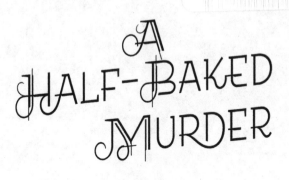

# A HALF-BAKED MURDER

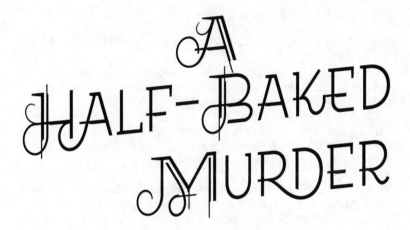

# A HALF-BAKED MURDER

## EMILY GEORGE

Kensington Publishing Corp.
www.kensingtonbooks.com

KENSINGTON BOOKS are published by
Kensington Publishing Corp.
119 West 40th Street
New York, NY 10018

All Kensington titles, imprints, and distributed lines are available at special quantity discounts for bulk purchases for sales promotion, premiums, fund-raising, educational, or institutional use.

This book is a work of fiction. Names, characters, businesses, organizations, places, events, and incidents either are the product of the author's imagination or are used fictitiously. Any resemblance to actual persons, living or dead, events, or locales is entirely coincidental.

To the extent that the image or images on the cover of this book depict a person or persons, such person or persons are merely models, and are not intended to portray any character or characters featured in the book.

Special book excerpts or customized printings can also be created to fit specific needs. For details, write or phone the office of the Kensington Sales Manager: Kensington Publishing Corp., 119 West 40th Street, New York, NY 10018. Attn. Sales Department. Phone: 1-800-221-2647.

The K and Teapot logo is a trademark of Kensington Publishing Corp.

ISBN: 978-1-4967-4049-6 (ebook)

ISBN: 978-1-4967-4048-9

First Kensington Trade Paperback Printing: March 2023

10 9 8 7 6 5 4 3 2 1

Printed in the United States of America

To Nan, for supplying me with "book funds"
every school holidays.
I miss you.

And to Mum, for being a fighter.

# CHAPTER 1

There's something you should know about me before we get into this. I grew up on a steady diet of romantic ideals—both of the Prince Charming and "you can achieve anything" variety.

It started with Disney, which not only gave me false expectations about how amazing my hair should look when wet (thanks, Ariel) but of how my "true love" would stumble across me when I least expected it. As I got older, cartoon fairy tales morphed into 2000s romantic comedies. I worshiped at the altars of Drew Barrymore and Reese Witherspoon and Cameron Diaz. I thought my life would be a fabulous montage of amazing outfits and adventure and charming men. But as I grew up, I came to a few unwelcome conclusions.

One, no woman should ever own a pair of pants with the word "juicy" written across the butt.

Two, my hair *never* looked good wet.

Three, dreams were fragile things easily shattered by the gritty truth of the real world.

Sometimes, when you kiss a prince they turn back into a toad. Sometimes, when you shoot for the moon in becoming a classically trained pastry chef in Paris, you do *not* land among the

Michelin stars. Sometimes, instead of making a perfect choux pastry you end up making pot brownies.

And sometimes, when you think you have everything worked out, a dead body ruins it all.

But let's rewind a bit.

I was strolling along my hometown's main strip. Like a lot of coastal towns, Azalea Bay was designed to echo the landscape. Sun-bleached wood, blue and yellow paint, images of starfish and seashells and dolphins. There were pretty scalloped awnings and eye-catching window displays with puntastic signs.

I could name the people who owned almost every single business along the strip, although some had changed hands in the five years I'd been away. My favorite café, Bean and Gone, had gotten a facelift and looked delightfully funky with Edison bulbs strung along the back wall and a new sign that mimicked vintage Las Vegas billboards. Thankfully, their coffee was just as good as I remembered.

A few doors down was one of two bakeries in town— Loafing Around, which was a more traditional bakery focused on fresh breads and rolls. Sweet Tooth was further up the strip and satisfied the town's dessert needs with cookies, pastries, and doughnuts. Plus it was the hot spot for special-occasion cakes. The surf shop, Offshore, brought color and vibrancy to the strip, with its rainbow racks of surfboards and swimsuits strung like a garland over the large front entrance. There was the ice cream parlor, Dripping Cones, which had a pink and yellow striped awning and a permanent line out the front, even when the weather wasn't that great.

Music always played in Azalea Bay—in this case a Beach Boys track, which floated on the air from the open doors of the surf shop and made me smile—and the slapping sound of flip-flops as people came and went from the sandy shoreline. No matter where you went, there were grains of sand tracked from the beach, and the balsamic scent of cypress trees mingled with sweet vanilla ice cream and coconut sunscreen, lightly salted by the ocean air, even when it wasn't hot outside.

I'd missed the laidback charm of this place when I was in Paris. Sure, seeing the Eiffel Tower from my bedroom—even if it was so far away I had to squint to bring it into focus— was pretty darn amazing. But I'd always felt out of place there. Not quite fashionable or cool enough. Even when I thought I'd started building a life with the man of my dreams, it turned out I was dead wrong.

You see, I had taken that "you can achieve anything" message to mean that any dream could be turned into a reality if a person was willing to work hard enough. I learned that from my grandparents. They were the best influences I could have asked for. Sadly, Gramps was no longer with us, but his impact— along with my grandmother's—was lasting. When I was eleven years old, my mother had announced that motherhood "didn't suit her" and that she was moving away with her new boyfriend. Since I'd been born out of an anonymous one-night stand, I'd never known my father. I didn't even have a name. And Mom had only ever seen me as a burden on her social life.

Anything I needed to know about the world, I learned from my grandparents. Grandma Rose, in particular, had peppered the years with glittering gems of wisdom.

*Nobody is going to gift you the future you want, Chloe. It's a house you must build yourself. Your grandfather and I will teach you how to mix cement and lay a strong foundation, but you're responsible for turning a pile of bricks into a life.*

Ambition became my cement, the pastry skills I'd honed in my grandmother's kitchen with her hand on my shoulder became my bricks, and I designed a dream that involved me leaving small-town life to study at Le Cordon Bleu in Paris in my early twenties. After receiving high praise from my instructors, I entered the workforce.

In a few years I was no longer dwelling in the bottom ranks of the kitchen hierarchy. I made suggestions for the menu, provided input into the flavor profiles of desserts, and worked in test kitchens to come up with innovative and unique dishes. I set my sights on a Head Pastry Chef position at a Michelin-star restaurant and one day penning a cookbook. The life my grandparents had taught me to build was coming together.

But I'd been too distracted to spot a crack in the foundation. Too laser-focused to even consider that what I had built wasn't strong enough to withstand a storm.

And I was so very wrong.

Shaking my head, I tried to dislodge the thought. There was no sense worrying about things that didn't affect me anymore. The second I'd found out my beloved Grandma Rose had been diagnosed with breast cancer, I booked a flight home and fled the smoldering ruins of my life and career in Paris. Which meant for now, I was planting my feet in Azalea Bay, and Paris would eventually become a distant memory.

After picking up some ingredients from the supermarket to make a shrimp scampi over the weekend, I headed back to my car. One good thing about being home was getting to cook for my grandmother. It was rewarding to return the favor for all the meals she'd cooked for me over the years. But just as I was heading back to my car, my phone buzzed with a message from my aunt, Dawn.

**Meet me at the corner of Shoreline and Cypress in 5 minutes. South side.**

I laughed. She was always doing stuff like this, spontaneously making plans and expecting people to roll with it. Well, today I was happy to roll with it . . . but only for a short while, because I needed to get home and pop my groceries in the fridge. I texted her back as I walked, saying I could meet for a few minutes. Despite the stress of the last month, I felt a spring in my step again.

It was good to be home and I was going to make the most of it.

As I slowed to a stop where my aunt had asked to meet, I suddenly understood why she wanted me to come here. A corner shop stood empty. It was painted a soft, sunset pink with white window frames. Big panes of glass revealed the inside, which was a blank canvas with the bones of a serving counter and little else. The front door was also white and had a vintage knob shaped like a flower, which was probably gold at one point, but it had developed a beautiful patina over time. A piece of paper that was taped to the inside of the window said FOR LEASE in bold letters.

I pressed a hand to the glass and peered in for a better look. The counter was built and there was sawdust on the ground. If I were to guess, it looked halfway through a renovation, like someone had abandoned their plans before the fit-out could be completed. What was here before? A smoothie bar, perhaps? Or maybe it was one of those custom salad places.

"Chloe!" Aunt Dawn rushed over and gave me a big hug. She smelled like rose and patchouli, and wore approximately six-hundred pieces of jewelry.

Okay, maybe not *that* many. But still, it was a lot.

She jingled like an army of house cats and the sound never failed to bring a smile to my lips. My aunt bucked almost all societal expectations—she was fifty-three, unmarried, and had zero interest in children. Over the course of my life she'd changed jobs like the wind, had her hair be every color in the rainbow (it was currently a rich, dark purple), and had dabbled in everything from tarot to tree-shaping to competitive duck herding.

Yes, competitive duck herding was a real thing.

"Every time I see you, I get a hug like I've just stepped off the plane," I said with a laugh. "You know how to make a gal feel special."

"It's hard to believe you're really back." She squeezed me and then cupped her hands around my face, like she was trying to make sure I wasn't a figment of her imagination.

"Believe it, I'm back."

"It seems like yesterday that I was listening to your grandmother yell at you for stealing the bike lock out of the shed to wrap around your diary." She chuckled. "How did you grow up so fast?"

"That was probably a bit excessive." I cringed. "Especially since every single entry was about Frankie Stewart."

My crush on him had been Azalea Bay's worst-kept secret for a time.

"He's married, you know," Aunt Dawn said. "Two kids."

"Don't rub it in," I grumbled. "His wife looks like a supermodel, too."

"So do you, dear." She patted my arm and I snorted.

A supermodel I was *not*. I didn't have any issues with how I looked, because I genuinely believed people had more to offer the world than their appearance. Besides, it was an impossible task to work as a pastry chef while retaining anything close to a model's physique. Or maybe that was simply my weakness for butter and sugar. Frankly, a life without pain au chocolat was not something I wanted to imagine.

"I'd need to have one hell of a growth spurt," I joked. "And at twenty-eight, I'm pretty sure that ship has sailed."

"Good things come in small packages."

"True." I grinned. "And what do you think you're doing showing me an empty shop like this?"

It was a rhetorical question. I knew *exactly* what she was doing.

"I had a brilliant idea." My aunt waved her hands energetically in the air, apparently to emphasize the "brilliant" part of her statement.

I couldn't help but raise an eyebrow. Aunt Dawn had a thing for brilliant ideas. She collected them like treasures and had started more businesses than I thought was possible for a single human being. Therefore, I knew to approach the conversation with more than a pinch of reservation.

"You always wanted to open a bakery, right?" she asked.

When I was a kid, sure. But now I'd set my sights on working in fine dining, not on running a small-town bakery. Unfortunately, my current situation was in direct opposition to that dream, because exactly how many fine dining restaurants were there in Azalea Bay?

That would be zero. A big fat zip.

Not to mention the fact that there were already two specialty places in town to acquire baked goods—plus the small selection at the local supermarket—and while I knew the locals here were always up for a tasty treat, we didn't have enough people to warrant any more than that.

My aunt didn't wait for an answer, however.

Instead she barreled on, "And you made those 'special' brownies the other night for your grandma, which I still claim were the most incredible thing I've ever eaten."

Talk about two things I never thought I would hear in the same breath—Grandma Rose and pot brownies.

Weed had been made legal for medicinal purposes over twenty years ago in California, so I hadn't been surprised to hear that Grandma's oncologist had suggested it might help with her chemo side effects. The nausea from the chemo treatments had hit her almost immediately and I could tell she'd been more anxious about it all than she was letting on. Frankly, I was glad she'd gotten past the stigma, to put her health first and accept the relief that cannabis offered. Relief that she *desperately* needed.

But pot brownies? My grandmother had made the request almost without being able to meet my eye. For my entire life, she'd been a straight arrow. She was the person who'd go back to a shop if they accidentally gave her an extra dime, and she'd grounded me once for making fake cigarettes to go with my Pink Ladies Rizzo costume on Halloween. So, when she'd turned to me in her kitchen and asked me to make "special" brownies, I thought she wanted me to make them with Valrhona chocolate.

Nope. Wrong again.

"Where exactly are you going with this?" I frowned at my aunt.

"You could sell them in a bakery." My aunt's eyes—which were rimmed with her usual smudgy and dramatic kohl—grew wide. "In *your* bakery. Well, I was thinking more café, because this would be a lovely spot to have people sit and enjoy a coffee with their weed brownies. But you know what I mean."

I shook my head. She couldn't be serious. I was a classically trained pastry chef bound for creating desserts that required tweezers and edible flowers and temperamental doughs. I was supposed to be wearing chef whites and working toward having my creations featured in *The Observer* and *The New York Times.*

Not making cannabis-laced baked goods.

"Get real," I scoffed.

"I'm not joking. Look, I might be an old lady to you, but I've tried my share of edibles. Most of them taste average at best. But yours were . . ." She mimicked the chef's kiss. "You have a gift."

"Some gift," I grumbled. "Didn't stop me getting butchered in *Le Figaro.*"

My aunt shot me a look. Okay, message received. The pity party was coming to an end.

"I know I make great desserts," I said. "But starting a business? I just got back."

"How else would you use your gift here in Azalea Bay, huh? Rolling cinnamon scrolls for the bakery counter at the supermarket?" She shook her head. "Or making wedding cakes at Sweet Tooth?"

I shuddered. As much as I appreciated the skill required to create towering cakes that fed hundreds, the idea of working on anything in the bridal industry made me want to puke. An image of my glittering diamond engagement ring popped into my mind. I'd left it on Jules's pillow as I'd walked out of his apartment while he was in the middle of a shift.

Jules had been . . . everything. Yes, he had the cliché chef's temper and sky-high standards. And yes, he had a capital R reputation. But we'd flirted during family meal—which was the meal that all the restaurant staff shared before service began—and he'd praised my humble American-style pies. He'd made me feel special. The first time he'd taken me out for a drink I'd kissed him in the foyer of my apartment building, hair damp from the spring rain. When he proposed, I was so happy I thought I would die.

Then it all came apart at the seams. I found out he'd gotten drunk and slept with one of the juniors. A one-time deal, apparently. A momentary lapse in judgment. Nerves about the wedding we were planning.

But she'd gotten pregnant.

"I am *not* making wedding cakes." I shook my head. "Honestly, I don't know what I'm going to do. All I know is that I need to be here with Grandma Rose. My career . . ."

Was in the toilet.

After finding out Jules had knocked someone up, I'd made a critical error: I'd stayed at work even though my head wasn't in the game.

Of course, it was *that* night a famous food critic showed up. When his review came out a week later, he'd called my raspberry and chocolate mousse cake *amateurish* and *a bitter disappointment better suited to a supermarket bakery than a five-star restaurant*. I wasn't sure I'd ever get over the shame. And like a healthy pinch of sea salt in the wound . . . that was the day I got the call about Grandma Rose's diagnosis.

Which is how I ended up back in Azalea Bay, sleeping in my old bedroom, with no plans for the future and my dreams lying like a pile of bricks around me. Coming home instead of staying to fix the damage I'd done to my reputation was as good as admitting I was a talentless hack.

I *knew* I wasn't a hack. But I did have bad taste in men and a tendency to bury my head in the sand, which made Aunt Dawn's prodding all the more painful—because I needed it.

"I thought I'd ask Sabrina for a job." My best friend ran her family's bed-and-breakfast on the outskirts of town, and she'd said they were always looking for good kitchen staff. "I could bake for them. Fresh bread and simple pastries for breakfast and fancy little cakes for high tea events."

For a moment I felt like my comments had disappointed my aunt. She shook her head. "And you're going to work at the bed-and-breakfast forever?"

"Not forever. Just while Grandma is . . ." I couldn't even think about the fact that there might be a time limit to consider. "I don't want to waste the time I have left with her by being somewhere else."

"I'm proud that you're such a family-oriented young woman. But if you put your life on hold for so long, you may find there aren't any opportunities waiting on the other side."

The comment struck ice-cold fear in my heart, because I knew it was true.

"A weed café, really?"

"Your brownies were *amazing*. I mean, we all know you're a talented baker." She grabbed my arm to emphasize her point. "But cannabis is a tricky flavor to work with and plenty of people get it wrong. I've *never* tasted anything as good as yours."

"You're trying to butter me up," I said, frowning.

"Is it working?" She offered me a charming, hopeful smile and I couldn't help but laugh.

"Maybe," I mumbled.

"Perhaps this might sway you." She stuck her hand into her pocket and pulled out a set of keys, jingling them like I was a kitten she was trying to distract. "Want a peek inside?"

I gasped. "How on earth did you get those?"

"Friends in high places." She winked. "I've been doing some work with the real estate office and I called in a favor. I have to drop them off first thing tomorrow, but if you want to take a look . . ."

I bit down on my lip and glanced at the adorable pink shop. It was *really* cute. Totally what I had envisaged at one point in my younger years as the ultimate life goal—a business selling my own baked goods. Something special and unique that would draw people from all over. But I thought I'd moved on from those dreams.

"Fine," I said, shaking my head. "Let me have a look."

I couldn't quite believe I was agreeing to hear her out. I'd only been home for two days and in that time I'd barely left Grandma Rose's side. But Dawn had a point. If I was going to stay here—which I was—then I needed a plan. My savings would only last so long and I refused to mooch off my grandmother.

There were two options: A, the safe route where I worked some okay job for okay money and counted down the hours each day. Or B, pivot.

Dawn looked almost giddy as she unlocked the shop and let me inside. "The people who leased the building unfortunately had to back out of their business plans due to a family crisis. The property agent wants to get someone in ASAP, because the owner is spitting mad about the broken contract."

I walked into the shop and pressed a hand to my chest. It was even *more* beautiful on the inside. I saw potential in the elegant molding on the walls and the space that was big enough to house a generous velvet-lined banquette. The counter was long and had plenty of space for a big display cabinet as well as an espresso machine.

Baking had always been a creative outlet for me, and now my head was spinning with ideas. I loved the challenge of trying something new, and when Grandma Rose had requested the "special" brownies, it sent me down a rabbit hole of research. For the first time since my life had fallen apart, I'd spent a few blissful hours in the kitchen completely free of my troubles. And Dawn's comments about how good my pot brownies were had got me thinking about all the baked goods I could infuse.

I could make different types of brownies, like salted caramel or chocolate cherry or peanut butter. My signature "everything but the kitchen sink" cookies would work perfectly as well, with bitter dark chocolate, salty pretzels and honeycomb pieces hiding the herbal nature of the cannabis. I could also do buttery herb scones, delectable praline dark chocolate spheres dusted with edible gold, or flaky savory pastries.

*This is crazy. You can't open a cannabis café.*

Why not? It was legal. And while it wasn't something I'd ever specifically considered, there was nothing else like it in Azalea Bay. I was sure it would make a splash. The only question was, how thin was the line between a splash and a belly flop?

*What would people say? Maybe it would be safer to stick to your comfort zone and open a regular old bakery or café.*

Instinctively, I knew Dawn's idea to use cannabis in my baking was the way I could differentiate myself. After all, Sweet Tooth had the market cornered for regular cakes and pastries and everybody knew Bean and Gone was the best place in town for coffee. They were both well established and had won a ton of local business awards. How could I compete with that?

What was the question my old boss had posed one time? Why compete in the part of the ocean where all the sharks were already feeding? You had to find the blue ocean—the untapped potential—with something fresh and new. Instead of poorly flavored gummies and dry chocolate squares, I could make the food as good as the high. Everything could have a touch of luxury—from gold detailing on the hardware to glamorous interior design to a unique menu. Parisian glamour meets West Coast chill.

I would be different than both regular bakeries and cannabis dispensaries—something that took elements of both those things, but was neither. I'd be in a class of my own.

"I can hear your brain working from here," Dawn said cheekily. "It's great, isn't it?"

I looked around. There was no denying the place had incredible bones *or* that my brain was running a million miles a minute. "I don't know if I can afford something like this."

"The lease has good terms and the price is fair. I've been looking for something to invest in, too." She came up beside me. "And I will always bet on you, Chloe."

I didn't want to be *so* tempted by her offer . . . but I was. If I built something incredible *here*, it could solve all my problems. I could be home permanently to take care of Grandma Rose and have a project to throw my career ambitions into.

My gut was telling me it was a good idea. The right idea.

But little did I know that by this time tomorrow, being cheated on and losing all my career dreams in one fell swoop would be the *least* of my problems. That dead body I mentioned earlier? Yeah, trouble was headed right for me and I didn't even see it coming.

# Chapter 2

I was about to open my mouth and respond when I saw a familiar face peer into the front window. Sabrina! I waved and rushed over to the door to yank it open.

"I *thought* that was you." She threw her arms around my neck and squeezed. Her curly hair rubbed against my cheek. We might look like polar opposites—with her dark brown hair, green eyes and tanned skin versus my pin-straight blond hair, blue eyes and vampire complexion—but we were as close as sisters. "I can't believe you're back. I'm so sorry it's taken me so long to catch you, but work has been—"

She broke off in an agitated huff.

"Everything okay?" I asked.

"Just busy getting everything prepared for the summer rush." She squeezed me again and then pulled back to give me the once-over. "Paris has been good to you, girl. You look amazing."

"I look like I gained ten pounds from eating my emotions," I quipped drily. "But I appreciate the kind words."

Sabrina knew all about the perfect storm of events that resulted in my coming home. We'd video-called each other every single week for the past five years, and I'd told her about the breakup even before my grandmother and aunt.

"Your body is beautiful, and I won't hear a bad word about it," she said. "Secondly, if a man doesn't see what a wonderful and worthy person you are, then his own shortsightedness is on him."

"I don't need the 'independent women don't need a man to make 'em happy' speech, okay?" I said with a laugh. "I know that. But having your heart broken sucks."

"It's his loss," Sabrina said. "But would it be terribly selfish to say I'm grateful his idiocy brought you home?"

"*Appallingly* selfish." I swatted her playfully.

"Excellent. Sometimes being selfish is just what the doctor ordered." She grinned. "I highly recommend it."

"Speaking of which," Dawn chimed in. "Don't you think this would make an incredible café? And since we have an internationally renowned pastry chef in our midst . . ."

Sabrina gasped. "You're opening a café?"

I shook my head. "No, I'm—"

"A *cannabis* café," Dawn interjected.

I glanced at her with narrowed eyes. "Your sales technique is a little pushy, you know?"

"Darling, I passed caring about being 'too much' before you were born." She lifted one shoulder into a carefree shrug. "If you want something, you have to put it out into the universe."

I looked around the half-constructed shop and my heart thumped in anticipation. It was way too easy to sketch in the details of what this place could be. What *I* could make it be.

"But I take your point," she said. "I'm going to grab some garlic bread from Casa Italiano's before they close up. Just lock the door from inside and pull it closed when you're done. I'll meet you outside in five minutes, okay?"

She patted me on the arm and headed toward the door, her maxi skirt swirling around her feet. Her bright purple hair gleamed in the warm evening light flooding in through the window, and the stack of bangles jangled on her arm when she pushed the door open.

Sabrina shook her head as the door closed. "Your aunt is a force."

"Tell me about it. She was ready to pack her bags and come to Paris so she could give Jules a piece of her mind. Or, as she put it, shove a stick of butter so far up his you-know-what that he'd be crapping croissants for a month."

Sabrina snorted. "That's very . . . colorful."

"It's very Dawn. Luckily she had one of her dance meets. If it wasn't for the lure of a first-place trophy, she would have gotten on a plane that night."

"Your aunt dances? I didn't know that."

"Canine freestyle dancing."

My best friend frowned. "Like, she dances with her dog?"

"I would argue Moxie dances with Dawn, and not the other way around." My aunt's border collie was one of the smartest creatures I'd ever encountered. She was also a giant diva. "Everybody knows Moxie is the real star. But yeah, canine freestyle dancing is technically a dog sport."

"So Moxie herds ducks *and* dances. Color me impressed."

"What can I say? We're a talented family," I joked.

"You certainly are. So, a weed café, huh?" Sabrina pressed a hand to her chest. "Don't think you're going to get out of telling me all about it! It's a freaking fantastic idea."

"You think?" I was curious to get her take on it, because Sabrina tended to have her pulse on things.

Despite always being a little alternative—she'd gone through a goth phase in high school and now prided herself on being an out-and-out nerd in her role as Dungeon Master with her local Dungeons and Dragons group—she had a knack for trends. In fact, she'd taken her parents' bed-and-breakfast business from being on the brink of bankruptcy to one of the most Instagram-worthy accommodation spots in all of Azalea Bay and the surrounding areas.

Thanks to her, they were always booked solid.

"It's a multibillion-dollar industry and most of the people who open those kinds of bakeries *aren't* bakers. Not trained like you, anyway." She bobbed her head. "I think it's incredibly smart."

"It's all Dawn's idea."

"Sure, but the idea doesn't mean anything if you don't have someone who can execute it. Trust me, if I can swap some crappy gummies for something that comes out of your oven, I'd do it in a heartbeat." She nudged me with her elbow. "You know I'll be a happy customer."

"You really think there will be demand for it?" I rubbed a hand over my chin. "I mean, I could come around to opening a regular bakery or café. But this . . ."

"Are you kidding me?" Sabrina laughed. "Weed is main-stream, Chloe. Netflix has baking-competition shows dedicated to cooking with cannabis. Heck, you can buy cannabis-infused skincare at Sephora now. Plus, there are no dispensaries in town and nowhere I can think of that would even come close to combining it with your cooking talent. It's a freaking golden opportunity and someone will eventually snatch it up. Besides, you've got a great flair for detail. I know you can make it classy."

Could this work? Instead of being something that people were wary of, I could make a space that was warm and enticing, with delicious products that would give people the chill-out experience they desired. The thought of breaking some stereo-types certainly appealed to me as well, as I'd always been the kind of person who hated when things were shoved into a box.

"This would be quite the deviation from my life plan," I mused. "To say the least."

"Girl, if you're back here then you've *already* deviated from your life plan." She patted me on the arm. "Now it's time to fig-ure out if you're going to correct course or keep heading toward the iceberg."

Sabrina and my aunt both had a point. I'd worked *so* hard to build my skills and experience. The last five years being away from my family would all be for nothing if I didn't do something with my talents.

But a cannabis café?

I was officially intrigued.

"I was going to ask you for a job," I said, only half joking.

"At the bed-and-breakfast? No way." She shook her head. "As much as I would *kill* to have someone as amazing as you in my kitchen, it wouldn't be what's best for you. So, consider yourself on my no-hire list."

I frowned. "Harsh."

"Not harsh. I'm being incredibly selfless *not* hiring you. Trust me." She sighed. "As much as I hate to do this, I have to run. Mom is waiting for me to get back so I can take over the front desk for the evening. But we're still doing lunch tomorrow, right?"

"Absolutely."

Sabrina gave me a hug and told me again that she thought the idea was brilliant. After she left, I stood in the middle of the shop and seriously considered my options. I was leaning toward saying yes—as risky as it felt—but I promised myself I would sleep on it first. As much as I was a person who loved to seize an opportunity, I wanted it to be the *right* opportunity.

It already felt like I'd made too many mistakes in the past year to throw myself into yet another.

I checked out the kitchen, which didn't appear to be brand-new like the front of the shop. It did, however, have solid mid-quality commercial appliances and a good, functional layout. There was a small commercial freezer and a decent-sized storage room with a desk wedged against one wall so it doubled as an office. All in all, it had everything my business could need.

After I'd snooped around, I exited through the front door, locking it as Dawn had instructed. Across the road, the line at the Italian deli was long, and she wasn't at the front counter yet, so I decided to check out the outside of the shop.

I walked around the corner and continued to snoop. The side was also painted that same warm pink as the front, though this time it was over brick, allowing some texture to come through. Maybe there would be enough space to fence off a small area and put some tables and chairs outside, if I could get the right permissions.

Behind the shop was a small alley, where several businesses had back entrances for deliveries and for staff to come and go. There was enough space for a car to drive though, though it would be a bit of a squeeze. I walked a little way down the alley so I could see all sides of the building. There was a single step flanked by a small accessibility railing that led up to the back door, which had a window at eye-level where you could see the kitchen.

"Chloe Barnes?"

The sound of my name had me whipping around. Ugh. I thought I recognized that voice. I forced myself to smile, despite wanting to pretend I was someone else. *Anyone* else.

"Brendan Chalmers," I replied stiffly. "It's been a while."

There were scant few people in my town that I disliked, but Brendan was one of them. A bully by nature with a sense of ego and entitlement more inflated than a kid's jumping castle, he'd been a pain in my rear ever since we were in elementary school. The last five years hadn't changed him too much. He'd lost his youthful pudginess and was now bulked with muscle like he spent a lot of time lifting weights. Sadly, maybe he'd lifted too many weights, because his neck had started to disappear into a pair of over-developed traps.

Yeah, I know some fitness terms. I went to a personal training session once or twice . . . like ten years ago.

He came toward me, walking with the swagger of a man who was used to getting his way. "I heard you were back in town."

He wore an orange polo shirt with a logo embroidered onto the chest that said Azalea Bay Furniture Removals. The garish shade was awful enough by itself, but it had the added down-side of casting his skin with a slight Oompa-Loompa glow.

"If you're looking to drum up business, I'm afraid I don't have any furniture that needs moving."

"Oh no, this isn't about business." He smiled and it sent a shudder through me.

You know how when some people smile, the expression goes all the way up their face? It pops their cheeks and crinkles the skin at the corners of their eyes and puts life into them. It's warm and inviting.

When Brendan Chalmers smiled it was akin to an animal baring its teeth.

"Then what do you want?" My question came out a little harsh, but this guy set me on edge. I was suddenly aware of the fact that I was in a quiet alley with a man who was at least a full head taller than me and probably weighed as much as a smart car.

"Did you lose your manners when you went to France?" He made a *tsk tsk* sound. "I always thought the Frenchies were rude."

I bit the inside of my cheek to stop myself from retorting that acquiring such knowledge would've required him to travel further than his mother's house. But there was no point poking the man-bear.

"I wasn't trying to be rude," I said calmly. "But I'm meeting my aunt and I'll be late if I don't get going."

"Everybody knows your Aunt Dawn is as flaky as old paint. She won't even remember what time she asked you to meet." Brendan took a step forward and I realized I was somewhat trapped on the single step that led up to the empty shop's back door. With the railing on either side, he was blocking my exit. A cold drip slid down the back of my spine.

*Don't panic. He's annoying and pushy, but he won't hurt you.*

It was starting to get late, the dusk falling with a quiet hush of lavender in the sky. But still, it wasn't exactly like the alley was shrouded in darkness. He wouldn't do something when anyone passing by could see . . . would he?

"She might not be punctual, but I am," I said. "So, if you'll excuse me—"

"Why do you have to play so hard to get?" His eyes slid over me. "You've always been like that."

If I wasn't feeling so uncomfortable, I would have laughed. In truth, I was anything but hard to get. That whole Disney-worship thing? I'd worn my heart on my sleeve with every single crush. Sabrina teased me about having stars in my eyes when I liked someone.

I did not like Brendan.

"Playing hard to get implies there's a level of interest," I said, speaking before I could think about the implications of antagonizing him.

"*You're* interested, I can tell." He winked and I felt a little like I was about to vomit in my mouth. "I have a seventh sense for those things."

"Oh? What's your sixth sense?" I replied smartly.

*Stop baiting him.*

He looked confused and then shrugged. "I dunno. Taste or something."

*Dumb as a post.*

"Anyway, I was thinking now that you're back, we can pick up where we left off." He placed his hands on the railings and leaned forward. My back bumped the door as I leaned away. "Go out for a nice meal, reminisce about old times."

"Reminisce about old times?" I shook my head. "Like when I said no to you taking me to prom?"

And no to his invite to go to homecoming together. And no to his numerous creepy notes left in my locker. And no to literally anything involving him.

"That was because you were mooning over Frankie Stewart. He's married now."

"I know," I said through gritted teeth. "Look, it's not personal. I just got out of a relationship and I'm not looking to date anyone new."

Except it was absolutely one hundred percent personal. Brendan gave me the creeps.

"The best way to get over a breakup is to get back on the horse and I am more than happy to be your horse." He gave me a sleazy wink. "I'm set up now, got my own place and everything, right on Pine Wood Lane. Come on, Chloe. Let me take you out to dinner. I'll be a gentleman and pay for everything."

I wanted to groan. *That's* what he thought being a gentleman meant? Why was I not surprised? He was probably the kind of guy who thought because he'd ponied up for dinner that I'd feel obligated to go back to his place for "a drink" afterwards. No thank you.

"Look, Brendan," I said, squaring my shoulders and trying to exude more confidence than I felt. "I'm not interested in dating anybody right now. I don't want a horse to get back up on or for someone to pay for my dinner or anything like that. I have bigger things to worry about than romance, so I'd appreciate it if you'd step out of the way so I can meet my aunt."

He blinked. It was like watching an old computer struggle to open a file as he processed the rejection. I could practically see the spinning beachball in the middle of his face. I also saw the exact moment his tiny lizard brain understood what I was saying. His face went hard—his jaw stiffened into a sharp line and his eyes narrowed under heavy brows.

"You don't know what you're missing out on," he said with all the unwarranted confidence of a man who grew up with people who were too afraid to give him constructive criticism. "This is a mistake."

"Like I said, it's not personal," I lied. "And no, it's not a mistake."

Initially, I thought standing up for myself had worked and I sensed a deflation in him. It was enough that I also relaxed.

Which was a tactical error. Because his lizard brain might not be great with nuance, but it smelled prey. He stepped forward, pressing me against the door and pinning me to the spot. My heart started banging like a toddler with a wooden spoon and a collection of pots.

"Get off me!" I tried to shove him away, but it was like trying to move a fridge.

"You need to see what you're missing out on, Chloe. I'm a nice guy." He leaned forward like he was going to kiss me and I shrieked at the top of my lungs. "If you give me a chance . . ."

"Stop!" I wriggled and tried to shove him away, but the grocery bag hanging on one arm was so heavy I couldn't lift it effectively. "I swear, I will knee you in the groin so hard you'll never have kids."

He had the audacity to chuckle as he tried to kiss me again. I smelled stale beer and cigarettes on his breath, and I wrenched my head away from him.

"Get off her, you animal!" There was a thump from behind Brendan and my knees almost sagged in relief as I recognized my aunt's voice. "Right now."

She was hitting him with something. I saw Brendan shake his head and he stepped back, a little dazed as he almost knocked Dawn over. Her face was red, and she was brandishing something in her hand. Was that . . . ?

"Are you hitting me with your shoe?" Brendan swatted at her like he was shooing a fly.

"Be thankful I don't have anything pointier on me." She swiped at him again, the flat sole of her sandal landing down against his arm with a loud slap.

"You bi—"

"What on earth is going on here?" A booming voice echoed down the alley and I saw a figure in a navy uniform standing a few feet away, a deep frown marring his face. Chief Gladwell, thank goodness.

"This oaf was assaulting my niece." Dawn pointed at Brendan, who glowered back at her. "I heard her call out and I came around here to find him pawing her."

"Is that true, Ms. Barnes?"

I froze. All three of them were looking at me and my face grew hot. I don't know why, but I suddenly felt ashamed for getting into this position. Why didn't I walk away from him the second I saw him? I knew what he was like. I should have bolted out of the alleyway before he could get a hold on me.

*This is* not *your fault at all. He's the one getting handsy without an invitation.*

"We were just having a conversation," Brendan interjected.

"Chloe?" The local police chief looked at me.

I tried to move my mouth, but nothing came out. It was like someone was shining a spotlight right in my face and all I wanted to do was to go home and crawl under my duvet and be left alone.

"This is ridiculous. You can't even ask a woman out these days." Brendan tossed his hands in the air and stalked out of the alley. At the end, he paused and threw a menacing look over his shoulder, directed right at me.

He disappeared around the corner and Chief Gladwell didn't go after him. Instead, he came closer, his eyes darting between me and my aunt. "Look, I know you probably want to go home now and forget this ever happened."

Tears sprang to my eyes and I nodded, feeling foolish and embarrassed. But I was also mad, because I *shouldn't* feel embarrassed. I hadn't done anything wrong. I certainly hadn't given him permission to kiss me. It was Brendan who should be slinking around with his tail between his legs, not me.

"Why don't you come with me?" the chief suggested gently. Chief Theodore Gladwell was in his fifties and I hadn't always been his biggest fan. He was uptight and as straight-laced as they came, and he'd given my aunt a hard time over the years because he thought she was a no-good hippie.

But nobody could deny he cared about Azalea Bay. And right now, I felt like he *did* care about what had happened to me.

"I can't do anything unless you make a statement, okay? I know it's unfair to put that pressure on your shoulders but that's how the law works." He scrubbed a hand over his gray-flecked beard. "I'm positive it's not the first time he's done something like this and I suspect it won't be the last."

I shut my eyes and sucked in a breath. The subtext of the chief's words was clear—if I didn't make a statement, there was a chance he'd come after me again or some other poor unsuspecting woman. But the law didn't allow the chief to go around warning or arresting people on suspicion alone, and while the chief wanted to do the right thing, he also wanted to keep his job.

At that point my phone buzzed in my bag. I pulled it out and my heart leaped into my throat. The text was from an unknown number, but the message was crystal clear.

**This is a small town, so I'd think very carefully about what you say to the chief. See you around, Chloe.**

How the heck did he get my number? Instead of scaring me, it filled me with a burning anger. This is what he did. What he'd *always* done. Intimidation was Brendan Chalmers's game and he'd been perfecting his technique for years.

"Okay," I said, nodding as resolve hardened in my gut. "I'll make a statement."

Dawn slipped an arm around my shoulder and kissed my head. "It's the right thing to do."

"Thanks for finding me," I said, looking up at her. I didn't even want to think about what might have happened if she hadn't come into the alleyway.

"Do you want me to come with you?" Dawn asked, her eyes brimming with worry.

"No." I shook my head. "If I leave this cream out for too

long, it'll curdle. And I promised Grandma Rose I'd make her something delicious this weekend, so I can't have that."

Dawn took the grocery bag from me with an air of reluctance. "The cream doesn't matter, hon. We'll buy another carton."

"I'm fine, I promise," I said to her, placing a hand on her arm and hoping I sounded a lot more grounded than I felt. I didn't want her to worry. "Tell Grandma I'll be home in a bit, okay?"

She nodded. "If that's what you want."

"Come on, let's head to my office." The chief motioned for me to walk with him. "I'll have you back to your grandmother in no time."

As I got to the end of the alley, I turned and looked back the way Brendan had gone moments earlier. The door to one of the other shops flew open, and two young men in jeans and T-shirts walked out, laughing. They were carefree and lifted their hands in friendly greeting. The alleyway looked completely normal. Completely safe.

Yet for some reason, a stone settled into the pit of my stomach. I tried to write it off as being shaken from the incident. It was understandable I'd feel unnerved by having someone invade my personal space like that. But the more I tried to justify the feeling as normal, the worse it got. My stomach churned and a deep sense of foreboding filtered through my system as I followed the chief to his cruiser.

It was almost like I knew this was the beginning of trouble, rather than the end.

# CHAPTER 3

The following morning I was up at the crack of dawn and already in the kitchen. I'd been on edge ever since the incident with Brendan and the threatening text message that I was *sure* was sent by him. I'd told Chief Gladwell I didn't necessarily want to press charges. Rather, I wanted the incident on record so he could be given a warning. That way, if it ever happened again, the chief would have grounds to act.

Frankly, I wanted to forget it ever happened. And the way I usually forgot about things was baking.

I crouched down in front of the cupboards, which were still painted a retro pistachio green with chips in the same places as when I left home. I rummaged through the well-stocked baking cupboard. Flour, white sugar, powdered sugar, baking chocolate, real vanilla extract, shredded coconut, molasses. I got my love of baking from my grandmother and she had all the basics neatly organized in her kitchen.

For some reason, I found myself wanting to experiment with cannabis treats that I might cook in the café. Aunt Dawn's suggestion had wormed into my brain and, backed up by Sabrina's enthusiasm and sage commentary about the wellness industry, I was seriously considering saying yes to this wild and unexpected idea. My gut was telling me that an ordinary bakery or café wouldn't cut it, especially not with all the established and popular competitors just down the road.

If I wanted to succeed, I needed to take risks.

I'd made some cannabis butter—or cannabutter, as some people called it—from scratch a few days ago when Grandma Rose originally requested the special brownies. Following a recipe I'd found online, I'd worked through the lengthy process, which required time to prepare the flowers in the oven and then three-plus hours to infuse the butter in a slow cooker. Thankfully, it could last up to three weeks in the refrigerator if stored properly, so I didn't have to make it from scratch for every recipe.

Weed baking is kind of a misnomer because you don't bake directly with the weed in a lot of cases. Often, it's infused into a fat like butter or oil and those items are used for the baking component after being decarbed—short for decarboxylation, which is the process of physically altering the chemical structure of the cannabis through heating, so that it becomes psychoactive. In short, this process is what helps people to experience a high. But it's also the process that allows cannabis to become a powerful anti-inflammatory and pain-relief treatment for people like Grandma Rose.

The possibilities are endless—cookies, slices, scones. Heck, you could throw some cannabutter into your morning omelet if you really wanted to.

I set about making another batch of brownies, this time a salted caramel version that used a traditional chocolate base recipe and had swirls of thick caramel sauce mixed through. I stood at the stove, stirring the sugar in a pot until it melted and became a lovely amber color. Next went some plain butter, which bubbled up vigorously, and I held the pot away from me to avoid getting splattered. Then came the cream, poured slowly and steadily until it was all incorporated.

I let it boil for a minute, watching the mixture rise and making sure it didn't bubble over. When it was done, I moved the pot to one side and added salt.

I let the caramel cool while I whipped up some more brownie mixture using the cannabutter. When it was done, I swirled the caramel sauce over the top to make a decorative marbled pattern. The flavor combination would be delicious, while also helping to mask the herbaceous taste of the cannabis. If I was making this in my own weed café, I'd add a touch of luxury as well. Maybe some gold dust with a stencil and Valrhona chocolate mixed into the batter.

I would want customers to feel like they were indulging *all* their senses.

When the timer went off, I pulled the brownies out of the oven and popped them onto a heatproof mat. It was getting lighter outside now. The sky was streaked with pink, warning that it would be a hot day ahead. I pottered around the kitchen, cleaning up after myself and trying to dispel my nervous energy. As tempting as it was to keep baking in the hopes it would eventually relax me, at this rate I'd clean out my grandmother's cupboards and have enough to feed an army.

Once the kitchen was sparkling clean, I was still as jittery as all get-out and I still hadn't come to a conclusion about the weed café. If I was being completely honest, I was scared. Because saying yes to this was as good as admitting I'd never get to chase my Michelin-star dreams. Being out of the fine dining industry for too long after getting trashed by a culinary critic was as good as waving a white flag.

Was I ready to give up that dream?

I decided to take a walk to the main strip to clear my head and get myself a coffee. Bean and Gone were usually open early, ready to serve the folks who wanted a caffeine fix before starting the hour-long commute to San Jose or Silicon Valley.

I changed into sneakers, a baggy T-shirt and my favorite Lululemon leggings. Yes, they were stupidly expensive and no, they had not seen the inside of a yoga studio. Ever. But I had few guilty pleasures in life, and buttery-soft Lycra was one of them. Outside the temperature was mild, perfect for a walk.

As I went to pop in my AirPods and blast my favorite pick-me-up playlist—hello mid-2000s Christina Aguilera, Destiny's Child and Paramore—something caught my attention.

Or should I say, some*one*.

The house next door to Grandma Rose's had previously been owned by a sweet older couple from Armenia. But now the garage door was up and inside was a vintage car and a guy about my age standing at a workbench with a small welding torch. He had a mask protecting his face, but I could see that he had a full head of thick brown hair that appeared slightly reddish in the glow of both an overhead light and the torch as he worked. He was tall and his muscular build was perfectly showcased in a pair of worn-in jeans and a fitted white T-shirt that cupped his biceps to mouthwatering perfection.

There was something about a muscular pair of arms that got me every time. Since when was there a certified dreamboat living next door to my grandmother?

At that moment—when I was probably staring open-mouthed like some child gawking at Disneyland—the hunky guy looked up and stared right at me. *Crap!* I seriously thought about diving into the bushes in Grandma Rose's front lawn. But A, I am not that athletically inclined; and B, I didn't want to risk getting a hole in my beloved leggings.

So I stood there like an awkward turtle, wishing the ground would swallow me whole. He switched his torch off and pulled off the mask, revealing a face that could make a person go weak at the knees. Kind eyes, strong jaw, proud nose.

And that smile . . . warm, genuine. See? A smile that goes all the way up a person's face is so flipping good. Zero creeper vibes, too, unlike the ones I'd gotten from Brendan Chalmers.

"Hi there." He held up his hand in a wave and started down the driveway toward me.

I glanced down at myself, wishing I'd thrown on something cuter than an oversized T-shirt that made me look like I was impersonating a yurt. "Hi."

"You must be Chloe." He stuck his hand out and I shook it. Even his hand squeeze was Goldilocks perfect—none of that "show 'em who's boss" bone-crushing crap. But no limp fish, either. "I'm Jake."

"Nice to meet you."

"I've heard you're quite the baker. You were living in Paris, right?" His hazel eyes shined with interest and I cocked my head, wondering how he knew about me. "Your grandmother and aunt speak very highly of you."

Ah, that explained it. I felt my face grow warm. By them speaking "very highly" of me, Grandma Rose and Aunt Dawn had been planting seeds for what they no doubt saw as "husband material." Since I'd never known my father and had nothing to do with my mother, I'd hoped that maybe I could avoid being pressured to get married and have babies.

Sadly, no dice.

My grandmother and aunt were one hell of a matchmaking duo when they wanted to be. I could sniff their work a mile off. Although I had to admit, they had good taste.

"Yeah, I lived in Paris for the last five years." I had to force myself not to grimace like I did every time I mentioned that part of my life. "But I moved back this week."

"I'm glad I finally got to put a face to the name. I've heard a lot about you," he said. I scrubbed a hand over my face and he laughed. "All good things, I promise."

"No doubt." My grandmother had probably been selling me like crazy. "Where did you move from?"

"New York. I got sick of the cold weather and frantic pace." He shoved his hands into the pockets of his jeans. "So, I packed everything up and moved here on my own. It's exciting, if a little lonely."

"I know that feeling."

My heart squeezed for the guy. His words carried a weight that told me there was a story hidden there, but I stopped myself from asking him about it. Yesterday, when I'd told Brendan Chalmers that I wasn't interested in going on a date with him, it *was* because I found him gross. However, I also didn't want to go on a date with anyone. Period.

My heart had been broken in the most humiliating way and I wasn't looking for a rebound. Especially not with someone like Jake, who appeared to be a truly decent guy.

*You don't know anything about him. Besides, you thought Jules was decent the first time you met him.*

Good point, brain. This was why I put my head in charge of making decisions and *not* my heart. Lesson absolutely learned.

"I'm sure I'll see you around," I said as nonchalantly as I could. "Being that we're neighbors and all."

"That does seem plausible." When he smiled this time, I noticed a dimple formed in his right cheek.

Ugh. Dimples were my *second* weakness after arms! I would have to be super careful around Jake. I was about to bid him a good day when a bloodcurdling scream pierced the air. It slashed through the quiet hush of the early morning and Jake and I both looked at one another before simultaneously breaking into a sprint toward the park across the road, where the sound had come from.

The park stretched all the way to the back of the main strip, and contained a barbecue and picnic area, a funky sculpture from a local artist, a gazebo that was often used for weddings, and a playground. The scream sounded as though it had come from the direction of the playground, and we headed toward the bright yellow slide and wooden fort.

I saw a woman frantically waving one arm in the air, trying to get our attention, while cradling a small white dog against her chest with the other. At first, I thought something might have happened to the animal, but it squirmed as if wanting to be set free and didn't appear injured. The woman's face was white as a sheet and her eyes were wide.

"What's going . . . oh no." Jake's sudden change in tone sent a chill down my spine and as we slowed to a stop at the edge of the playground, I finally saw what had caused the woman to scream.

A body was lying facedown in the bark chips.

"I . . . I found him like this. My poor little Izzie ran straight over and . . ." The woman's voice trembled and she had tears in her eyes. "I think . . . should we call nine-one-one?"

The body wasn't moving. There was something off about the color of the skin and I had a feeling there wasn't much the paramedics would be able to do for this poor person. For a moment I stared, hoping to see some signs of life. The twitch of a finger or foot. Something.

But he was still as a statue.

He appeared tall and bulky, with short hair, large hands and thick wrists. From this angle, it looked like he barely had a neck. And that's when something else caught my attention—he was wearing an ugly orange polo shirt.

"Oh my god." I pressed a hand to my mouth.

I walked around to the other side of the body, while Jake consoled the distraught woman. My heart was beating a million miles a minute as a trickle of foreboding crawled down my spine. A dark stain coated the bark chips around the man's shoulder and head. That wasn't a good sign.

As I got a better look, I could see his head was turned to the side and his eyes were open, staring blankly into the early morning. There was no mistaking his identity. It was Brendan Chalmers, and there was a pocketknife sticking out of the side of his neck, embedded all the way to the hilt.

He was undeniably dead.

# CHAPTER 4

Within minutes there were EMTs and uniformed patrol officers on the scene. The flashing blue and red of the ambulance and police vehicle lights drew Azalea Bay residents from their homes, some still in their pajamas and fuzzy slippers. Soon there was a crowd at the edge of the park. I stood with Jake and the woman who'd found the body, Nancy, looking on as it became clear the EMTs would not be able to help Brendan Chalmers. The police asked people to stay back as they cordoned off the area with yellow crime-scene tape.

I spotted Chief Gladwell talking on the phone, and a woman wearing plastic gloves and plastic covers on her shoes crouching down by the body.

Nancy clutched her fluffy, white dog to her chest, her hands trembling. The chief had asked us to stay close so one of his people could ask us a few questions as soon as they'd secured the scene. "Do you think it was an accident?"

Jake and I exchanged glances. I wasn't exactly sure that a pocketknife to the neck could be classified as an accident. Self-defense, maybe. Especially knowing what Brendan had been like with me. Perhaps he'd been aggressive with someone who was armed to defend themselves. Or maybe it was a mugging gone wrong.

It seemed crazy to think of a murder happening in Azalea Bay. It was a small town where most people knew one another, especially when, like now, the tourism season hadn't yet kicked off for the year. Our population would swell in a month's time, as people flocked to the rugged surf beaches and lush hiking trails and the boutique vineyards our part of the world had to offer. But it was still too early for that.

And no matter how hard it was to believe there was a murderer in our midst, *nothing* about Brendan's wound looked accidental.

"I don't know," I said, figuring that was the safest answer. I didn't want to upset the poor woman more than she already was. "Despite watching every crime show with an acronym, this is quite outside my area of expertise."

Seriously, I *loved* those shows. *CSI, NCIS, FBI, Chicago P.D., Law and Order SVU* . . . the list went on. I could make a whole alphabet out of those shows. Now, though, having seen a dead body in real life I wasn't sure I would find them quite so entertaining anymore.

Nancy bit down on her lip. "My husband and I moved here a year ago because we'd heard it was safe and idyllic. But now . . ."

"Chief Gladwell will figure out what happened," I said, reassuringly. "He's good at his job."

"I hope so."

Jake stood quietly beside us and for some reason, I was glad of his presence. He struck me as a steady sort of guy. Reliable. Calm in a crisis. He'd been swift to dial 911, explaining the situation and giving our location in an even, controlled voice. Much more controlled than I would have been.

My stomach churned at the thought of Brendan's gray-toned face. I'd never seen a dead body before. Blood didn't make me squeamish—work in a kitchen long enough and you'll end up seeing all kinds of nasty injuries—but it was the contrast of how he'd been yesterday, red-faced and full of bluster. And now, so pale that it looked like he had ash in his veins.

Time felt like molasses, and it seemed an age while we waited for the chief to come speak to us.

Eventually, a woman approached. She was the same one who'd been inspecting the body, though now she'd removed the plastic gloves from her hands and the covers from her shoes. I guessed her to be around mid-to-late thirties. She had long dark brown hair pulled back into a braid, clear olive skin and wide brown eyes that looked almost owlish behind a pair of oversized blue glasses, a funky style which felt a little at odds with her bland tan slacks, dark blazer and sensible black shoes.

I didn't recognize her.

"Which one of you found the body?" she asked, direct but not confrontational.

"Me," Nancy squeaked, clutching Izzie the dog so tight I was worried she might squeeze the poor thing to death.

*Maybe now's not a great time to use that expression, huh?*

"And you called nine-one-one?" the woman asked Jake. "I was told a male called."

"That's right." He nodded.

"I'm Detective Adriana Alvarez." Her gaze flicked across the three of us. "The chief wants me to take a statement from each of you about what happened this morning."

Nancy whimpered beside me, so Jake took the lead. "Chloe and I were talking in my driveway," he said, pointing back toward his house. "We heard a scream coming from the park and we ran over. That's when we saw Nancy."

The detective scribbled notes on an electronic device that looked like a small tablet or digital notebook of some kind. "What were you talking about?"

I raised an eyebrow, unsure why that was relevant. But I figured it was better to be forthcoming than evasive. Given what had happened yesterday between Brendan and me, I didn't want to make myself look like a suspect.

Unless I already did? I gulped.

"Uhh . . . I was introducing myself to Jake, because we're next-door neighbors now that I've just moved back in with my grandmother."

The detective nodded, apparently satisfied with my answer. "And you, Nancy? How did you come across the deceased?"

So that was confirmation then. Nothing could be done for Brendan Chalmers.

"I was walking my dog, Izzie," Nancy replied, her voice trembling. "We walk every morning bright and early."

"Do you always come through this park?"

"Most days." Nancy nodded. "I like how quiet and peaceful it is . . . usually."

"And where were all three of you last night?" she asked.

A breath stuck in the back of my throat. Was that a normal question to ask or did they think that one of us might be responsible for Brendan's death? Surely not. Detective Alvarez must have figured out we were taken by surprise when no one jumped in with an answer.

"It's standard procedure for us to ask this question," she said with a warm smile. "It helps us to know who might have seen something, that's all. Nothing to be worried about."

"I was home last night," Nancy said. "My husband and I had friends over for dinner."

"About what time did they leave?" the detective asked.

"Around ten p.m."

Nancy supplied the names of her dinner-party guests and gave their phone numbers when the detective asked. Then the detective looked at Jake.

"I was home all night," he said, his expression difficult to read. "But I ordered a pizza which was delivered around seven thirty, and I was on Skype with my sister until after eleven."

"And you?" Detective Alvarez turned to me.

"I was with Chief Gladwell until eight thirty," I said, biting down on my lip as the curious stares of both Jake and Nancy swung in my direction. "Then I went to the bed-and-breakfast to see my best friend. Her family owns the business. She drove me home around ten."

I'd been too upset about having to file the report to go straight home. Grandma Rose and Aunt Dawn had been worried about me, but I knew they would fuss, and frankly, I'd wanted a distraction rather than to be coddled. Sabrina, and her tales of all the crazy things that happened in the bed-and-breakfast, had been the perfect choice. She'd made me a coffee with a healthy splash of Irish whisky and I'd sat behind the front counter with her, listening to her chatter until my muscles started to loosen.

"You were with Chief Gladwell?" Detective Alvarez raised an eyebrow. Heat rose into my cheeks and I dropped my gaze to the ground.

"I was making a statement at the station." Did I really have to go into this in front of two people who were—for all intents and purposes—strangers?

Thankfully, the detective seemed to sense I was uncomfortable. "I'll corroborate that with the chief directly."

"Thank you."

"I'll need to get each of your contact details, in case we have any further follow-up. But for now, you're free to go." The detective took a moment to get our names, phone numbers and addresses before snapping the cover closed on her tablet.

"Do . . . do you think he was murdered?" Nancy asked, a deep line forming between her brows.

"That's for the county coroner to determine. He's on his way now, so hopefully we'll know more soon." The response was delivered with a friendly tone, but there was a definite line in the sand. The detective played her cards close to her chest and we would get nothing out of her. "But if you happen to remember seeing anything strange in the area recently, please give me a call."

She slipped a card into each of our hands and bid us a good

day before ducking back under the yellow crime-screen tape and heading toward where the police chief stood, his arms folded tightly across his chest and an intense expression on his face.

Something told me this was not the last I was going to hear about Brendan Chalmers.

"He's *dead*?" Sabrina gaped at me across the table. "No way."

"Way." I nodded.

We were seated at Sprout, an LA-inspired health and wellness café. In truth, this place wasn't really my thing. If there were to be a type of food diametrically opposed to my beloved butter-laden French cuisine, it was Sprout with its antioxidant crystal-charged smoothie bowls.

Yes, that was a real menu item.

But Sabrina liked it here, and who was I to argue? Besides, the best thing about lunch was seeing her. I could always order a sandwich and then make myself something more substantial or satisfying later.

I had to admit, the café *was* cute. It was painted in a dreamy combination of soft white, peach sherbet, millennial pink and a powdery light blue. The back wall had the word "joy" spelled out in pink neon lights and the tables were all a pale blond wood, with chairs and the banquette seating covered in peach velvet cushions. Talk about an Instagram photoshoot waiting to happen.

It was also proof that a new business could find success if they did something to stand out, which Sprout absolutely did. I could admit it, even if I'd rather starve than eat anything for the sake of healing my chakras.

"How did you find out?" Sabrina asked.

I relayed the details of hearing Nancy's scream and finding Brendan's body in the park, and her eyes grew wider by the moment. I kept my voice down, but word was already spreading through town that something untoward was going on. After all, it wasn't every day in Azalea Bay that we saw crime-scene tape and multiple emergency vehicles. And while it had happened quite early in the morning and the police had secured the scene promptly, plenty of town residents still witnessed an investigation going on.

"I heard the chief was at the park and there was a lot of activity, but I would never have guessed *that*." Sabrina shook her head, her dark curls bouncing around her face. "I mean, the fact that you saw him alive yesterday and now he's dead is . . . wild."

"I know." I was still reeling from shock myself. "It looked . . . intentional."

Sabrina leaned forward. "You mean, you think he was murdered?"

"He had a knife sticking out of his neck," I said, holding my menu in a way that obscured our view from the rest of the café. I'd arrived first and had snagged the table in the back corner, so we had some privacy to talk. "Unless he has the worst luck in the world to trip and accidentally kill himself, someone did it."

"What are you two whispering about?" The female voice dripped with unconcealed curiosity as the owner of Sprout approached us.

I looked up. Starr Bright—not her real name—hovered over us, face alight. I fought the urge to roll my eyes. For as long as she had lived in Azalea Bay, which was over twenty years now, she'd *thrived* on gossip. And while she claimed that it was the special açaí berries she sourced for her smoothies which kept her skin and hair in great condition, part of me wondered if she was some kind of vampire who fed on the misery of others. I had seen her entire being light up at the news of an affair or divorce, almost like she gained vitality from knowing people's sordid secrets.

"Just catching up," I said with a forced smile. "It's been a long time, so there's a lot to talk about."

Starr tilted her head to the side, as if she was trying to figure out whether I was telling the truth. Her waist-length blond hair was a gleaming shade of platinum—thanks to a talented hairdresser, rather than berries—and her skin was tanned, with a small tattoo of a dolphin gracing the inside of her arm. She was a little over a decade older than Sabrina and I, putting her in her late thirties, and she acted like she was better than everyone else because she'd "grown up" in LA.

Meanwhile, I knew for a fact that her family had moved when she was five and she'd actually spent most of her childhood and teen years in Idaho.

"Were you catching up about what happened this morning in Azalea Park?" A smug smile pulled at her lips. It looked like she'd had fillers recently, giving her a bit of a trout-like appearance. "A source told me you were totally chatting with one of the officers."

Great. The last thing I needed was Starr snooping around my business. For someone who'd been quite the open book my entire life, I suddenly had a lot to hide. Getting cheated on in Paris, the crushing review of my work, the fact that I'd reported Brendan's predatory behavior to the cops last night . . .

*Don't get rattled, that's only going to make her curious.*

"My grandmother's house is across the road from the park. It was hard to ignore what was going on."

Starr didn't seem convinced. She reached for one of several necklaces layered around her neck, fingering a piece of rough-cut stone in a pretty shade of periwinkle blue. "That's not really a reason to speak with an officer during an investigation."

"Sure it is. They wanted to know if I'd seen anything." I shrugged, hoping that my dismal results in high school drama class wouldn't come back to bite me now. "Frankly, with how connected you are, I'm sure you know *way* more than I do."

This comment landed exactly as I'd hoped it would. Starr drew her shoulders back and fluffed out her hair like a peacock fanning its tail. "I do, like, know *everything* that happens in this town."

"Exactly. I should be coming to you for answers instead of the other way around." I smiled sweetly, and caught Sabrina burying her face in her menu to stifle a smirk.

"Well, I heard that there was a body. A *male* body." Starr leaned forward conspiratorially, her necklaces swinging forward and almost hitting me in the face. "And I don't think the cops would be there unless there were some suspicions about it being, like, a homicide."

Her eyes were wide and her cheeks were flushed, the thrill of something so salacious seeming to have her almost vibrating with excitement. It made me sick to my stomach. A man was dead. It was nothing to be excited about.

"Say any more and you're going to put us off our food," Sabrina interjected. "That wouldn't be good for business, now would it?"

"Not my fault you have a weak stomach. Or maybe that's because I grew up in LA, you become a little wiser about the world living in a city like that." Starr shrugged. "It's totally sheltered here."

I opened my mouth to remind her I knew about the Idaho thing, but Sabrina kicked me under the table. Then a small group came into the café and lined up at the bar, which thankfully drew her gaze away from us.

"But business is booming, so I can't stay and chat," Starr said. "It's hard running a place that's so full all the time."

"You poor thing," I said drily, but she didn't seem to catch my sarcasm.

"What can I get you gals?" she asked, pulling a small notepad from the tie-dyed half apron wrapped over her floral maxi dress. "Our lunch special for today is the small-batch fair trade organic chocolate smoothie bowl—we have one with toasted cacao nibs, which has been charged with black tourmaline to prevent bad vibes, or we have one with goji berries and twenty-four-karat gold dust, that has been charged with jade for good luck. Our soup of the day is artichoke and lemon, and our salad is the hand-massaged kale and with wild foraged herbs."

*This* was the reason I would never live in LA. Their food culture was ridiculous.

"I'll take the chocolate smoothie bowl with the cacao nibs," Sabrina said. "And a cold brew, please. Black."

Starr turned to me. "And for you?"

I glanced at the menu, trying to find the most normal thing on there. "The farm-to-table chicken wrap, please, with hummus on the side. And I'll take a glass of the fresh-pressed orange juice as well."

"Coming right up."

As Starr disappeared to serve the people who'd just walked in, I turned to Sabrina. "I have no idea why you wanted to come here."

"I like to try different things," she replied with a shrug. "And increasingly our customers are asking for this kind of food, so let's file this under research."

"Really?" I knew Sabrina had given the family business a much-needed facelift, but their menu had always been more on the greasy spoon side of things. I could hardly see them adding twenty-four-karat gold dust to someone's waffles.

"The wellness trend isn't going away and as much as you think you're above it, Miss French Patisserie Chef, you're going to capitalize on that when you open your weed café."

"If," I corrected her. "*If* I open it. I'm still thinking about it."

But I had promised Aunt Dawn an answer, so I really needed to figure this out.

"What's holding you back?" she asked.

"Oh, I don't know. Maybe the fact that I had my whole life mapped out and it didn't include making pot brownies for people in my hometown."

"What are you *really* afraid of?" Sabrina asked. "Is it that you're worried how people are going to react to the weed element?"

"I guess that has something to do with it," I admitted.

Increased legalization across the country hadn't convinced everyone that cannabis was safe, despite all the research that pointed to its medicinal benefits. Not to mention the positive impact on the economy in terms of tax revenue and employment, *and* the fact that having production be regulated protected people who chose to use it. But yeah, maybe part of me was worried about the blowback and stigma of running a weed café, from some of the folks in town who hadn't yet come around to the idea.

"Here's the thing," Sabrina said. "No matter what you do, someone will *always* react negatively. The only way to avoid being criticized is to never do anything with your life."

"That's a good point." I nodded. "But part of me wonders if it might be safer to do something a little less . . . controversial. Like a regular café. I could still put a Parisian spin on it and make it my own. I make excellent macarons."

"Sure. You *could* take the safer route." Sabrina nodded. "But do you think yet another cute café, even a Parisian-inspired one, is going to draw anyone's attention?"

This was exactly the question I'd asked myself, and I already knew what my gut had to say about it. People wouldn't come from three towns over simply for macarons. But they *might* come from three towns over for macarons with weed-infused buttercream.

And Sabrina had touched on my core problem: I hated drawing attention to myself. I was never that kid who liked being on stage or who wanted to stand out in the crowd. But when it came to business, it was better to have people talking—even if some comments were negative—than to have no one talking at all.

"Would *you* judge someone for opening a weed café?" Sabrina asked.

"Of course not." I shook my head.

I'd dabbled a bit after recreational use became legal in California, more out of curiosity than anything else. I wasn't a regular user, because I craved control—it was the very reason baking suited me. I found pleasure in perfecting small details. But it was also that need for control which had caused me to turn to a joint in the past when the stress of perfectionism got too much.

"Honestly, that's only one part of my reservation," I said. "I'm not trying to convince anyone to do something they don't want to do."

It was no different from alcohol in my mind—some people like to dabble and others didn't, and both were legitimate personal choices.

"Then what?" Sabrina prompted.

"I guess when I thought about being a pastry chef, I would be tucked away behind the scenes. I'd spend my time in the restaurant kitchen or in a test kitchen, dreaming up creations and maybe getting interviewed on occasion. Here . . ." I shook my head. "People will know who I am. It will be *my* business, with my name on it. If I walk down the street, people will know who I am."

"Ahhh." Sabrina nodded, looking like a puzzle piece had clicked into place. "So if it fails, the failure will be public."

"Bingo."

Having a food critic shred my work in a print publication was bad enough. But when I left the restaurant, nobody knew who I was. Heck, I doubt the critic himself would have recognized me if we'd walked past one another in the street. I was simply a name. And yes, if I rose in the ranks I would become more well-known. But how many people would instantly recognize the chef from their favorite restaurant in person? Not many.

Yet here, any misstep would be fodder for people like Starr Bright. People *would* recognize me in the street, and I was terrified of being a laughingstock.

"I know what happened in Paris really knocked your confidence, but none of that diminishes your talent in the kitchen." My best friend shook her head. "Working for someone else where you'll be making the same things over and over isn't going to satisfy you."

She was right.

"You've always wanted to make your own creations and now you have an opportunity to do it. The weed thing is a smart way to differentiate. And, yeah, some people might get their pitchforks out. But the wellness trend is only growing and if you don't fill this gap, I guarantee someone else will in the future."

"I'm not going to charge any of my stuff with crystals," I grumbled, and she laughed.

"You can leave that to Starr. I doubt you'd want to get in her line of fire, anyway."

"Truth." I sighed. "And I like the idea of reducing the stigma around it for people like Grandma Rose."

In my mind, food wasn't simply something to eat. It was connection and education and joy and growth and love. Would a regular French-inspired café help me achieve those things? Probably not. The weed café was a chance for me to do something different. To make an impact.

And there was something deeply appealing about that.

"It's time for you to bet on yourself." Sabrina nodded emphatically. "You should *seriously* consider taking your aunt up on this. There are plenty of people who want to see you succeed, myself included."

"I am," I said. "Seriously considering it."

"Good."

But Brendan's murder had occupied me all morning. I couldn't seem to get the image of his lifeless body out of my head, especially not the knife sticking out of his neck and the blood pooling around him.

I shook my head, as if trying to physically dislodge the visual.

"Still thinking about this morning, huh?" Sabrina asked, as if reading my mind. She'd always been intuitive like that, ever since we were kids. "You holding up okay?"

"It was a shock." I sighed. "I'm trying not to think about it, but we don't even know if it's a one-off thing."

Sabrina reached for my hand and squeezed. "We're not the kind of town to have a serial killer running around, and with everything we know about Brendan, I'm honestly not shocked that he pissed off someone enough that there was an altercation."

"There's having an altercation and then there's murder," I replied with a sigh. "Those are *not* the same thing."

"You're right. But I would be surprised if it was a random attack. *Seriously* surprised." She paused as one of Starr's staff members delivered our drinks. "Seems too much of a coincidence that they would pick someone who'd upset *so* many people."

"Like other women he's harassed?"

"Not only that," Sabrina replied. "I know for a fact that he had beef with one of his colleagues at work and did some shady crap to get her fired. She's a regular in our Dungeons and Dragons crew and was always complaining about Brendan's behavior. I'd wager that there were dozens of people he's bullied."

"He was a bad egg, through and through." I reached for my orange juice and took a sip. "Chief Gladwell is going to have his work cut out for him."

I just had to hope that my incident with the murder victim not too long before he died wouldn't make it into the Azalea Bay gossip circles, or else my business could be sunk before it had even begun.

# CHAPTER 5

After lunch with Sabrina, I headed back to my grandmother's house and let myself inside. There was a note on the kitchen counter saying that she'd gone to pick up a prescription from the pharmacy—something I absolutely would have done for her. But Grandma Rose was independent to the core and she still liked to get out and run her own errands, even if there were a dozen people lining up to help.

I placed the note back on the counter and smiled. I'd inherited so many things from her, most of all my stubborn independence.

Heading into my old bedroom was like stepping into the twilight zone. I was thrust back into my pink-toned teenage years, and Grandma Rose had kept it exactly as I remembered from my last year of high school, right down to the lipstick stain on the white carpet near the foot of my vanity unit and the photos of my friends wedged into the frame of my mirror. It was hard to believe it was approaching ten years since I'd packed my bags and left for college, and five since I'd headed to Paris with stars in my eyes.

I heard the front door open and close as I fingered the edge of one of the photos, which featured me and Sabrina with wide smiles, skin pink from a long weekend spent at the beach. We'd looked so . . . hopeful. Obliviously positive. Products of being raised by strong women with big hearts who really believed we could conquer the world.

Right then, I wasn't sure I could conquer anything.

"Chloe?" Grandma Rose knocked on the open door. Today she was totally living up to her namesake by dressing in her signature rosy hues with a pair of loose, light pink slacks and a dusky rose-colored T-shirt with fine white stripes.

"You're back." I smiled. "Good timing, I just got home."

"Can I come in?"

"It's your house, Grandma." I laughed. "You're allowed in every room."

Grandma Rose made a huffing sound. "I remember a precocious young lady once telling me that all humans deserved privacy."

That *did* sound like something my sassy teenage self would have said. Looking back, however, I'd never gone through the typical rebellious phase like many of my peers. There'd always been part of me that was afraid if I acted out too hard that my grandmother might abandon me like my mom did.

That said more about me than it did about her, however.

"I was thinking we could spruce up your room, if you want," she said. "We could give it a fresh coat of paint and get a new bed and . . . well, make it however you like. I don't want you to feel like you're here as a guest, sleeping in a kid's room. I want it to feel like home."

"Of *course* it feels like home." I was touched by the kind suggestion. "But this room could use an upgrade. The pink is a little . . ."

I searched for the right word.

"Obnoxious?" she suggested and I laughed, nodding. "We should be able to paint it ourselves."

"So long as we get a decent stepladder, because these ceilings are high and I am short."

"You're taller than me," she pointed out.

"*Everyone* is taller than you."

My grandmother was five foot one on a good day. She might have been taller at some stage, but age had shrunk her down so that her head barely passed my shoulder. She had brilliant blue eyes that didn't miss a trick and her hair was a fluffy silver cloud around her head, though it looked much thinner than I remembered, likely from the chemo. I swallowed, emotion clogging the back of my throat.

"I know that look." She waggled a finger in my face. "You've been home three days and I have seen you cry more now than ever before."

"Well *that's* not true." I folded my arms over my chest. "I cried a whole bunch when I was a kid."

"Well, I'm telling you, don't cry now." She pulled me in for a hug, which didn't do much to help the situation. Tears rushed up hot and angry inside me, but I did my best to tamp them down for her sake.

Grandma Rose was one of the good ones. My mother, meanwhile, was a careless, neglectful person and yet was healthy as a horse, last I'd heard. It didn't seem fair.

"I *will* get through this, my dear girl. I will." She squeezed me. "Now, I forgot to mention that the ladies are coming over for cards tonight."

"Really?" I pulled away and swiped the back of one hand over my eyes. She wasn't wrong—my eyes had been leakier than a badly fitted pipe lately. It wasn't only the cancer diagnosis that had rocked me, but all the things that had led to me coming home. And now a murder in town . . .

It was a lot.

"What time?" I asked, drawing my shoulders back and forcing myself to be strong. She shouldn't have to look after me, it should be the other way around. "Would you like me to bake something?"

My grandmother's eyes lit up. "Oh, would you? I know the

ladies have all missed your talents in the kitchen while you were gone. But I don't want to put any pressure—"

"Please, baking is my love language." I slung an arm around her slight shoulders. We walked down the hallway and I avoided the same squeaky floorboard that had been there ever since I was a kid. "Who's coming?"

"Just the usual group—Betty, Luisa and Ida. I'm going to take all their money."

I couldn't help but laugh. Seriously, I had never met a group of women more fiercely competitive than my grandmother and her friends. Their euchre games involved the kind of smack talk I'd expect to see in a rap battle . . . minus the cursing. These ladies could cut a person down with only a well-intonated *oh, honey.*

"And Lawrence St. James is coming, too," she added as though it was only an afterthought. But I knew better than to let that information slip by me.

"Lawrence St. James the crime author?" I raised an eyebrow.

"*Retired* crime author," she corrected me. We made our way into the kitchen and Grandma Rose set about making a pot of tea. "His last book came out two years ago."

"And now he fills his time attending ladies' euchre night?" I teased.

My grandmother flushed. I knew she'd had a crush on Lawrence for as long as I could remember. My grandfather—bless his soul—passed away almost two decades ago and Grandma Rose had remained single ever since. Lawrence was the brother of her friend Betty, and he was quite the silver fox. Well-read and well-spoken, too. Thoughtful. Just her type. But she'd spent a long time denying her attraction to the man. So, to find out he was crashing their evening piqued my interest.

"He fills his time with many things," she replied primly, shooting me a look over her shoulder that told me not to push it. She might be pocket-sized, but she could clip a person's ear like nobody's business. "But yes, playing cards is one of those things."

Stifling a smirk, I nodded. "Fair enough."

"Now, I saw that you've already done some baking today," she said, her eyes still avoiding mine.

"Salted caramel brownies."

"The special kind?" she asked, and I nodded. "Would you mind if we served some tonight? I was talking to Betty about how the . . . alternative medicine is helping my pain. She has a persistent back injury, you know."

"Grandma, you can say the word. Cannabis." I hated the idea that she was embarrassed by something that was helping her. "There's nothing to be ashamed of."

Her lips tightened. "I don't need a lecture from you, too."

Ah. Aunt Dawn had already gotten in her ear about it, no doubt. Though my aunt's persuasion style was a little less gentle than mine.

"How about I whip up a plain batch, too, that way anyone who wants to try the special brownies can try them and anyone who doesn't can have a piece of the plain one?" I suggested. "That way no one will feel left out or uncomfortable."

"You're a good egg, Chloe." She patted my arm. "That would be wonderful."

A few hours later my grandmother's friends had all arrived. They'd had a bi-weekly cards night for as long as I could remember and I'd grown up listening to the sounds of their cackling laughter every second Tuesday, often sneaking down to watch the women in their element. The sink had always been full of glasses, with empty wine bottles stuffed into the recycling bin and plates scattered with cake crumbs piled onto the countertop.

Recently, the cards night had been "rebranded" to "Screw Cancer Night." Aunt Dawn had started attending, too, wanting to join in the fun but also to make sure Grandma Rose didn't tire herself out when it was her turn to host. In many ways, these women taught me what it was like to be part of a community. I may not have had a mother who cared about my existence, but my glorious consolation prize was this vibrant, outspoken, sharp-minded band of female role models.

Luisa Fusco was a retired restaurateur and had the most finely tuned BS radar I'd ever seen. Betty St. James had managed the perfume and cosmetics counter at our local pharmacy for years and had taught me how to apply makeup when I was a teenager. And retired teacher Ida Smith could sweet-talk a lollipop right out of a child's hand.

They were all fabulous and it was like being blessed with three extra grandmas. I loved them dearly. That being said, the motto of cards night was "take no prisoners" and I had been roped into a game of euchre. I'm not ashamed to say they were whipping my butt.

"You should come to all our games, Chloe," Luisa said. She wore her hair in a fluffy dark brown perm, and despite being in her late sixties, had hardly any gray hair at all. "I like an easy target."

I knew my thirty-dollar buy-in was blown the second I handed the bills over. "I'm more than happy for the opportunity to learn from such experienced card sharks."

"That's a good attitude, dear." Betty threw down a pair of red queens, causing Luisa to groan. Her nails were painted a bright sparkly silver and they distracted me every time she moved her hand, which I suspected was not an accident. "There is always something to be learned from hardship."

"Losing isn't hardship," I said, and all four of the older women looked at me. "What's wrong with playing for fun?"

"Winning is fun." Betty glanced around the table and when it was clear nobody could beat her pair, she claimed that trick.

"I swear that woman keeps extra cards up her sleeves," Ida

grumbled. She had smooth dark brown skin and was always dressed like she'd taken inspiration from a painter's palette. Tonight, it was a vibrant royal purple and a rich cherry red.

"How about we break for some dessert?" Grandma Rose suggested. She looked extra pretty tonight, swapping her earlier outfit for a fuchsia blouse and a light pink cardigan. She'd also swiped on some lipstick and added a little blush to her cheeks, which she didn't often bother with.

I'd noticed her and Lawrence casting furtive glances at one another. It was freaking adorable, but she'd made me promise to be on my best behavior, so I would keep my trap shut.

Reluctantly, I might add.

"Would anyone like coffee or tea?" I asked, pushing back on my chair.

"I'll help." Dawn joined me in taking everyone's orders and in the kitchen she took care of the drinks while I sliced up both types of brownies.

I arranged them on two beautiful china plates from my grandmother's collection. She hardly ever used the fancy china that she'd had for decades, always wanting to save them for a special occasion. But I believed in making use of what we owned, especially now.

Life was short.

It was a cliché, sure, but along with growing up on romantic ideals I was also partial to a little Instagram wisdom here and there. And part of me felt guilty for being away from her these past five years, even though she'd assured me many times that I should chase my dreams. Still, now that she was sick I felt more than a twinge of regret. I'd never get those years back, so the next best thing would be to be the perfect granddaughter now.

I arranged the brownies in an appealing formation, dusting the normal ones with a little extra cocoa powder and some fine edible glitter that I'd found in the back of the baking cupboard. On the other plate, I left them plain so the caramel swirls would shine and so they wouldn't be mixed up.

With butterflies in my stomach, I took the plates of brownies out to the group.

"Oh, are these the *special* brownies I've heard so much about?" Betty clapped her hands together. "I'm excited."

I explained which brownies were which and made sure that nobody felt pressured to try the cannabis ones, if they weren't comfortable. Most of the group, however, was eager to test them out.

"You know, I tried pot brownies once on a trip to Amsterdam. Such a wild time we had back then," Betty said, as she reached for one of the cannabis-infused caramel-swirl brownies. I could easily imagine the glamorous older woman partying her way through Europe when she was younger. "They take a while to get going."

"Yes," I said, nodding. "That's a good tip. If you're still feeling a sweet craving after one square, have a plain brownie instead because it's easy to overconsume before the effects fully kick in."

"Darling, I'm sure they're wonderful, but I would prefer a plain one if that's okay." Ida touched my arm. "I'm on some medication and I don't know how it might interact."

"No worries. It's precisely why I made two options." I put a regular brownie on a plate and handed it to her with a smile. "I didn't want anyone to miss out."

Grandma Rose, ever the sweet tooth, helped herself to one of each and Lawrence tried a small bite from his sister's plate.

"My goodness, they're delicious!" he said. "Your grandmother told me what a talent you have in the kitchen, but this is even better than I could have imagined."

"You understand balance and flavor," Luisa added, nodding while she wiped a smudge of chocolate from the corner of her mouth. "Bellissima!"

"And the texture . . ." Betty made a chef's kiss gesture. "Perfectly gooey on the inside and crispy on the outside. It has none of the funky taste I remember, either."

I sat back and watched the group enjoy my food. There was no greater moment for me than when someone's eyes fluttered shut as they enjoyed a treat that I had created. It was the ultimate form of connection for me, a way for me to show care and love for those around me.

"You could sell these, you know," Betty said, licking some chocolate off her finger. "They really are very good."

"Oh yes!" Ida nodded emphatically. She was already reaching for another square of the plain brownies. "I bet people would line up down the street."

I felt Aunt Dawn's elbow dig into my ribs. I hadn't even seen her return. "See," she said. "Told you."

Knowing people like my grandmother and her friends were supportive of our business idea and weren't treating me with judgment bolstered my confidence. Views really were changing when it came to cannabis and people were becoming more open-minded. I *could* make this work. I could take a risk and find success, even if it looked a little different than my original career plan.

"I'm glad you're all enjoying it," I said graciously. "Don't forget to pace yourselves."

I stood to help Dawn with the drinks. The kettle whistled as we walked back into the kitchen, where a few mugs were lined up with tea bags waiting. Two cups waiting for the coffee to finish brewing were off to one side.

"I never thought I'd see my mother asking for pot brownies for her girls' night," Dawn said, shaking her head and laughing. "I still remember the time she caught me smoking after school one day. My hide was so raw I couldn't sit for a week."

"I'm lucky I never got caught," I replied with a wink. "Honestly, I'm glad she's listening to the doctor. There's no sense suffering for the sake of worrying about what people think."

*Hmm, shouldn't I take a bit of my own advice there when it comes to the café?*

"As I always say: opinions are like backsides, everyone has one but we don't necessarily want to hear it."

I snorted. "So true."

"Besides, other people don't have to see her struggling like we do. The first two sessions of her chemo treatment were rough." Something dark passed across Dawn's face. "I hated seeing her so sick like that. I hope the next round is easier."

A lump lodged in the back of my throat.

*You promised her you wouldn't cry.*

"She's going to be okay." Dawn wrapped an arm around my shoulders and kissed the top of my head. "Your grandmother is a strong lady and she's going to fight with everything she has. The oncologist seems positive, too. It's a good prognosis, all things considered."

"You're not sugarcoating it for me, are you?" I looked up at her.

"You know I'm a straight shooter," she said, and I nodded. "You being home has lifted her spirits immensely. She loves you more than anything."

I swallowed and nodded. I never had any concerns about whether I was loved when it came to Grandma Rose or Aunt Dawn.

"Now, being that I'm your favorite aunt . . ." Dawn said cajolingly.

"My *only* aunt," I teased in response.

"Darling, sometimes perfection only requires one shot." She grinned. "I want to talk about the café."

I sucked in a breath. The conversation with Sabrina played on my mind and the question she'd asked me looped in my head.

*What are you really afraid of?*

Failure. Embarrassing myself publicly. Judgment.

But were those really good reasons to hold myself back?

I'd always been the kind of person who dreamed big. I

*prided* myself on it, in fact. In high school I'd been voted "most likely to get a Food Network TV show" because I was never shy about letting my work ethic or my dreams shine. But now my confidence had been shaken and the ground still felt unsteady beneath my feet.

"The real estate agent wants an answer," she said softly. "Despite what you say about my persuasion tactics, I'm not going to push you into anything. I want you to be happy."

"What if I don't know what's going to make me happy?"

Ugh, if that wasn't a cliché millennial question then I didn't know *what* was.

"If it were so easy to figure that out, more people would *be* happy." She smiled. "All I know is that when you're in the kitchen being creative, you glow."

"And you think that's enough to make a café successful?" I asked.

"Goodness no. We'll need marketing and processes and business acumen." She ticked the items off her fingers. "But we're two smart women with contacts around town. Between your baking talents and creativity and my ability to get what I want, I think we have a great partnership."

I couldn't help but laugh. Aunt Dawn *was* good at getting her way.

"Besides, to even be able to apply for a cannabis retail license you need to have a place of business. So that's the first step." She nodded. "It's a risk, sure. But this isn't an idea that just popped into my head. I've been thinking about it and doing some research for quite a while."

"Really?"

"It's a good idea and there's no competition here yet," she said. "I wanted to be prepared in case you were interested."

"Yes." The word popped out of me, powered by a strike of intuition to my gut.

My aunt was right. Sabrina was right. I would never be happy pumping out generic cinnamon rolls and vanilla cupcakes for someone else's business. I needed an outlet for my ideas. I needed to create.

"Yes?" Dawn's eyes lit up. "You know that's my favorite word!"

"Yes, I want to open a weed café with you." I barely got the words out before laughter overtook me.

I couldn't believe I was taking such a huge leap, veering so far away from my life plans that I was standing at the edge of a cliff face. It was terrifying and exhilarating and I had no idea what would come from it.

But I was ready to bet on myself.

"Let me call the agent right now." Dawn reached into the deep pockets on her maxi skirt and pulled out her cell phone. "You're making the right decision."

"I hope so," I said, my stomach swishing and tilting with a mélange of excitement, anxiety and anticipation.

I bounced on the spot as she spoke to the agent, confirming that we would come by the office tomorrow to discuss next steps. We'd need to meet with the bank and find people to continue the store renovation and I'd have to learn the process of how cannabis was sourced for a business and maybe register . . .

*Stop panicking. You can figure this all out.*

"She says congratulations." Dawn dropped her phone back into her pocket. "And I can already see you freaking out, but I promise this is going to be amazing. I've done plenty of research and—"

A knock at the front door cut her off. Strange. I wondered who had stopped by, because everyone who'd been invited to Grandma Rose's Screw Cancer card night was already here. Being that the kitchen was closest to the front of the house, I went to answer the door.

To my surprise, Detective Alvarez was standing on our doorstep and she seemed to have lost a little of the easygoing, albeit guarded, appearance I'd seen earlier that morning. Instead, now she had a look of determination on her face. I felt Aunt Dawn come up behind me and Detective Alvarez looked over my shoulder, almost as if I wasn't even there.

"Dawn Barnes?" she asked.

"That's right," my aunt said. "Can we help you?"

"I'm going to need you to come down to the station and answer some questions in relation to the murder of Brendan Chalmers."

# CHAPTER 6

I couldn't stop fidgeting. It had been two hours since Detective Alvarez had shown up at our front door and whisked my aunt away. In that time the euchre competition had ground to a halt while my grandmother's friends tried to comfort us. Even my delicious brownies couldn't help. I'd only taken a single bite because it tasted like sawdust in my mouth.

Ida had taken over making the drinks, and she'd pressed a warm mug of milky black tea with a squeeze of honey into my hands. But it had gone cold and now I could only stare at my dazed reflection in the pale liquid surface.

"What could they possibly want with her?" Betty smoothed a hand over her coiffed silver hair and a stack of fine gold bangles tinkled on her wrist. Her movements were a little slow now, as the brownie had kicked in. I hadn't eaten much at all, so my mind raced. I told the group about the encounter with Brendan last night, and how Aunt Dawn had come to my rescue, sandal in hand.

"Chief Gladwell seems to think she's some kind of . . . ruffian, but I don't understand it." Betty shook her head. She reached for one of the remaining squares of plain brownie, some crumbs dropping onto the table. "Gosh, I'm hungry tonight."

"I wonder why." Luisa snorted, stifling a giggle.

"That man has a stick up his you-know-what," Ida said, frowning. "One time he gave me a lecture because I was parked on Shoreline Street for three minutes past my ticket. I said I thought he would have more important things to do than to issue parking fines to old women."

"Not to mention that they should never have implemented timed parking spots, anyway. At least not in the off-season," Lawrence grumbled.

*That's* the kind of town we were—where parking restrictions were the biggest issue we had to worry about. Not murders!

"She will be fine." Luisa patted my arm, her dark brown eyes crinkled with concern. "And if the chief does not come to his senses, I know a guy."

Ever since I was a kid there'd been a running gag about Luisa's second husband being a mobster, which I'm sure was nothing more than a story.

At least, I assumed it was a story.

I tried to muster a smile and failed. "This is all my fault. I should have walked away from Brendan the second I saw him! He was trouble personified from the first day of elementary school and he's only gotten worse with age."

I felt guilty the second the words popped out of my mouth, because Brendan wouldn't be aging any more. Really, even though I didn't like the guy, his younger sister Andrea had always been nice to me. And their parents, while they perhaps hadn't done the best job wrangling their difficult son, were also polite, respectful folks who contributed to the town. I felt sorry for them.

"It is absolutely *not* your fault," Grandma Rose said resolutely. The color had returned to her cheeks with a hot cup of tea and now, instead of worried, she appeared angry. "I don't know who Chief Gladwell thinks he is—"

Her words were cut short by the sound of a car door slamming in the driveway, followed by the distinct slap of flip-flops and the jingle of keys. I put my tea down and rushed to the door, heart in my throat. I yanked it open before Dawn had a chance to get her key in the lock.

She looked like she'd aged a decade in two hours.

Dark circles ringed her blue eyes, giving her skin an almost bruise-like appearance, and her dark purple hair was ruffled as though she'd run her hands through it repeatedly. Nobody said a word as she walked through the front door. You could have heard a pin drop.

I couldn't take the silence a moment longer. "What did they want?"

Her eyes slid to mine, worry creating fine grooves in her skin. "They wanted to know where I was last night, between the hours of eight and ten."

That must be the window for the time of death. Now I knew why they hadn't wanted to speak to me—I'd been at the police station for the start of that window and then at the bed-and-breakfast until after it. Footage from both places would easily corroborate my story. But knowing I couldn't possibly be a suspect brought me no relief if my aunt was on their list thanks to helping me out.

"And?" I asked. "You were here, right?"

"I came straight here to update your grandmother after you went to the station." She smoothed her hands down the front of her skirt.

"Well, then they can't possibly believe . . ." I shook my head.

"I think everybody should go," Grandma Rose said quietly. "I want a moment alone with my family, please."

A somberness settled over the group, and there was quiet shuffling and whispered reassurances as my grandmother's friends packed themselves up, their night abandoned. Ida was the designated driver and was dropping the others home. Since she had only eaten the plain brownies, there was no need for us to call a cab. Betty came past and gave me a big squeeze, the scent of rose and violet perfume wrapping around me like a fluffy pink blanket.

"You can call me for anything, okay?" she said. "Especially if that chief does anything stupid. I have the means to help."

I didn't know what she meant exactly, but I was momentarily comforted by the fierce tone of her voice. My grandmother's friends were a tight group and they had all seen one another through a lot. Ida gave me a wordless hug on her way out and Luisa followed, pausing to pat me on the shoulder.

"I'll make you a lasagna," she declared.

As the group filtered through the doorway, I caught Lawrence looking at my grandmother, his eyes brimming with worry. But Grandma Rose was doing what she did best in a time of crisis—drawing her shoulders back and keeping her chin high and telling the world that nothing would keep her down. I remember her looking that way at my grandfather's funeral, only crying once she was home and her bedroom door was shut. She was the rock of this family. *My* rock.

As the front door closed with a soft click, and footsteps headed down the driveway, I turned to my aunt. "Tell us everything."

"A detective was running the interview, but Chief Gladwell was there." She walked over to the couch and flopped down. "They asked me how I felt after seeing Brendan grabbing at you and I told them I was furious, naturally."

Grandma Rose's lips tightened and she came to stand beside me, looping her arm through mine. "Surely that's not cause to be a murder suspect."

"Uh no." Dawn sighed. "That would be due to the fact that the murder weapon has my initials on it."

"What?" I squeaked.

"They showed me. It was a pocketknife with the initials DB engraved on the side, but I don't think they believed me when I said I'd never seen it before."

"That's pure coincidence. How can they make you a suspect because of something so circumstantial?" My voice climbed higher with each word, and Grandma Rose squeezed my arm. I drew in a deep breath to settle myself. "How many people have the initials DB anyway? There's probably dozens of people in town and that's only *if* it was some who lived here."

"It's not so much a question of how many people have those initials, but how many people have those initials *and* had a run-in with the victim the night he was murdered *and* have motive to kill him."

"You don't have motive." I shook my head.

My aunt could certainly be described as "passionate" or even "fiery" by some people, but killing a person in cold blood? No way.

"He tried to hurt you, Chloe," she said softly. "And the chief says you showed him an anonymous threatening text that you received after the incident."

Grandma Rose's head whipped toward me. "You never mentioned that."

"I didn't feel the need to," I replied defensively. "Especially not after . . ."

As of this morning, Brendan Chalmers was no longer a threat to me. But from the chief and the detective's eyes . . . yeah, protecting a family member probably *did* seem like motive.

"Well, Detective Alvarez was under the assumption I *had* seen it, because what reason would you have to hide anything from me? She questioned me extensively about how close we are and whether I felt responsible for protecting you." She lifted one shoulder into a tired shrug. "Therefore, I'm a suspect."

"A suspect or *the* suspect?" The distinction was important. Were Detective Alvarez and Chief Gladwell simply doing their jobs by looking at anyone and everyone who might have a reason to hurt Brendan Chalmers? Or had they decided my aunt was an easy target?

Dawn scrubbed a hand over her face. "I honestly don't know."

A hard lump settled into the pit of my stomach, but I tried my best to ignore it. I wouldn't help my aunt by freaking out or overreacting to anything. The police were simply doing their jobs. Someone had murdered a man and they were turning over all the rocks required to find out who did it. In theory, it was a positive.

I simply had to hope that they had plenty of other rocks to look under.

The following day, the Barnes family behaved how we always did in a crisis—we got on with life. Because what better way was there to keep your mind off things, than getting shiz done? Nothing. I may dabble in special brownies from time to time, but productivity was my true drug of choice and it was absolutely a family activity.

Grandma Rose had an appointment at the nail salon, and then she was due to pay a visit to a friend of hers who lived nearby. Dawn and I spent the morning at Bean and Gone, going through ideas for the weed café, including walking through all the topics she'd researched—such as the best way to obtain cannabis for commercial use, what licenses we would need to serve it, and everything we needed to finish fitting out the café itself.

By the end of the discussion, I'd had three cups of coffee and my head was spinning. We'd sketched out the broad strokes of our business plan and familiarized ourselves with the license application process. It was overwhelming and exciting, and I felt like everything was moving so fast. I wasn't the kind of person who made decisions on a whim . . . at least, not until recently.

But along with the enthusiasm from my grandmother and her friends, as well as Sabrina telling me I would be hopping on a hot trend, my gut was telling me this was the right thing to do. Go big or go home, as they say.

*You already took the "go home" option. Now it's time to go big.*

"Are you really sure you want to put all your money into this business?" I asked my aunt as we walked out of Bean and Gone. I noticed I had some powdered sugar on my T-shirt from the almond cookies I'd eaten, and I dusted the white particles off with my hand. "I mean, I have a bit to contribute given I'd been saving for a wedding and all . . ."

My bank account was healthier than ever, in fact. I'd sold everything I owned in Paris, which had more than covered the airfare back to the States, and since I was living rent-free in my childhood home, I hadn't touched the little nest-egg that was supposed to fund my future with Jules. We'd been planning a big celebration with a honeymoon in Cinque Terre, and I'd squirrelled away every spare cent I had.

But I still wouldn't have been able to start a business on a whim without *some* financial backing.

"But it's a big ask," I finished.

"Well, technically you didn't ask. *I* suggested." She smiled. "And I might have bounced around a bit in my life, but I never had anyone to spend my money on."

A look of fleeting emotion flashed across her face, but it was gone before I could decipher what she was feeling.

"It means the world to be able to help you build something wonderful," she said, touching my arm. "Besides, I figure if I invest in you financially then you'll feel obligated to stay and look after me when I get old."

I snorted, knowing she was joking. Mostly. "Very manipulative."

"You say manipulative and I say . . ." She waved her hand around in an exuberant way. "Proactive."

Despite Aunt Dawn appearing to be her usual upbeat self, I knew her better than most people and was, therefore, able to detect the subtle signs that she wasn't taking yesterday's events as lightly as it seemed. Dark shadows peeked through under her eyes, not quite hidden by her concealer and heavy eyeliner. The corners of her mouth drooped when she thought no one was looking, and she'd been playing with the pendant around her neck more than usual.

I wanted to ask her if she was okay, but I'd already asked three times and gotten nothing out of her.

"Come on," she said. "Stop trying to figure out how you can chicken out of this."

My mouth popped open. "I am *not* trying to figure out how to chicken out of this! I'm just . . ."

My aunt raised an eyebrow.

"I think it's wise to anticipate risks and problems." Ah, I sounded mature rather than scared. *Good work, brain.* "And that means making sure that my business partner isn't having second thoughts."

"Business partner." She fluffed out her purple hair. "I like the sound of that."

"We'll need to put a plan together so we can apply for a loan," I said. "It could take more than a month to have it approved. What are we going to do about the café in the meantime?"

Aunt Dawn might joke about me wanting to chicken out, but after only one visit I'd grown attached to the space. I was already sketching in the details of how it would look and smell, of how customers would line up around the block to taste my creations. It was all too easy to fantasize, and this building was the *perfect* place to make those fantasies a reality.

Besides, in order to file for the license required to sell products containing cannabis we needed to supply a business address.

"When I spoke with Diane, she said we could do a short-term lease to cover the period of the loan and license approval processes, with an option that allows us to move into a longer-term lease when we get the green light," Dawn said. Diane was the woman who ran one of the local real estate offices and she and my aunt had been friends for many years. "Apparently having 'pop-ups' is all the rage, so they've done a number of these short contracts recently and she managed to convince the owners of the building to sign off."

"And what happens if we don't get the loan? Or the license?" I wrung my hands. I'd never done anything so grown-up like getting a loan before. Well, other than my student loans. But this felt different. "They *could* say no."

"Then I'll have lost what we paid for the short-term lease and Diane will be pissed at me." Dawn grinned. "But they're not going to say no. Everything we brainstormed this morning is fantastic and the data doesn't lie. This industry is growing like weeds. Get it?"

I couldn't help but laugh at her cheesy pun. "Very funny."

"Between the capital I'm willing to invest and your great ideas and experience . . ." She linked her arm through mine and pulled me close, bringing the scent of her rose and patchouli perfume to my nose. "It's a recipe for success."

"I admire your confidence," I said as we started in the direction of the real estate office. "I wish I had more of that myself."

"It comes with age, girlie. And I'm happy to sound like a broken record telling you how great you are." She gave me a squeeze. "Never doubt yourself, Chloe. Never ever."

A little bell tinkled overhead as we entered the real estate office. The space was bright and airy, mostly decorated in white and silver with a touch of bright yellow in the throw cushions dotting the couch by the reception desk, and in a vase of sunflowers sitting on one of the tables.

"Am I looking at Azalea Bay's newest business superstars?" Diane came out of one of the glass-fronted offices with a big smile on her face. She had frizzy hair and wore a pantsuit in a retina-searing green the approximate shade of Mike from *Monsters, Inc.* "I sure hope so!"

"So do we," I replied with a nervous laugh.

"It's wonderful to see you again, Chloe." Diane came over and kissed me on both cheeks in a sensory overload of expensive floral perfume, wild hair and large tinkling earrings. It was easy to see why she and my aunt got along—they were both confident, vibrant women in their fifties who'd chosen adventure and business over building a family. "We're so glad you're home. Frankly, this place needs someone to shake things up. We've got the same old people making the same old things. It's time for something fresh and new."

I liked the "same old" aspect of my hometown, in truth. There was comfort in sameness and predictability—a comfort which I felt like I needed with all the recent upheaval in my life. But at the same time, nobody ever found success doing the same thing everyone else was doing. As much as I hated to be the center of attention, opening a weed café would make me stand out . . . and for business, that was a positive.

"Not everybody likes fresh and new," a voice grumbled from a desk nearby. An older man with gray hair meticulously combed over a bald patch even bigger than I remembered sat at a desk that was devoid of any personal effects.

"Nice to see you, Mr. Bottom," I said politely, shooting my aunt a look when she rolled her eyes.

Bertram Bottom was the epitome of "old man yells at cloud"— if there was something insignificant for him to be upset by, he was. One time, he requested that we chop down a whole tree in front of Grandma Rose's house because he happened to slip on a twig that had fallen onto the sidewalk. Needless to say, my grandmother held her ground and the tree stayed. But Bertram Bottom had hated us ever since.

"I would say the same, Miss Barnes. But I hear you are bringing our wholesome town into disrepute with your drug café."

How had word gotten out already? Panic seized my stomach. I hadn't even secured the loan, let alone outfitted the shop or tested many recipes. My fear of the speed at which things were moving rushed to the surface, filling my face with warm, prickly shame. What if the café was a failure before I could even open its doors and the whole town knew I'd fallen flat on my face?

As soon as the question came to fruition in my mind, I heard the voices of Grandma Rose and Aunt Dawn and Sabrina all encouraging me. Yes, there would be naysayers like the curmudgeonly Bertram Bottom, but I had to try. Because if I didn't, what would become of me?

I would be a hack who'd proved her critics right by doing nothing and being nothing.

"Cannabis café," I corrected him firmly. "Cannabis is an effective relaxant and can be a wonderful remedy for stress levels, as it elevates one's mood. You might enjoy that aspect."

Beside me Aunt Dawn snorted and didn't even bother attempting to hide her amusement.

"We support all types of legal businesses," Diane said, her tone sharp as she looked at her employee.

Bertram made a sound of disgust and turned back to his computer, shaking his head and muttering under his breath. "What has this world come to?"

"I'm thrilled for you, Chloe. It's wonderful to see young, ambitious people using their talents here in town. It stops us from feeling stale. And," Diane continued, jabbing her finger into the air, "it's good for tourism, which means it's good for all of us. Now, step into my office and we can go through the paperwork for the short-term lease."

By the time we were done with the paperwork, I was giddy with excitement. It was clear why Diane owned the premier real estate business in Azalea Bay, even though there were several others around—her infectious enthusiasm could make even the most hardened cynic sign their life away, because there was nothing inauthentic about it. She genuinely loved this town and wanted to see it and its residents thrive.

"Shall we walk over together? I was planning to pop out for a bit anyway," Diane said, handing me a set of keys.

They felt weighty in my hands. Resonant. I had approached

a fork in the road of my life, and now I was striding down one path. "Sure."

I was grateful to see that Bertram Bottom had left the office, so I didn't have to look at his sneering face during this important moment. Diane let her assistant know she would be back soon, and then we headed out into the mild, sunny air.

"How are you feeling?" Dawn asked as we walked the short few blocks to where our new business would be located.

"Nervous, excited, anxious, eager . . . did I mention I'm nervous?" The words flooded out of me, a giddy laugh following close behind.

"That's because you want everything to be perfect and it won't be. We'll make mistakes along the way, but any time we do we'll learn and get better." Dawn nodded. "Besides, *how* many people do you know in the restaurant industry?"

"Tons," I admitted. If I had any questions at all about how to run an effective food business, then there were at least fifteen to twenty people whom I could call for advice. In fact, I'd left Paris with a fistful of favors I could cash in, too. "That's a really good point."

My nerves immediately eased. She was totally right. My last boss, Claude, had been a huge supporter of me going out on my own at some point, and he'd explicitly told me that whenever I was ready he would make sure I started on the right foot.

As we approached, my stomach fluttered with excitement. I was already working through an idea for a "flight" of miniature macarons featuring different buttercream centers made with cannabutter. I could have some flavors lean into the herbaceous nature of the cannabis—options for aromatic ingredients like lavender, thyme or rosemary abounded—or I could use warm, rich flavors to mask it—like salted caramel, cinnamon, ginger or dark chocolate.

*You're doing the right thing.*

I almost skipped as we got to the corner where my café would be, the keys jingling in my hand. Diane bid us good luck, telling me she wanted to know the second we got our loan and license approvals. My face was stretched wide with a big grin as I crossed the street, eager to get inside the shop and have another look around. But as we got closer, I noticed a white piece of paper taped to the window and the smile dropped off my face.

In scrawled red letters was the word "murderer."

# CHAPTER 7

I snatched the piece of paper off the door, looking around to see if anyone was watching. Nobody was. The word was written in red marker, but there was nothing distinct about the block lettering or the paper, which appeared to have been torn off a spiral-bound notebook.

"What was that?" Dawn frowned and she reached for the paper, but I kept it away from her. "Give it to me, Chloe. I'm not playing."

I sighed and let her have it. The blood drained out of her face, leaving her looking hollowed out like she'd been last night. Her lips pursed and she crumpled the paper in her fist.

"It's probably someone playing a prank," I said, knowing the suggestion was weak. "Who even knows this is our shop?"

"I might have told a few people we were looking to rent it," she admitted.

"Aunt Dawn!" She was an incredible woman, but when she got excited about something there was no hope of her keeping it secret.

She folded her arms defensively across her chest, trapping some of the billowing fabric from her orange and white tie-dye blouse. "What's wrong with that?"

"I don't want the whole town knowing about our business until I'm sure we can open our doors. What if it falls through?" I shook my head. Right now, my fear of public failure wasn't the important thing here. It was the fact that someone was looking to spread a rumor that we were responsible for Brendan's death. "Never mind. I can't believe someone would think we were involved."

"Not *we*, darling. Me." She sighed. "Although I have to say Dawn Barnes, Murderess of Azalea Bay, has quite a ring to it."

I could tell she was trying not to let on how worried she was, but I knew better than to fall for her self-deprecating banter. She was seriously concerned. With a shaking hand, I unlocked the door to the shop and we went inside.

"Even putting aside *why* someone might think you capable of such a thing, I'd like to know how anyone even knows you're a suspect," I said, placing my purse on the unfinished serving counter. Word had gotten around that Brendan Chalmers's untimely death was the cause of all the police tape and flashing lights at the park, but how would anyone know who was on the suspect list?

"I saw Starr walking her dog past the police station when I got out of the car with Detective Alvarez and Chief Gladwell," Dawn replied.

"Great. Now the whole world probably knows you were there." My fists clenched by my side. "People like Starr make me so mad. Why can't everyone mind their own freaking business?"

"Because some people have nothing in their own lives to keep them occupied."

"That doesn't give them license to scrutinize us." I harrumphed.

"Let it go, Chloe." My aunt slung her arm around my shoulders. "I'm sure this will all blow over once they get further into the investigation."

But her words did little to reassure me. As much as Chief Gladwell had years of experience under his belt, how many homicide investigations had he been part of? It wasn't like people were murdered in our little seaside town all that often. In fact, the biggest killer around here was the riptide that caught swimmers unaware when they drifted beyond the flags or went out against the warnings. There was also a fatal shark attack when I was in high school, where a surfer was bitten by a great white. But that was it.

Was Chief Gladwell up to the task? What if the police department had pressure from the local media and Brendan's family to get the case closed quickly, and my aunt ended up as the scapegoat?

I would drive myself crazy with wondering and the best cure for that was keeping busy.

"What do you think we can do in here during the short-term lease?" I asked, looking around. "I mean, it seems risky to go ahead with furnishing the place until we know for sure we're approved for both the loan and license."

"I agree." Dawn looked relieved that I'd changed the topic of conversation. "But we can clean the place up."

I nodded. It was dusty as heck and there were small piles of sawdust dotting the floor. It looked like someone had come in on a rainy day and large, muddy footprints were tracked through the open space I envisaged as the dine-in area.

"Maybe we can clean and prime the walls, too," I suggested. The warm peach paint was too bright for my personal aesthetic, and it had been scuffed in several places. "This color has to go."

"There's plenty for us to do. Why don't we take a trip over to the hardware store for supplies? Then we can head home, change into something more appropriate for cleaning work, and come back."

"Sounds great to me."

I would try to put the awful note out of my mind, but something told me that the gossip wheels were turning in Azalea Bay, and if Starr Bright was involved, then I could only imagine just how far word had spread. There *had* to be other suspects, surely? Because if the police were coming up empty, that was *not* good news. Especially not for my aunt.

Later that day my muscles ached from sweeping, dusting and scrubbing, but the shop was already looking so much better. The job was far from done, but an afternoon of hard work had helped ease the stress. There was nothing like getting one's hands dirty to quiet the mind, in my opinion. For the evening I had an invite from Sabrina to join her Dungeons and Dragons group, who were meeting at one of the member's houses. She picked me up on the way over, and riding shotgun in her car reminded me of old times rolling the windows down, blasting Lady Gaga and singing at the top of our lungs.

"I need to save my voice," Sabrina said, reaching for the volume knob and turning Lady Gaga down after we'd belted out "Poker Face." "Being a DM means a lot of talking."

"I expected you to be dressed a little different for being a dungeon master," I teased, looking over at Sabrina's graphic tee—which was black with a picture of a multisided die with the number 20 in the middle—and jeans. It was chilly enough that she'd thrown a leather jacket over the top, giving her a tough edge, which matched perfectly with her unruly dark hair and burgundy lipstick. "Where's the chains and studs and patent leather corset, huh? And I don't see a whip anywhere."

She laughed. "I'm sure Cal would *love* that."

Cal—short for Calix—was Sabrina's boyfriend. They'd met at Comic-Con a few years ago when they'd been cosplaying characters with a romantic history. After posing for photos together, they'd gone for a drink and talked all night. Only a month later he'd moved to Azalea Bay to be with her—it was love at first con! He was a computer programmer by day and avid D&D player by night. I'd only ever seen him a handful of times when he popped his head over Sabrina's shoulder to say hello during one of our Zoom calls. I liked his vibe instantly and he'd struck me as friendly and laidback.

"I'm excited to meet him in person," I said, looking out the window as the houses rolled past. It was getting dark and a warm glow emanated from most front windows. "I'm glad you've found someone who's into all the same things that you are."

"Comic-Con is a great place to find a nerdy boyfriend." Sabrina grinned. "But I will try not to be that awful person who gushes over their partner ad nauseam."

"Gush away," I replied, waving my hand. "I'm glad you're happy."

For a moment Sabrina didn't say anything. The streetlights flickered over her face as she kept her eyes on the road, but I could tell she was toiling with something in her head.

"I'm not bitter toward people in love just because my relationship crashed and burned," I said. "You should know me better than that."

"Always a romantic, even when things don't go your way. I love that about you."

"I might be a romantic at heart, but I'm *not* looking for a romance right now. That's for sure."

My mind flicked to Jake for a moment and I remembered the way my heart had skipped a beat when we made eye contact in his driveway. I hadn't seen him since we'd parted ways after chatting with Detective Alvarez, which was probably for the best.

Sabrina pulled her car to a stop in front of a simple single-story bungalow. There were three cars parked in the driveway and I could see figures moving inside through the front window. As I got out of the car, I caught a whiff of tangy ocean air mixed with the fresh, slightly resinous and sweetly balsamic scent of cypress trees. Lord, how I'd missed that smell these last five years. I sucked it in, filling my nose with the familiar aroma and letting it remind me I was truly home.

We walked up the driveway, shuffling between parked cars and some overgrown bushes. I ran my fingers through my hair, feeling a little self-conscious that I hadn't dressed up more. I'd been so tired after the cleaning session that I only threw on a loose pink tie-dyed T-shirt dress, a denim jacket and a pair of white sneakers, letting my hair air dry and skipping makeup altogether.

I couldn't remember the last time I'd been to a social event. Back in Paris, the most social part of my week was "family meal" before the restaurant opened, where I'd sit and eat and chat with colleagues. But restaurant hours were unsociable, and Jules and I worked late and slept late, sometimes not leaving the house at all during the day. Instead, we'd make love and eat amazing cheese and bread in bed.

A lump caught in the back of my throat and I banished the memory from my mind. I would *not* be a sad sack tonight. Pulling my shoulders back, I pasted on a bright smile as the front door opened and a big bear of a man filled the doorway.

"Come here, asteráki mou." Cal pulled Sabrina toward him and the smile that lit her face struck me in the chest. I knew that smile and had worn it myself at one time.

"Hmm. I love it when you speak Greek to me," she murmured, pressing up on her toes and pecking his cheek.

"And you must be Chloe. We're so happy to have you join us." Cal's smile was so genuine it immediately lifted my reservations about crashing their game night.

"It's great to finally meet you in person."

I stuck a hand out to shake his, but he laughed and pulled me in for a hug. "It's great to meet you, too. We usually grab a drink and a bite to eat before we get started, so that should give you a chance to get to know everyone. And don't worry about not knowing the rules."

"I told Sabrina I would be observing tonight," I replied, as Sabrina and I followed him inside.

"I give it one session before you want to jump in." She laughed. "It's addictive."

"Let me introduce you around." Cal motioned for me to follow him into a cozy living room, where several people were standing around a table filled with bowls of chips, a platter of meat and cheese, and beer bottles chilling in a bucket filled with ice. "Everyone, please welcome Chloe Barnes. She's new to Dungeons and Dragons."

The group smiled and waved.

"This is Matt Wilson and Ben Wong," Cal said, motioning to two men. Matt was tall and roguish, with floppy blond hair, an easy smile and a full arm of tattoos. He wore a leather vest over a white T-shirt and jeans with rips in the knees. Ben, on the other hand, wore a pressed blue button-down and tan slacks, and had his jet-black hair neatly styled. "They both work in the video game industry."

"G'day." Matt stuck a hand out and I shook it. "Nice to meet you, Chloe."

I spotted the Australian accent almost immediately, as I'd worked with an Aussie in one of my earlier jobs after graduating from Le Cordon Bleu. I shook hands with Ben as well. "Lovely to meet you both. The video game industry, huh? That sounds exciting."

"Matt's job is exciting. Mine, not so much," Ben said with a warm smile. "He composes soundtracks for games and gets to spend his days making music. I test for bugs."

"No point having a great soundtrack if the game is unplayable." Matt slung an arm around Ben's shoulder and looked at him adoringly. "Your job is *way* more important than mine."

"It sounds like they're both very important jobs." They made such a cute couple and it warmed my heart.

"And these two fine people are Archie Schwartz and Erica

Simms," Cal said, indicating toward the two other people in the room—a tall, lanky guy with wire-rimmed glasses and a petite woman with pixie-cut blond hair.

"Of course I remember Erica." I grinned, relieved to see a familiar face. "Mrs. Simms was my softball coach back in the day. It's good to see you."

Erica was two or three years behind me in school, but she used to attend all the softball practice sessions and matches with her mom. My time in the sport was short-lived—I wasn't good at hitting, catching *or* running, sadly—but I remembered her having the same short, almost spiky blond hair and big eyes.

"Nice to see you, too. And I feel like I need to clarify that we're not a couple," Erica said with a smile, nodding toward Archie.

"Good call. You know how the rumor mill works around here," Archie joked.

Erica nodded. "We've got enough lovebirds in this group as it is."

"Well, I can help to even things out," I joked back. "One more for the singles team."

"That will make a team of two, then. I'm married, but my wife is home with the kids tonight," Archie said with a smile, as he reached for a bottle of Corona. "Beer?"

"Yes, please." I took it readily, happy for a little liquid courage to ease my shyness.

It seemed like everyone here had been friends for a long time or, at the very least, that they were a highly compatible group. I got no sense of tension or in-fighting, and I felt good about my decision to come along. The fact was, apart from Sabrina, I didn't have a lot of friends in Azalea Bay. I'd been shy in high school and the small group of friends I *did* have were now dispersed. Two had moved to other parts of the country after college and another, like me, had done a stint overseas. Only she hadn't returned.

Sabrina was the sole person from our friendship group who'd stayed in Azalea Bay this whole time.

"What do you do for work?" I asked, drawing on one of several pre-canned topics I kept up my sleeve for small talk.

"I'm the HR manager at Azalea Bay Furniture Removals," Archie said. "Well, actually I'm the *entire* HR team. Kind of like a one-man-band situation."

I tried not to let the surprise show on my face. He was a colleague of Brendan's, emphasis on the *was*. I noticed then that Archie's gaze flicked over to Erica, and something about her expression seemed a little off. Her lips tightened and her eyes became cold for a second.

"I *used* to be an employee of Azalea Bay Furniture Removals," she said, her voice tight.

*Oh yeah. Sabrina mentioned Brendan had gotten one of her D&D pals fired.*

Sabrina and Cal were chatting with Matt and Ben, and they appeared oblivious to our conversation. Unable to curb my curiosity, I asked innocently, "But you left?"

"I was fired." She looked over at Archie, her expression softening. "Don't worry, I don't blame you. You were only following orders."

Archie raked a hand through his hair and let out a sigh. I could tell he wasn't comfortable with the topic at hand, but then suddenly his expression shifted and I felt his intelligent eyes lock onto me. "Wait, Chloe Barnes. Why do I know that name?"

"I grew up here." I pegged Archie to be a good six or seven years older than me, so we probably hadn't been in school at the same time if he was an Azalea Bay lifer. I scanned my memory for his surname, but came up empty. It might be a small town, but there were plenty of people who came and went—the tourism town attracted some and repelled others. The lifestyle wasn't for everyone. "But I moved away for college and then lived overseas for five years."

"I moved here about eight years ago, after I met my wife. Elena Nowak? Well, now she's Elena Schwartz."

"Oh, I know the Nowak family." I nodded. "They lived down the street from us."

"You're not thinking of . . ." Erica's eyes darted to Archie and something passed between them. They clearly had the kind of friendship where things could be communicated without the use of words.

"Oh." He blinked, his eyes widening. "Right."

I let out a nervous laugh as unease coiled in my gut. "Now you have to say what you're thinking."

"You found . . ." Archie swallowed. "You were one of the people who found Brendan Chalmers's body, right?"

"News really does travel fast here." I took a swig of my beer, trying to distract my senses from remembering the pale, clammy look of his skin and the dried blood caked around the knife embedded in his neck. "Technically, someone else found him and when they screamed, I came to their aid."

"How awful." Archie shook his head and beside him, Erica made a snorting sound as she dug her hand into one of the bowls on the table and came up with some chips.

"I know it's callous for me to say this, but good riddance." She popped a chip into her mouth and chewed. "Brendan Chalmers was a blight on this town."

Archie frowned and looked like he was about to say something that might shut her down, so I interjected, "Why do you say that?"

"He was the one who got me fired." Her face—which a moment ago had been open and happy—turned dark. "I was kicking his butt in the company 'employee of the month' competition and he hated being beaten, especially by a woman. He thought I didn't belong there, simply because I couldn't lift a fridge on my own. But if it wasn't for me, there would have been way more broken items. I took care of the customers' things when he wanted to rush through jobs. I reassured the customers that we would treat their items like they were our own."

"And he thought you slowed him down?"

"Yep. But the customers always mentioned me in their feedback—what a great job I did and how I made them feel comfortable." Pride shone in her eyes. "But when it looked like I was going to beat him, he decided to take matters into his own hands by planting one of the customer's items in my bag."

"What?" I gasped. Archie looked at the ground and shook his head.

"It was an heirloom item—some little crystal figurine that had belonged to the woman's great-grandmother. Brendan planted it in my bag and then made sure the woman knew it was missing, so we would have to do an inspection with the boss. But he didn't believe me when I said I didn't take it."

"Ross knows you better than that," Archie said. I could see the guilt written all over his face—as HR manager, he was probably the one who had to do the firing. "I tried to talk to him. The guy wouldn't listen to reason."

"It's not your fault." Erica reached behind her head and messed with some of the short strands of her hair, a nervous habit no doubt. "I mean, it's not like I thought furniture removal was what I wanted to do with my life. But now word has gotten around that I was fired and . . ."

My heart clenched as I saw the worry and frustration streak across her face.

"I've applied for a bunch of jobs and they all seem to have better candidates than me, even though two of them reposted the job ad." She tossed her hands in the air. "So, am I sorry that Brendan is dead? Not even a little bit."

"You should be careful where you say that," Archie advised, placing a protective hand on her shoulder. "You don't want anyone thinking you might have done it."

Erica didn't say anything in response. Was it strange that she chose not to clarify that she hadn't done it? Perhaps it was simply because her friends would never suspect her of such a thing. But she had motive.

Brendan's actions had caused her to not only lose her job, but prevent her from finding other work. Financial pressures would have to be mounting. Azalea Bay was a small town, but like in most places across the country rent was going up, bills were getting more expensive.

And revenge was a heck of a motive for murder.

# CHAPTER 8

The following morning, I headed out to do some research for my business plan. Aunt Dawn was taking Grandma Rose to her next round of chemo infusions and I'd offered to go, but was promptly told that I wasn't needed. My grandmother was clearly trying to shield me, but it didn't make me worry any less. The cancer was in her lymph nodes as well as her breast, which was why they had suggested chemo rather than a straight lumpectomy or mastectomy.

I couldn't even think about losing her.

Without my mother, Grandma Rose and Aunt Dawn were all I'd ever had. We were the three musketeers. A flock of our own making. I loved these women with all my heart. For Grandma Rose's sake, I had to be strong. And to me, strong meant working.

I set off in the morning to track down the closest cannabis dispensary. There wasn't one located directly in Azalea Bay, but a short drive to a nearby town would do the trick. However, I hit a snag before I'd even left the driveway. My grandmother's car, which she barely ever drove and thus was mine to use, wouldn't start. The powder-blue Fiat 500—which we jokingly called the Jellybean—was almost cartoonishly small, but Grandma Rose had never been a confident driver and you could throw this thing sideways into a parking spot and it would still fit. Too bad the engine was less reliable than a politician's promise.

I turned the key in the engine, groaning when it made a wheezing noise that made it sound like it had smoked too many cigarettes. I tried again. No dice.

A knock on my window startled me and I whipped around to see Jake standing outside, a crooked smile on his face and his dimple threatening to turn me into a pile of goo. He looked like he was going somewhere nice, because he had a light blue shirt on with the sleeves rolled back and a pair of dark jeans with a tan leather belt at his waist.

I rolled the window down. "Uh, hi."

"Hey." He leaned on the window and I caught a whiff of a delicious, light cologne—citrus notes, lemon perhaps, and thyme. Maybe a little mint. "Having some trouble there?"

"You could say that." I sighed. "The Jellybean is giving up on me."

"The Jellybean?" He cocked his head, causing dark hair to flop over his forehead and into his hazel eyes. He scraped the strands back with one sweeping movement.

"She's small and colorful, like a jellybean." I cringed. Was it weird to name your car?

"Cute." Jake nodded. "Do me a favor and tell me what the clock says."

I glanced over at it. "It says twelve fifteen."

Which was wrong, because it had only just gone ten a.m.

"Hmm sounds like a battery issue. Put the key in the run position and flick the headlights on."

I did what he asked and noticed the lights on the clock dimmed in response. "Weird."

"It's common for a battery to do that when it's about to die," he said. "Want me to take a peek under the hood?"

"Only if you have time. It looks like you've got somewhere to be." I indicated to his put-together outfit. "And I'd hate to make you late."

"I've *been* out somewhere already and I'm actually free all day now." His smile widened and the dimple in his cheek deepened. Was it suddenly hot in the car? I glanced at the air-conditioning button but figured it probably wouldn't work what with the car not starting. "Pop her open."

I did and got out of the car while he had a look around. It gave me a moment to observe Jake, and there was something methodical about the way he checked the engine. His fingers drifted from one part to another, looking for things that were totally foreign to me, and asking questions I didn't really know how to answer.

"The battery is old," he said. "Generally, they last about four or five years, and this one is close to six. So that's probably the culprit, but I'd suggest having the timing belt looked at as well. If that fails it can really screw up the engine and it's an expensive fix. When was the last time it was properly serviced?"

I shrugged. "No idea. It's my grandma's car and she doesn't drive much these days. Her eyesight is not so good, especially in the dark."

He nodded. "Does she have roadside assistance?"

I cringed. "I swear, I do know *some* things but not anything about this car, apparently. She's out and she never turns her phone on."

Not only that, but I didn't want to bother her about something trivial while she was getting her treatment.

"I guess I'm stuck here for the day." I sighed. I had really wanted to get out and distract myself from everything going on, but it seemed like fate had other plans. "It's fine. I can figure it out later."

"Or I could give you a jump start and get you to the mechanic shop off Shoreline. You never know when you might need a working vehicle if there's an emergency or something, and the guys there are good. They'll get the Jellybean up and running in no time," he said. "And then maybe I could take you wherever you were planning to go?"

I looked at Jake. *Really* looked at him. Was he genuinely a nice guy or was there something else going on here? I mean, what motive could he possibly have to be so darn chipper and helpful?

"That's a way more skeptical expression than I was hoping for," he said with yet another delightfully lopsided smile.

"Sorry, it's been a long . . . couple of months." I let out a breath. "And you're a relative stranger who's being super nice and for some reason my brain is trying to come up with all the ulterior motives you might have for being so sweet."

"You've been away from small-town life for too long." He laughed and the sound was rich and deep, like dark chocolate ganache and blackberries and truffle. "Although you did call me sweet, so it's not all bad."

There was something playful in his voice, like he didn't take himself or the world too seriously. Which made him the polar opposite of me . . . and of Jules. For some reason, I found that utterly refreshing and it made my heart thud a little harder in my chest. In recent times, life had made me wary of people and things who seemed too good to be true.

But something in my gut told me I could trust this man—at least for an afternoon.

"I guess I did call you sweet," I said, a warm bubble growing in my chest and a flush rising up into my cheeks. "And if you don't have anything better to do with your day, then I would be super grateful for a lift."

His eyes sparkled. "I'll go get my jumper cables."

The Jellybean got going with some assistance from Jake and he followed me to the mechanic shop in his own car, a simple silver sedan and not the impressive-looking vintage car I'd seen him tinkering with in his garage. After I'd left the Jellybean to get fixed, we punched the address for the Greener Pastures dispensary into the satnav in his car and set on our way.

"So, a dispensary trip, huh? That's not what I anticipated." He pulled the car away from the side of the street and performed a tight U-turn so we were headed in the right direction.

"I, uh . . ." Well, if he was kind enough to chauffer me around, the least I could do was be honest with him. "My aunt and I are looking to open a cannabis café. This trip is market research."

"Oh." His eyebrows shot up. "How did that come about?"

I laughed. "It's a long story."

"Well, we have exactly . . ." He glanced at the satnav. "Forty-two minutes before we're due to arrive. Can you get the story out in forty-two minutes?"

I couldn't even tell you the amount of dates I'd been on where the guys were more than happy to dominate the conversation, bragging about themselves and barely letting me get a word in, and here was Jake being unexpectedly sweet again.

*This isn't a date.*

Clearly, I needed the reminder.

"How about I give you the abridged version?" I offered. "I trained to be a pastry chef in Paris and I was working my way up in the world. Then plans changed and I had to come home."

"Plans changed?" He glanced at me as we rolled to a stop for a red light.

"My fiancé and I parted ways." Ugh, it sounded so sterile when I said it like that. "He, um . . . he cheated on me. But then I found out I needed to come home to help my grandma. I wasn't sure what I was going to do for work since there aren't any fine-dining restaurants here. My aunt suggested that we go into business together . . . and now we're looking to open a weed café."

Jake blinked. The words had rushed out of my mouth so fast he was probably still catching up.

"My friend Sabrina said the wellness industry is booming, and adding cannabis to high-quality baked goods is a really business-savvy way to stand out," I added, hoping he would focus more on the business aspect of my story than the fact that I'd been cheated on and fled with my tail between my legs. "I couldn't find any other comparable businesses nearby to research. So, I figured dispensaries were the next best thing."

*Take a breath, would you?*

"Smart." He nodded.

"When life gives you lemons, you make tarte au citron, right?" I watched as Azalea Bay rolled on by outside the window, the view of the ocean fading into the background as we drove further inland.

"You have to." There was a seriousness to Jake's words. "You have to find a way to keep going."

"Did something happen that made you leave New York?" I couldn't help myself, the man had snagged my curiosity despite my better judgment.

"You could say that." His eyes flicked to me and then back to the road. "Working on Wall Street takes a toll on a lot of people. Long hours, high stress, impossible targets. It's not healthy. My, uh . . . my best friend had a heart attack at thirty-five."

I gasped. "Oh my gosh, that's so young! Is he okay?"

"Yes, thankfully." Jake nodded. "He ended up quitting the firm where we worked to move back to Nebraska with his family. I stayed on for a while, and then I ended up in the ER one night with palpitations and pain in my chest. I thought I was going to die. Turns out it was a panic attack—I'd never had one before."

"They're awful," I sympathized. "You poor thing."

"It was a much-needed wake-up call," he said resolutely. "I knew it could have just as easily been me in the ER having a cardiac incident and that, if I wasn't careful, some day it *would* be me."

"So you quit and moved here."

He nodded. "Yeah. My gramps was born around here, before the family moved over to the East Coast. He passed some years ago and he left me his 1968 Chevy Camaro, because I've always had an interest in cars. He was a mechanic and I used to help out in his shop for extra cash while I was getting my finance degree."

"And now you're living in the area he's from and working on his car." If I was a character in a Jane Austen novel I would have swooned. A family-oriented guy who loved tradition? Happy sigh.

"I sure am." He nodded. "A decade on Wall Street taught me what was important in life and I wanted to get the hell away from there as much as possible."

"Where's the rest of your family? Are they all still on the East Coast?"

"My parents split when I was in college. My dad and step-mom moved down to Florida when he retired last year. Mom is younger, so she's still working. She moved out to Phoenix a couple years back with her boyfriend, and my sister lives in the UK."

"Wow, you're all spread out."

"Yeah. It meant nothing was tying me to New York and I could go anywhere I wanted, so I came here." He glanced over at me, the edges of his eyes crinkled with a warm smile. "So far, zero regrets."

For some reason, the words made my belly flutter.

*No fluttering allowed. You're taking a break from relationships to focus on building your future.*

I changed the subject again, asking him about the vintage car restoration project and Jake's whole face lit up. He chatted happily, telling me all the things he needed to do to get the car running in tip-top condition and I listened, totally absorbed by his passion and excitement even though cars didn't interest me personally. But I loved people who were obsessed with something as much as I was obsessed with baking.

Eventually we arrived in Twin Parks, the closest town to Azalea Bay that had a dispensary. The main strip was simple, without the beachy touches that I loved so much about my home. But it was pretty and leafy, and I immediately spotted the storefront for Greener Pastures. The sign had neon-green lettering on a black background, with the logo containing the quintessential leaf motif.

Jake parked his car in an empty spot, and we walked toward the dispensary. Inside, the vibe was modern, with sleek white counters and lots of glass. The wall behind the cash register was a reflective black, highlighting the boxes of tinctures, packets of edibles and other cannabis-related tools like pipes, etc. There were space-age-like ordering stations made of glossy white plastic and a waiting area with lime-green plastic chairs and a neon cannabis leaf on the wall.

The only thing I could think was how passionately Grandma Rose would *hate* this place. It was stylish, in its own way, but it was also the antithesis of the warm, inviting and decadent vibe I wanted to create with my café. At least on first glance, it felt like we would be catering to different clientele.

"I'm not planning to let them know about the café," I said to Jake as we looked around. A woman and a man were behind the counter, speaking with a customer. "I just want to see what they offer and how it all works."

"Fair enough. I'll keep my mouth shut." He grinned. "Do you ah . . . partake?"

"I've tried it before," I said, nodding. "I'm not a big user. I'm not a big drinker, either, truth be told. Carbs and butter are my vices of choice."

"Spoken like someone who lived in France." He laughed. "What drew you to the idea of it then? For the business?"

"My grandma uses it for pain relief," I replied. "I don't really want to say more than that, because it's her business. But it's helped her immensely."

"I won't pry," Jake promised.

"Thanks." I looked up at him and placed a hand on his arm. "And thanks for coming to the rescue this morning. The Jellybean would still be sitting like an oversized paperweight in my grandma's driveway if it wasn't for you."

"I'm always happy to help out a neighbor." He winked and I wondered if there was more to it than that.

Before I could analyze him any further, the female dispensary employee came over to us. "Hi there, welcome to Greener Pastures. I'm Cindy and I'll be your budista."

"Oh, like a barista but for weed. Clever." I nodded.

Cindy had long dark hair which was swept back into a ponytail and eyelash extensions that were so big it looked like she could make a breeze every time she blinked. She wore a tight black T-shirt with a green apron over the top, which kind of gave off a slight Starbucks vibe, though she had a leaf embroidered in black at her chest rather than a coffee cup.

"I wish I could claim that little bit of creative genius, but it's a common term in the industry." She smiled and clapped her hands together, showcasing that her long, fake nails were painted green and black to match the store's decor. I appreciated the attention to detail and her dedication to the theme. "Could I see some ID before we get started?"

"Sure." I fished out my driver's license. I still got carded occasionally if I wasn't wearing any makeup. Aunt Dawn said I had a baby face. "Here you go."

"Thank you." She glanced at my ID and then at Jake's. "Great! Were you looking for anything in particular? We've got some new sublingual oils in and a fresh batch of our bestselling pomegranate jelly edibles. We also have a bi-monthly—or *high* monthly, as we like to say—sampler box where we feature designs from local artists and a selection of our most popular products for people who want to try it all. We do the boxes both for CBD-only products and for those who prefer THC."

"Wow." I blinked. "I had no idea there was so much choice." My experience with weed had been limited to the basics, and I could see why Sabrina and Aunt Dawn were so enthused by the possibilities of the industry. In the reading I'd done over the last few days, my mind was buzzing with ideas.

"How about we start with edibles," I said, given that was probably the closest comparison to what I would be doing.

"Sure. Follow me." Cindy led us to a section which contained lots of colorful packets and containers. "We have a great selection here—gummies, soft chews, chocolate, cookies and more. What type of experience are you looking for?"

Hmm, I probably should have thought about how I might answer these questions before I came here, but I'd planned to figure it all out on the drive over. Only, I'd been distracted by Jake.

"Well, I like something to help me relax. I'm not a great sleeper." This was true. The downside of having high ambitions and perfectionistic tendencies was often an inability to shut the mind down at night. I'd suffered with my share of anxiety-induced insomnia over the years.

"Oh, these are great." Cindy plucked a small silver container off the shelf. "They're made with a pure CBD isolate to ensure there's no THC content, *plus* they contain some melatonin, which helps to improve sleep cycles. So, you won't get any kind of high from these, because there are no psychoactive ingredients. But they work a treat if you're struggling to either fall asleep or stay asleep."

Given how restless I'd been the last few months, I would kill for a decent night of shut-eye.

"And what would you recommend for pain relief?" I asked. "My grandmother is suffering with some side effects of a medical treatment, so I want to get some for her as well."

"Oh, I have just the thing. My pops has terrible arthritis and he was in a lot of pain before he started taking these." A wave of emotion washed over Cindy's face and my heart squeezed for her. I knew that feeling—the helplessness that comes with watching a loved one suffer. It was a unique kind of pain. "Let me go grab them for you."

As Cindy headed to a different part of the store, I looked around. There were posters on the wall advertising several different products, including birthday-cake-flavored cookies that were supposedly one of their biggest sellers. I'd grab some of those as well, to test them out and see what other companies were producing.

"Are you from around town or just passing through?" Cindy asked as she brought back a packet of gummies specifically aimed at pain relief. They had several flavors, and I selected the pomegranate ones.

"I'm from Azalea Bay," I replied. Jake had wandered off to inspect some of the art near the shelves with their subscription boxes. "Not too far away."

Cindy's eyes widened. "I heard about the murder there."

"Wow. Word travels fast." I shook my head.

"My cousin lives in Azalea Bay. He *knew* the guy that got . . ." She shuddered. "Not that they were close friends or anything, he was just a client."

I leaned forward on the counter. "Where does your cousin work?"

"At the Iron Works gym. He's a personal trainer."

Would it be weird if I asked what her cousin's name was? He might know something about Brendan outside of what I'd heard about his issues at work. What did I have to lose? It wasn't like I would be coming back here as a frequent customer.

"What's his name? I'm actually looking to get back into the gym." I smiled. "I spent the last few years living in France and it's time to work off those croissants."

If Cindy thought the turn of conversation was weird, she didn't let on. In fact, she was so helpful that she fetched the guy's business card from her purse in the back room. Bless people like her. She returned with the card and passed it to me.

Jay Donaldson, personal trainer and nutrition coach.

Going into a gym was not my idea of fun, but if it might help my aunt then I'd suck it up *and* suck it in.

"Is there anything else I can help you with?" Cindy asked with a bright smile.

"That's everything. Thank you! You've been super helpful."

We moved to the counter so she could cash me out and she sweetly wished my grandmother well with her pain management. In the short time I was in the dispensary the steady flow of people surprised me, not just in terms of the volume that came through but in that no two patrons were alike.

There were customers of all ages, races and persuasions. There was a mother seeking some CBD products to help with her son's anxiety disorder and a man in his thirties who suffered with seizures. There was another guy with long hair who got into a hearty discussion with the other budista about his favorite cannabis strains and the different experiences they provided. He was an artist.

As I walked out of the store, something told me I was onto a very good thing.

# CHAPTER 9

"Hey, uh . . . so there was something I wanted tell you," Jake said as we carried our road trip sustenance to a small round table.

After the trip to the dispensary, we'd decided to stop for a snack. Now we were in one of Twin Parks' cafés, a small place with modest décor and the delicious aroma of coffee beans and freshly baked cookies wafting through the air. I'd ordered a cappuccino and a white chocolate macadamia cookie, and he'd opted for an Americano and a classic chocolate chip.

"Sure." I placed my items down on the table and slid into my seat. "What is it?"

Jake raked a hand through his hair as he took the seat across from me. So far, I'd found him to be warm and open, with a ready smile and crinkle-edged eyes, but right now he could barely look at me. Had the trip to the dispensary made him uncomfortable? He certainly hadn't seemed like it in the store.

"You're making me nervous," I said with a self-conscious laugh. I took a sip of my coffee and put the cup back on the saucer, a little bit of liquid sloshing over the edge. He handed me a napkin before I even had the chance to look for one.

What a gentleman.

"It's about . . ." He sighed. "Detective Alvarez came to see me yesterday."

"Oh." I looked up. "What did she want?"

"She wanted to see the footage from my home security system for the night of the murder."

"Right." I nibbled on the edge of my cookie. It was nice, but could have done with a little extra salt to balance out the sweet white chocolate and creamy nuts.

"Mr. Avagyan, the previous owner of the house, had a security system set up after some kids trampled through his wife's roses."

"That sounds like Mr. and Mrs. Avagyan. They were always so proud of their beautiful garden. Grandma Rose used to call her the flower whisperer, because she could get anything to grow even if the climate didn't really suit it." I smiled. "Do the cameras show much?"

"They're positioned in a way that you can see my driveway, the sidewalk, the road and the very edge of the park where anyone might be coming or going in front of my house."

"That's great." My eyes widened and I took another gulp of my coffee. "You might be able to see the killer! Have you checked the footage?"

"I have." He nodded. "I was actually at the police station this morning dropping off a copy of it on a USB."

Jake didn't seem excited at the chance to help the investigation. In fact, there was a definite line developing between his brows that made ice-water slide through my veins.

"Why did you want to tell me about it?" I asked, suddenly unsure whether I wanted to know the answer.

"There's something on the footage, Chloe." He let out a long sigh and the bites I'd taken out of my cookie threatened to come up.

"Tell me," I croaked.

"Your aunt. The camera clearly shows her walking across the

road and going into the park on the night of the murder." He swore under his breath and I gripped the edge of the table, my breathing turning shallow. "I'm so sorry."

When Jake pulled back into his driveway forty-something minutes later, I barely said goodbye before I raced into the house to see if Aunt Dawn was there. She wasn't. Instead I found Grandma Rose sitting on the couch looking completely washed-out from her treatment. There was an empty bucket by her feet.

"Nauseous?" I asked.

She nodded. "A little."

I couldn't tell her about Jake's footage now, not while she was feeling fragile. But my nerves were frayed because I knew how it would look for my aunt to be entering the park around the time of the murder. Why hadn't Aunt Dawn told us she was there that night? I knew in my heart of hearts there was no way she was involved, but still . . .

This would absolutely look suspicious.

Did they know about Erica and the incident at the removal company? Were they looking at other suspects? Or were they focused on the initials on the knife, and now that they knew my aunt had been near the scene of the crime . . .

"Stop looking at me like that," Grandma Rose said, frowning. "I'm not dead yet."

"You have a way with words." I plopped down onto the couch beside her and reached for her hand. Her nails were painted a glorious hot pink and the ring fingers had a layer of sparkle over the top as a pretty accent. "I like your nails."

"Me too." She smiled. "The nurse said I have spunk."

"You *do* have spunk." I snuggled up close to her and put my head on her shoulder. Her clothes had a faint whiff of perfume on them, like they always did, and I was transported back to being a child, cuddled up on her lap. "In fact, I would wager you're the spunkiest grandma in all of America. Possibly the world."

"And don't you forget it." She kissed the top of my head. "Can you stop worrying, Chloe? Please?"

"No."

"At least you're honest." She sighed.

"How was the treatment today?" I asked.

"Hard. But I took some of the leftover special brownies with me."

"Oh, you did?" What twilight world was I living in where my dear, sweet little grandma was taking pot brownies to her friends at the cancer treatment center?

"I hope you don't mind."

"Not at all."

"I mentioned them to one of the ladies I've seen there a lot, and she said she didn't like the idea of smoking or anything like that. She tried to go to one of those . . . what do you call them? Like a pharmacy for cannabis?"

"A dispensary?" I supplied.

"Yes, that." She nodded. "But she said it was intimidating and there were too many options and it smelled funny. She said to me last time, 'Oh, I wish I could just have it in something where I didn't even notice it was there.' She had a little nibble and said they were delicious!"

My heart warmed, not only from the praise but also from knowing it might help someone having a difficult time of things. "I'd be happy to make her a whole batch if you want to take them next time."

"You have a good heart, Chloe."

"It's all because of you. All the times you spent the day in the kitchen, preparing great meals for me . . . Food is love. I'll never forget that."

Nor would I forget the times before I'd lived with Grandma Rose, scrounging the cupboards and the refrigerator, my young tummy growling with hunger. Not because we couldn't afford to eat, necessarily, but because my mother had forgotten to do the shopping again, too occupied with her own wants and desires. Too neglectful to think about the daughter she'd brought into the world.

"It was my job to feed you," she said resolutely. "I never thought of my food as a gift. It was the bare minimum."

But to a child who knew what it was like to be unwanted and forgotten, it had meant everything.

"*You* are a gift, Grandma." I hugged her tight. "Now, how's that stomach feeling?"

"Not great," she admitted. "I'm feeling very weary."

"Well, I picked up something for you today." I got up from the couch and fetched the bag of goodies from Greener Pastures. "Speaking of dispensaries, I went to one in Twin Parks and the lady recommended these for pain. But I noticed the packet also says they're good for nausea and muscle cramps. I got the pomegranate flavor, because I thought that might be tasty."

"You're a good girl." Grandma Rose leaned back against the couch and closed her eyes. Her skin looked a little pale and she didn't have her usual pep about her.

I checked the dosage information on the back and determined that a single gummy would be the right amount for her, based on what she'd been taking previously. I opened the bag and popped one into her hand. Slowly, she brought it up to her mouth and chewed, making a slight face.

"No good?" I asked, putting the rest of the packet away in the cupboard with all her other medicine.

"I'm sure it will work fine but the taste . . ." She shook her head. "It's just okay. But I always get a bit of that funkiness, you know?"

I nodded. The herbaceous and medicinal taste of the cannabis was not an easy thing to mask. Perhaps for some that wasn't a bad thing, but I knew my grandmother had a sweet tooth. I planned to ensure that all my cannabis baked goods delivered on the flavor promise.

"See how you go with that, and later tonight I can always bake something with the rest of the cannabutter, if you need it."

"I *much* prefer your way of doing it," she said. After a moment, she looked at me with a slight frown. "I don't want to be rude, Chloe. But I need to sit alone for a while. I sent Dawn home for the same reason."

"Of course. That's not rude at all." I bent down to kiss her forehead. "I'm going to head out for a walk, but I'll have my phone on me. Call me if you need anything, even a glass of water. I'll come right back."

"You're fussing over me like you're the grandma and I'm the granddaughter." A smile lifted her lips momentarily.

"You took care of me for years, now let me return the favor. Please."

She nodded and kept her eyes closed, and I took that as my cue to leave her alone. I changed into my favorite pair of Lululemon leggings, a pink T-shirt with white stripes and my Converse sneakers. I had no idea where I was going, but I didn't want to potter around the house and disturb Grandma Rose while she was trying to rest.

A walk to the beach might clear my head and I wanted to check in on Aunt Dawn, anyway. I headed outside and dialed my aunt's number, but it rang out and I left a voicemail asking her to call me back. I tried not to let my imagination run wild. She often got wrapped up in her own activities and didn't call back until hours later.

Letting out a long breath, I turned west, toward the water. Hopefully the beach would help calm my nerves.

One of the most amazing things about Azalea Bay was the view of the ocean from the high points of town. As I walked over a gently cresting hill, the view revealed itself in spectacular, near-monochromatic glory. The sky was bright azure and the ocean a vibrant jewel-toned blue with a hint of green. Silver foam capped the waves and I could spot tiny flecks of color from the surfboards of a few souls who sought to tame the swell and claim it as their own. Down on the golden sand, toddlers played along the shoreline, leaving messy footprints as they waddled after a group of seagulls. The birds' cries echoed in the air, along with the crash of a forceful wave against the sand, sending the children skittering back up the beach and squealing with joy.

Following the path that led to the boardwalk, I sucked in the clean, tangy air and let it fill my lungs. A group of women about my aunt's age, who wore brightly colored athleisure outfits and Fitbits, were gathered by a wooden bench, stretching. They were clearly gossiping about the murder.

". . . always thought she was a bit weird . . ."

". . . no way a woman could have done it . . ."

". . . what if they don't . . ."

Were they talking about Aunt Dawn? None of the women paid me any mind as I approached, as not everyone recognized me after my return. I'd been a skinny girl in my youth and Paris had given me some extra jiggle along with life experience, filling my body out with dips and curves that hadn't been there before. In truth, while I noticed the changes, they didn't bother me. I was strong from the physical work of being in a kitchen and that was what mattered to me—what I could *do* with my body, rather than how it looked.

". . . stabbed him in cold blood . . ."

". . . she's the prime suspect . . ."

". . . Rose must be devastated . . ."

I hurried past the women, head down. They *were* talking about Dawn! Was it Starr Bright who'd leaked the information or someone else? And to think, the detective and chief were probably toiling over Jake's security footage, getting ready to nail my aunt for a crime she didn't commit.

I pulled my phone out and just as I was about to try calling my aunt again, I saw someone familiar coming toward me. "Andrea!"

The woman startled at the sound of her name, her hand flying up to her chest. She'd been lost in her own world. But as her eyes settled on mine, recognition flooded her face. "Chloe Barnes, it's been a while."

Andrea Chalmers, Brendan's sister—younger by two years—was the polar opposite of him. Softly spoken, kind and well-liked, she had curly brown hair, big eyes and a tall but slim build. In fact, she looked even slimmer than I remembered, a pink sweatshirt with the words *Eat. Sleep. Yoga.* swamping her frame. While I was prone to stress eating myself, I knew for some that difficult times turned them away from food.

"I'm so sorry about your brother," I said, dropping my eyes to the floor momentarily. I wondered if she knew about my last encounter with him.

"Thank you."

"Are you . . ." I let out a breath. "I'm sure you're *not* okay but I feel compelled to ask."

"I don't know how to feel, honestly." She pulled a hair tie off her wrist and yanked her thick hair back. "It's a strange time."

As another walker came past with a small white dog on his leash, we moved to the side so we weren't blocking the path. I got the impression she wanted to get something off her chest. Andrea had been an excellent student when we were young and had skipped two grades—so, despite being younger we'd had some classes together. I wouldn't have said we were friends, exactly. But we'd been lab partners for a whole year and shared a homeroom more than once. I'd always liked her.

"Brendan and I . . ." She knotted her hands in front of her body and looked out to the ocean. "We didn't have the best relationship, as I'm sure anyone who went to school with us would know."

I *did* know. I'd seen him shove her into a locker on the first day she'd moved up into his grade—he wasn't happy having everyone know his little sister was smarter than him. Another time, he'd tripped her during a soccer match and claimed it was an accident, but I wasn't the only one who'd seen a look of intent.

"Sibling rivalry?" I suggested.

"Perhaps that's what it was. Older brothers can be like that, I'm sure, but . . . he was cruel." She shook her head. "God. I don't know why I'm telling you this."

"It's easier to talk to someone outside the situation," I said. "I've been there."

"Perhaps you're right." She nodded. "My parents are devastated, obviously. And we had a huge fight because apparently I'm not acting the way they think I should. They said I wasn't grieving him enough and then Steve stepped in and . . . what a mess."

"Steve Boyd?" I blinked. "As in the hunky center of the Azalea Bay High basketball team?"

"The one and only." Andrea blushed. "*My* one and only."

That's when I noticed the sparkling engagement ring on her finger. "Congratulations, that's wonderful news."

Andrea's face completely transformed. Her eyes lit up and her whole body seemed to pull itself into a more upright, engaged position. "Steve has been an absolute lifeline. After I came back from college, things with Brendan were rough. He thought the family made a fuss over me because of everything and that he got no attention at all."

I wasn't sure exactly what she meant by "everything," but I didn't want to interrupt her.

"His bullying got really bad and my parents kicked him out of the house for a bit, which only made him angrier. He took a baseball bat to my car." Andrea's eyes filled with tears, but she blinked them away. A slender hand hovered at her throat and her engagement ring slumped to the side, like it was slightly too big. "Steve was actually the one who caught him in the act. He took me to the police station and then out for a coffee. We clicked. He wouldn't have looked *twice* at me in high school, but as adults we're perfect for each other."

I made an *aww* sound. "You sound utterly in love."

"I am. Needless to say, things with Steve and Brendan were tense. Now Mom and Dad think we're happy he's gone, and Steve stormed out of dinner the other night. We're supposed to be getting married this summer, but everything feels so tumultuous."

"I'm so sorry." I reached out and touched her shoulder. "If there's anything I can do . . ."

"I appreciate that, but there isn't." She shook her head. "Well, other than you simply saying hello and then kindly letting me spill my emotions all over you."

I laughed. "Hey, that's what old lab partners are for, right?"

"True." Andrea glanced at her watch. "Sorry, but I have to run. We should get coffee sometime."

"I'd love that."

With a wave, she hurried off in the direction from where I'd come. I wasn't sure if the coffee invite was a genuine invitation or one of those platitudes people gave when they hadn't seen an acquaintance in a long time, but I hoped it was the former. In fact, maybe I would reach out to Andrea in a few days and make the connection myself.

Something about what she'd told me today had my intuition prickling. A wedding coming up, tension between the groom and the future brother-in-law, a history of violence . . .

Perhaps there was more going on behind the scenes than Andrea was letting on.

# CHAPTER 10

I tried calling my aunt one more time as I walked along the boardwalk, but it went to voicemail again. Maybe this would be a good time to pop into the gym and see if I could make an appointment to see Cindy's cousin, Jay.

I double-checked the address on my phone and headed over. Iron Works had opened in the time I'd been away from Azalea Bay, and appeared much flashier than the other long-standing gym in town. The front of the building was mostly glass, showing neat rows of treadmills where a few beautiful people bounded along in their perfectly coordinated activewear. Behind the treadmills was a weights area.

Two women exited the studio and walked past me, wearing leggings and cropped T-shirts that showed off their washboard stomachs. Both had artfully applied makeup and freshly styled hair that gleamed in the afternoon sun. I couldn't look that put-together on my best day, let alone right after a sweaty workout.

I hesitated by the front door, feeling like an imposter. *This* was why I never went to the gym. I found the atmosphere intimidating and this seemed like the kind of place where someone went to be seen, which was the last thing my tomato face wanted when I exercised.

"Chloe?" A voice broke through my internal tornado of self-doubt.

I turned around and saw a guy about my age wearing an Iron Works T-shirt walking toward me and smiling. At first, the dark hair, green eyes and muscular physique didn't register. But he knew who I was, so . . .

"Oh my gosh." I blinked. "Jamie."

"It's Jay now," he said with a friendly smile.

Jay Donaldson. I almost laughed at myself for missing something so obvious—I already knew Cindy's cousin . . . just by a slightly different name. But the name wasn't the only reason I hadn't put two and two together. The Jamie—sorry, Jay—I knew hadn't exactly been the physical type in high school. He'd been a smaller guy back then, slight in build and barely taller than me, and he'd spent most of his time in the computer lab.

Not the person I would have assumed to end up as a personal trainer and nutrition coach.

"I'm so sorry, I didn't recognize you at first." I laughed awkwardly. "You're taller now."

"Are you a client?" he asked. "I don't remember ever seeing you here."

"I just moved back home, actually. So I, uh . . . well, I thought now that I'm back I should get into fitness and stuff."

*Fitness and stuff? Wow. So articulate.*

"That's great." He smiled and I was almost blinded by how perfectly white his teeth were. That was also new. "Come on in and I'll give you a look around. That's good timing, I just got back from lunch."

I spied the Sprout bag in his hand. "Don't tell me you're into the crystal-charged smoothie bowls," I joked.

He laughed. "Not really. I know some of the menu items there are a bit wacky, but it's a good place to get a nice healthy lunch."

I followed Jay into Iron Works and he waved at a colleague

as he motioned for me to follow him around the corner. He stashed his Sprout bag into what looked like a staff room and then turned to me.

"So, what are the goals you're hoping to achieve with a gym membership?" he asked.

"Uh, general fitness." I nodded. "What do people usually say? They want to get shredded for summer, right?"

"We have clients with all types of goals here and weight loss is definitely one of the popular ones." Jay nodded. "I work with my clients on shifting the mindset to be about making small, sustainable improvements to flexibility, strength and cardio-vascular fitness rather than just focusing on the weight loss, though. We're here to help you live a longer, healthier life."

"Oh." I blinked, a little surprised by his answer. "That's very refreshing."

"Come on, let me give you the grand tour."

I followed Jay through the gym as he explained all the different areas and services they offered. Suddenly, seeing the place through his eyes, it became a little less intimidating. I spotted a young female personal trainer working with an older gentleman who was trying to improve his mobility. There was also a curvy woman standing in a squat rack getting cheered on by two guys as she hauled a very impressive load of weight onto her back.

My initial impression of this place had been colored by my own insecurities and I was adult enough to admit it. Jay showed me the studio where the classes were held, plus the spin room, locker rooms and they even had a massage room as well.

"Let's sit while I run through some of the membership options," Jay said, as he led me to a few empty tables by the reception area.

"This place is *huge*." I shook my head in wonder as I grabbed a seat. "No wonder I know so many people who come here."

"Oh yeah?" Jay raised an eyebrow as he pulled a clipboard

from a section of shelves containing brochures and other marketing materials. He took the seat across from me. "Like who?"

This was my moment.

"Oh well, it seems a bit weird to say now, but . . . I know Brendan Chalmers was a member."

"Oh." Jay nodded. "Yeah, he was."

"Was he a client of yours?" I asked, putting a sympathetic tone in my voice. I knew Jay wasn't a fan of Brendan when we were in high school, but I also didn't want to come across as callous in case things had changed.

"No." He shook his head. "Brendan worked with one of my colleagues, Anthony. Two peas in a pod those two."

I detected a note of sourness in his voice. A memory rattled around in the back of my mind—Brendan knocking Jay over in a basketball game in high school, then saying something horrible about Jamie being a girl's name and him having skinny little chicken legs. I wondered if that had anything to do with Jay's name change and career of choice.

"Sorry." He shook his head. "That was unprofessional."

"Please." I waved my hand as if shooing a fly. "We're old friends. I'd rather you didn't put on airs and graces, frankly. It makes me more comfortable."

"Still, it's not nice to speak about someone who . . ." He screwed up his nose. "Well, I guess you know what happened. It's all anyone is talking about."

"I know what you mean." I nodded. "So he and your colleague Anthony were friends?"

I hoped the gentle prodding might yield something useful. Jay and I might not exactly be the "old friends" I'd claimed us to be, but we'd talked at parties and school events on occasion. Hopefully he wouldn't see me as someone trying to stir up trouble.

"Yeah, they hung out a lot. Mostly here, because Brendan would work out five or six nights a week. Although he spent as much time sitting around trash-talking as he actually did doing any reps." Jay shook his head. "We try so hard to make Iron Works a welcoming and inclusive environment, but Anthony and Brendan were the antithesis of that."

"Trash-talking?" I asked. "Like, making fun of people?"

"Yeah." A line formed between his brows. "I reported it to management on multiple occasions and I know Anthony got a warning once or twice. But they didn't do much about Brendan, because he was a paying client."

"What did he say to people?"

"Stupid things. Like, that guy, Tate." Jay inclined his head toward a guy who was walking between the weights area and the men's locker rooms.

He was on the shorter side, maybe five foot seven, and had a slender frame, with a shock of boot-polish-black hair that looked too dark to be natural, fair skin and a weak chin. He had a silver earring in one ear and kept having to hitch up his baggy shorts every few steps.

"The poor guy was always trying to impress them by lifting heavier than he could manage. It was like he became obsessed with getting their approval."

"That's sad."

"It's *dangerous.*" He let out a breath. "Tate almost got stuck under a barbell one time while Brendan was supposed to be spotting him, and then he refused to help Tate out, claiming he just needed to push through."

"Oh my gosh." That seemed very on-brand for Brendan. "Was he okay?"

"I stepped in before it went too far. Tate was furious but unhurt, and I tore into Brendan." He let out a humorless laugh. "Thank God I was at a team-building evening with the rest of the Iron Works folks the night he got murdered, or else the cops might be looking at me. *That's* how much of a ruckus I made about the whole incident."

"I'm glad you're sticking up for people," I said. "Someone needs to."

"I was the scrawny kid once, I know what it feels like." He bobbed his head, but a faint reddish tint colored his cheeks and he scrubbed a hand along his jaw. "I hope I didn't scare you off. I swear, everyone else who works here is great. I shouldn't have told you that story."

"It's fine, seriously. Let me take all the paperwork home so I can have a think about it." I smiled. "Thanks so much for showing me around."

"It's good to see you again, Chloe."

Jay walked me to the door and said that he hoped I'd be back. I wasn't sure that a big gym like Iron Works was the place for me, but it *would* be nice to do something for fun and exercise. Maybe a class of some kind where I could blend in with the crowd.

I made a mental note to ask Sabrina if she wanted to join me. In the meantime, I wondered if this Tate guy might be another name for my suspect list. Like many people around Azalea Bay, he'd been publicly bullied by Brendan. Not just bullied with words, either; it sounded like Tate had almost been physically harmed, too.

Maybe he wanted to get revenge on Brendan by flipping the tables and making him feel powerless. Being ashamed could make people do extreme things.

I tried calling my aunt again but *still* didn't get an answer. Now I was getting worried and my mind wouldn't rest until I'd checked in, so I headed to her house.

Aunt Dawn lived in a bungalow that was a mirror image of my grandmother's, only her front garden was filled with a wild, tangled array of flowers and had a slightly overgrown, witchy vibe. There was creeping jasmine, which released a heady perfume into the air, a wild golden-orange spray of California poppies and fat bushes of lavender, which had bees buzzing around them. Knowing she wouldn't mind, I paused at one of the lavender bushes and removed a few sprigs. They would be handy for some experimental baking I wanted to do.

Music floated into the air and I was pretty sure it was coming from her backyard—"Killer Queen" by Queen, a very Dawn song but perhaps not the best thing to be playing as a murder suspect.

Knowing my rebellious aunt, there was a good reason that's *why* she was playing it.

I headed to the side gate, which she'd once painted a vibrant royal purple, though it was now flaking, and pushed. It rattled against the hinges, locked. Interesting. Azalea Bay wasn't the kind of place where people tended to worry too much about security, and I wondered when that had changed. I climbed up onto a retaining wall and poked my head over the top. The music was definitely coming from the yard and it was so loud I was sure Dawn hadn't even heard her phone ringing.

She and her border collie, Moxie, were mid-dance routine. Aunt Dawn tapped her heel against the ground, shimmying her arms overhead in time to the music. I could see her lips moving, subtly issuing commands to Moxie, who circled in front of her—first clockwise and then counterclockwise. Dawn walked sideways, crossing one foot in front of the other, and Moxie moved in the same fashion, stepping perfectly in time.

Freddie Mercury belted out the lyrics, and Dawn and Moxie both turned away from me, sashaying up the yard and then coming to an abrupt stop, before turning back around. Dawn took long strides back the way she'd come, only this time Moxie wove in between her legs, almost like how the dogs did in those obstacle courses at the Westminster dog show.

As the song hit its crescendo, Dawn and Moxie came back to back, and moved in a slow circle, with Moxie on her hind legs. Then the finale. The final pose was a big deal for canine freestyle dancing, or so my aunt had told me.

*You want to leave a magnificent impression, Chloe,* she'd said. *When you're trying to impress, the very last thing you do or say will linger in people's minds.*

Dawn and Moxie faced one another, and Moxie sat in a begging position, bringing her front paws up so that my aunt could clasp them. Then Moxie leaned back, throwing her head back so far I was amazed she didn't topple over and my aunt threw her head back too, in a mirror image.

Balancing as best I could, I clapped loudly as the song ended. Moxie raced over to the gate, barking and wagging her fluffy black-and-white tail. She scraped at the wood, wanting to get closer.

"What are you doing here?" Dawn asked with a smile as she walked over. She was wearing a vibrant pantsuit in cobalt blue, with a band of matching sequins running down the outside of her legs and the arms of the cropped jacket. Underneath, she wore a silky white top.

"Grandma Rose wanted some quiet time, so I came out for a walk." I hopped down from the retaining wall as my aunt unlatched the gate. "I love your outfit."

"We're doing a dress rehearsal."

When the door opened, Moxie rushed forward, burying her nose in my hand and slobbering me with her tongue. "Hey, girl. You did such a good job!"

"She was late on the sashaying," Dawn said, frowning. "We can't have that if we want to make it to the regional competition."

"I think you're perfect." I crouched down and hugged the dog, smoothing her ears back and squeezing her. "Such a clever girl."

"It's lucky she doesn't live with you," Dawn quipped. "She'd never learn a thing because you'd give her treats for simply existing."

"I can't really argue there," I replied with a shrug as I stood.

"So, are you going to tell me the real reason you came by?"

My aunt held the door open and I went into the backyard, bringing Moxie with me. I noticed that she secured the latch right away.

"Can't a gal visit her favorite aunt?" I offered up my most winning smile, but that only made Dawn narrow her eyes in suspicion. "Okay, fine. I was worried, so I came to check on you."

"Never lie to me, girl. I have a BS detector that's sharper than any knife in your kitchen." She folded her arms across her chest. "Now, why are you worried?"

"Oh, I don't know. Maybe because I recently witnessed the dead body of someone I knew and the local authorities seem to think you did it. That might be causing some slight concern."

Her frown deepened. "Don't sass me."

"I saw Jake earlier today."

Dawn's expression immediately changed from annoyed to excited. "Hunky Jake? Did he ask you out?"

"No!" I waved a hand. "It wasn't anything like that."

*Even though you wanted it to be like that.*

I cursed my inner voice for stirring up trouble, because I did *not* want it to be like that. From now on, my head was in charge of things, not my heart. And certainly not any body parts lower than that.

"He . . ." I sucked in a breath.

I *had* to tell her. There was no sense keeping the information to myself, because sooner or later, the police would come knocking. And I figured a little extra stress now was worth it for the sake of being prepared.

"Jake had to give footage from his security cameras to the police and it shows you entering the park the night Brendan was murdered." The words came out in a rush and I deflated like a balloon.

There, I'd said it. Come what may.

"Oh, I know," she replied breezily, leaning down to pat

Moxie's head. The dog nuzzled the leg of her pant, her treat-seeking signal, and Dawn reached into her pocket and palmed her one.

"You know?" I shook my head. "How?"

"The detective came to see me this morning."

"But you didn't say anything when you came by to pick up Grandma Rose."

Dawn took a seat at her outdoor table setting and motioned for me to do the same. Moxie wandered off into the yard, nose to the ground as she went sniffing for something more interesting.

"Firstly, I didn't see that there was any point upsetting my mother right before her chemo infusion. They're tough enough as it is."

I nodded. "Fair."

"Secondly, it's my issue to handle. Not yours, young lady." She nailed me with her mama-bear stare. "You have other things to worry about."

"Family is my top priority," I shot back. "I care about you. I can't imagine what would happen to Grandma Rose if you were . . ."

I couldn't even finish that sentence.

"Everything will be fine." She inspected the sequins on her costume, frowning when she noticed one had come loose. A snapped thread dangled and she toyed with it. "It's not a big deal."

"Not a big deal? You're a suspect in a murder investigation!"

"Don't be so dramatic, the police are just doing their job."

I could tell she was more worried than she was letting on—because no amount of concealer would hide the bags under her eyes and no amount of nail polish would hide the fact that she'd bitten her nails down to their quicks. One might accuse her of not taking this whole thing seriously, but I knew better. She *was* worried.

She was simply trying to shield Grandma Rose and me from it.

"Do you know who else is on the suspect list?" I asked. "What did the detective say about the footage? Why were you at the park at that time, anyway?"

My aunt looked at me and raised an eyebrow. "Want to jam any more questions in before I have a chance to answer?"

"Hardy-har." I folded my arms across my chest. She was right, of course, but I didn't want her keeping things from me. We were a family unit and families stuck together. I wasn't about to go on with my life acting like this wasn't happening.

"I don't know if there are other suspects. The detective wasn't very forthcoming this morning when I spoke with her. She said the footage proved I was in the park around the time of the murder, which I haven't denied. In fact, the first time they interviewed me, I told them I went out for a walk to clear my head because I was stressed out waiting for you to come home," she said. "And lastly, I have every right to go for a walk in a park, even at night. It's a safe town, so there's nothing suspicious about that."

"Not *that* safe," I grumbled. "A man ended up dead."

"A man who gave a lot of people a lot of reasons to want him gone." Dawn patted my arm. "They might not have said it to my face, but I'm *sure* there are other people for the police to look at. In fact, I'd say the list of people who liked him was far shorter than the list of people who'd be happy never to see him again."

Based on what I'd learned at Iron Works, that certainly seemed true. The more I looked into Brendan's life, the more names I added to the list of people he'd hurt.

*Speaking of which . . .*

"I bumped into Andrea Chalmers today," I said.

Dawn's expression softened. "How's she doing?"

"It's a lot to work through. They didn't have a good relationship and it sounded like things were very tense between her fiancé and him." I drummed my fingers against my thigh. "I wonder if the detective has spoken with them."

"Don't they always look at family members in cases like this?"

"True." I nodded. "But there was also an incident where he had a coworker fired from the removal company. Not to mention a man he almost seriously injured at the gym."

"How do you know these things?"

"The woman who was fired is part of Sabrina's Dungeons and Dragons group."

"And the gym?"

"I was thinking about getting a membership," I said, though I'm sure my tone gave me away.

She looked at me closely. "What are you doing, Chloe?"

"Nothing, just . . . talking to people." I sounded like a liar, even to my own ears.

Aunt Dawn sighed. "Stay out of it, okay? Let the professionals do their job. This is what they're trained to do and I'm confident they'll find who did it."

I, on the other hand, wasn't so sure. The fact that the detective had gone to my aunt so soon after receiving the footage from Jake told me that they were looking very closely at her. Between the footage, the knife with her initials, *and* the fact that Chief Gladwell had witnessed the altercation between Aunt Dawn and Brendan the night of the murder . . .

Evidence was mounting.

And to make matters worse, my gut was telling me that my aunt wasn't being entirely honest about *why* she was in the park the night of the murder.

# CHAPTER 11

The next few days passed without incident. I buried myself in pulling together the business plan for the cannabis café, which involved Skyping with an old boss who gave me a ton of helpful information on how to calculate startup costs and lay it out clearly in the plan. I researched the closest farms where I could establish a business relationship for buying raw cannabis flowers, leaves, and trim, and I then came up with a basic menu of things we could offer on opening day and once we were more established. I knew from working in the industry that the more curated a menu, the easier it was to budget for ingredients and minimize waste.

Oh, and we came up with a name: Baked by Chloe.

I did love a good pun.

Dawn and I submitted the licensing request along with our business plan, and celebrated with a bottle of champagne and a test batch of honey lavender macarons, with homemade blueberry lavender jam and cannabis-infused buttercream. That night I slept like a baby.

But worry still played on my mind.

The murder investigation became a taboo subject in the house, with my aunt clamming up anytime I mentioned it. Grandma Rose was acting like everything was fine, which I knew was her trying to cope with it all. She'd done the same after my mother left.

*This is okay, Chloe. Sometimes people need a break, but she'll be back once she sees sense. She'll be back . . .*

Spoiler alert: she did not come back.

"I feel like I'm living in a twilight zone," I said to Sabrina. "They're both acting like it's not happening, and meanwhile I'm pretty sure there was an unmarked cop car parked outside our house last night."

We were sitting on a bench in the beautiful outdoor area of the bed-and-breakfast while Sabrina had her break. I'd picked up prosciutto-spinach-and-brie sandwiches from Casa Italiano's for our lunch, cleaned and de-stemmed some strawberries and packaged up some of the leftover macarons (for her to consume after work, of course). Sabrina had snagged some bottles of sparkling water from the kitchen and we were having a sort-of picnic outside in the sunshine.

"You think they're tailing your aunt?" she asked.

"She noticed a black car in several places she's been the last few days."

"Could be a coincidence," Sabrina offered. "Black cars aren't exactly uncommon."

"Maybe." I tilted my head. "But I suspect this isn't going to stop until someone else is the prime suspect. The *right* someone else."

"Who do you think did it?" she asked, popping a strawberry into her mouth.

"I honestly don't know." I relayed what I had found out about Erica, Tate, Andrea and Steve. "But I'm sure that's the tip of the iceberg."

"No way Erica did it." Sabrina shook her head, a few wiry curls loosening from her ponytail. "She's been part of our D&D group from the beginning and I've never seen anything that would make me think she was capable of something like that."

"Isn't that usually the case when they interview neighbors

and friends of killers? Nobody saw it coming. They were such a good person. Blah, blah, blah . . ."

"She didn't do it." Sabrina remained staunch in her defense.

"Does she have an alibi for the night?"

"I don't think so." Sabrina shook her head. "I'd texted her that night to see what she was up to right before you called me, and she said, quote, 'quality time with my PlayStation.' But I didn't exactly ask her if she had an alibi, because that's not really something people ask their friends."

She had a good point. That wouldn't come across as supportive. "Do you know if the police have questioned her?"

Sabrina shook her head. "I'm not sure. But even if they did, I don't know how she'd end up on the suspect list."

"Maybe someone at work mentioned she was pissed about getting fired?"

"Perhaps." Sabrina frowned. "Now that I think about it, we went out for drinks one night and she got tipsy and said she'd thought about slashing Brendan's tires . . . but she didn't do anything. It was just venting. Besides, you saw her. She's a hundred and thirty pounds wet. How would she take down a big guy like that?"

"Element of surprise?" I said, but Sabrina had a point. She *was* small, especially in comparison to Brendan. "How the heck does she move furniture then?"

"She tends to do the jobs where the clients want items packed for them or if they have a lot of delicate things. Half the time she works the reception desk and manages bookings, and then she goes on the jobs that need her skills. That's why Brendan was pissed that she was leading the internal employee competition, because he thought she was some desk bimbo who didn't want to break a nail."

I couldn't think of a more *inaccurate* description of the woman I'd met. Erica had struck me as tough and forthright, someone who spoke her mind and didn't shy away from conflict. And the way she'd played her D&D character—a sorcerer with an intimate knowledge of the arcane—she'd come across as intelligent, pragmatic and quick-witted.

*Doesn't really sound like the profile of a murderer, does it?*

"I *really* don't see her being the one who did it." Sabrina shook her head. "Call me biased because she's my friend, but I can't wrap my head around it."

"It's kind of shocking that she could go from leading an employee competition to being fired for theft. I know she said Brendan planted the stolen item, but you'd think her bosses would have given her the benefit of the doubt."

I bit into my sandwich and chewed. The bread had a great resistance and the prosciutto was perfectly salty and chewy, which paired excellently with the creamy cheese. Despite all the craziness that was inhabiting my life right now, there was something special about sitting in the sunshine with my best friend and chowing down on a delicious lunch.

We sat in silence for a few moments, lost in thought.

"One time she made a comment about how she thought there was something funky going on at work," Sabrina said. "With her boss, I mean."

"Funky like what?"

"She was complaining about Brendan and how she couldn't believe he still had a job. Apparently, she found him sleeping at work, literally tucked under a desk in one of the meeting rooms. Happened more than once." Sabrina snorted. "He always *was* lazy."

"So she reported him?" I asked.

"She went to her boss and told him about it, but . . . nothing. No reprimand. No warning. Nothing. In fact, it got back to Brendan that Erica reported him and he started leaving gross things in her desk drawer like rotten banana peels and stuff. One time she found a whole bunch of dirt and worms there."

"Ew." I wrinkled my nose. "And he didn't get fired for *that*, either?"

"Nope. She joked that he must have pictures of the boss doing something scandalous, because he seemed untouchable. Nothing he did got him in trouble. No matter who he bullied or how slack he was, he somehow still got bonuses and awards."

"Interesting."

"Doesn't matter now, anyway." Sabrina reached for the Tupperware container of strawberries only to realize we'd eaten them all. "That's for the police to figure out."

"I'm not sure I feel so confident in their abilities." I sighed. "They seem fixated on my aunt, and if they're tailing her . . ."

"You have to let them do their job, even if it means them looking at your aunt. She didn't do it, so they won't find concrete evidence against her."

"Yeah, because nobody was ever imprisoned for a crime they didn't commit." I shot her a look. "Mistakes happen."

Sabrina nodded. "I understand why you're worried, I really do."

"I just needed to get it off my chest." I sighed. "But I should let you get back to work."

"Thanks for bringing me lunch."

"Any time. I may as well enjoy being a free, unemployed woman because the second we get the go-ahead for the café I'm going to be a busy bee."

"I'm so glad you're home," she said with a smile. "Azalea Bay wasn't the same without you."

"I'm happy to be back here."

And I was. But there was also a lot of turmoil in my world and I feared that it wouldn't be too long before the police intensified their efforts in surveilling my aunt. Yet the more I learned about what had been happening in the years I was away from this town, the more it seemed like Brendan Chalmers had enemies in every corner.

Enemies that the police might not know about.

After I picked up the newly serviced Jellybean—which now started like a dream—I decided to make a stop at the shops before heading home. First, the convenience store for some milk and then . . . Sprout. As much as seeking out Starr Bright for local gossip felt a *lot* like selling my soul, I wanted to arm myself with as much information as possible before I went to the police.

It would be easy for them to fob me off as a worried and interfering relative . . . which I absolutely was. So, if I had any chance of getting them to take me seriously *and* look at someone besides my aunt, I needed solid evidence and a legitimate suspect.

Despite discussing Erica with Sabrina today, my gut was telling me the chance of it being her was slim. First, there was the massive size difference. Second, her initials didn't match the knife. Third, well . . . she just seemed too smart to stab someone and then leave evidence behind. That could be an indication of several things:

—someone who was so enraged they forgot about the evidence.

—an unplanned attack.

—a potential witness who scared the murderer off.

Perhaps my aunt's presence interrupted the murderer from cleaning up after the deed was done. But besides Erica, who else could it be? Tate from the gym? It sounded as though there could be a motive, but motive alone was not enough and given his first initial was T, it didn't match the knife. Steve Boyd was another possibility, although his initials didn't match, either. What about the sister, Andrea? Still no match. Maybe the knife didn't belong to the killer. And it sounded like there was something strange going on with Brendan's boss, as well.

I walked into the convenience store to grab some milk and toothpaste for Grandma Rose. As I entered the store, a funny chime played to the tune of "Another One Bites the Dust." It made me laugh. Behind the front counter, I saw the owner reading the newspaper.

"Now there's a face I haven't seen in a long time," he said, looking up and smiling. "Good to see you, Chloe."

"You too, Mr. Collins." I grinned. "I see you still have your fun welcome chime going."

"That I do."

Over the years, he'd switched up the tunes for very recognizable melodies and even doing fun things for holidays, like ghost noises on Halloween and sleigh bells at Christmas. I walked past the counter and pay phone to grab a carton of milk from the big refrigerator on the side of the shop and hunted around for some toothpaste, bringing both items to the front counter.

"How's your grandmother doing?" he asked as he processed the sale. "I haven't seen her for a while."

"She's good."

"And your aunt?" There was a hint of curiosity in his voice that made my stomach turn.

"Also good."

I pasted a smile on my face and grabbed my items, hustling out of the store before he thought to ask any specific questions. A bad feeling coiled in my gut as I headed toward Sprout. Something told me that my aunt's reputation might not be in the best standing right now. But if anyone had heard the gossip floating around town, it would be Starr.

Now I had to hope that if I sucked up to her enough, she might be willing to share.

Feeling slimier than a bag of past-its-prime spinach, I pushed open the door to Sprout. The café was nearly empty, since it was at that weird time of day when the lunch rush had died but people hadn't yet popped in after work. Starr was behind the counter, playing around with one of those boards with the movable letters. She looked up as I approached.

"Chloe Barnes, now that's a face I wasn't expecting to see!" Her platinum hair was pulled up into an enormous bun on top of her head. It was so large a family of squirrels could have nested in there.

"Why is that?" I asked. Given I'd eaten lunch here once already since returning home, I was curious as to why my presence was surprising.

"Well, it must be, like, *so* embarrassing for you to go out. What with all the . . ." She waved her hand in the air. "Speculation."

"Speculation?"

"That your aunt totally killed Brendan Chalmers."

I swallowed. Maybe this was a bad idea. I knew people were talking about my aunt—the piece of paper left on our shop was indication of that—and if people were talking, Starr was involved. After all, it was the very reason I was here. I licked my lips and they suddenly felt parched.

"She didn't do it," I said, unsure how else to respond.

"Babe, of course you would say that. You have to defend your family." She leaned her forearms on the serving counter and cocked her head. The giant squirrel's nest slumped to one side. "But everyone knows she's quite passionate."

"You're passionate," I pointed out. "Have you ever killed anyone?"

"Touché." Starr nodded, giving me a look of grudging respect. "Now, did you come in here to make a purchase or to gossip?"

At least she knew what her role was in town. "Would the gossip come easier if it was accompanied by a purchase?"

"It might."

A smile lifted the corner of Starr's lips. They were lacquered with a bright pink gloss that matched the tropical flowers on her dress and the tips of her French manicure. Her ring fingers had little pink gemstones stuck on, which looked cute. It was also how I knew she didn't do much work in her own kitchen—ninety-nine percent of the people I'd encountered in a professional kitchen setting had their nails cut short and kept free of decoration.

The last thing you wanted was to serve someone a pot de crème with a rogue diamanté.

"I'll take half a dozen of the mind-balancing energy balls and a slice of the antitoxin charcoal bar." I hated myself for even saying those words aloud. I hated myself even more for the fact that the energy balls looked pretty darn delicious.

The stress was clearly getting to me.

"Excellent choice," Starr said with an approving nod. "Now, what do you want to know?"

Hmm, where to start? Should I ask her what she knew about the people who owned the furniture removal company where Brendan worked? I wanted to find out if there was anything weird going on between Brendan and his boss, like Erica intimated. Or perhaps if she'd heard about the tension between Brendan and his future brother-in-law? Or if she'd heard of any *other* suspects beyond that? I decided to keep it broad and see what she said.

"Are people talking about anyone *besides* my aunt when it comes to the murder?"

She reached for a small pair of tongs and began placing the energy balls into a peach cardboard box with Sprout written in scrolling glittery white letters. Starr really did have her branding down pat.

"Well, your aunt is suspect number one," she said, looking up for a moment. "But I *had* heard about a conflict between Brendan and his neighbor, Darius."

That was a new one. "Oh?"

"Apparently Brendan poisoned his dog."

I gasped. A liar, groper *and* an animal abuser . . . wow.

"I know. Absolutely despicable," Starr said without even giving me the chance to ask more. She placed my box down on the counter, the purchase momentarily forgotten, and her eyes sparkled. "One of my regulars lives on the same street as them, and she told me that Darius and Brendan had a full-on screaming match in Brendan's driveway three days before the murder."

"Yikes."

"Worst of all, my regular says that she's pretty sure Darius has a record of some kind. He moved to town about a year ago but he's, like, a complete mystery. He doesn't talk to people or try to make friends. Nobody knows what he does for work. It's all very strange."

Starr was practically glowing. It made me sick to my stomach, since I'm sure this poor Darius guy hadn't done anything wrong besides being reserved. As much as I loved small towns for how people banded together to help one another—like Jake had done the day the Jellybean wouldn't start—there was also a tendency toward judging people who didn't immediately assimilate into the community.

Personally, I didn't think that was right. Just because someone kept to themselves didn't mean they had something to hide.

"What do you know about the people who run Azalea Bay Furniture Removal?" I asked, and Starr wrinkled her nose.

"Ross and Maisey Brent? Why on earth would you want to know about them?"

I made a mental note of the names.

"I heard there was something fishy going on with Brendan at work."

"I don't know much, other than that Ross could do with one of my healthy reset smoothies, stat. He smokes like a chimney." She shrugged. "Oh, and their marriage is *totally* on the rocks. A little birdie told me they saw her exiting a divorce lawyer's office a few towns away, but they're still acting like everything is fine."

"Any idea why they're splitting up?"

"No clue. I wondered if one of them might be having an affair, but Maisey is kind of an ice queen. And Ross . . ." She wrinkled her nose. "Let's just say he hasn't got a lot going for him. He definitely married above his station."

That didn't seem like information that would help me, so I decided to change my tactic before Starr started asking *me* questions.

"Out of curiosity, have the police talked with you about the murder? I mean, given that you know everything that goes on around here."

"Uh, no. In fact, I tried to give Detective Alvarez some information when she came in one day—I was trying to be helpful!—and she told me that gossip wasn't evidence. Like, excuse me. I'm *not* gossiping. Can you believe it?"

"You would think they'd want to hear from someone with their ear to the ground," I replied, although I could certainly understand why the detective might be a little wary of Starr. Even before I left for college, she'd perpetuated some rumors about an affair that turned out to be false.

"Thank you." Starr threw her hands in the air. "You know, I always thought you didn't like me, Chloe."

"Now what could have given you that impression?" I asked.

*Uh, maybe the fact that it's true?*

I couldn't help it that Starr had rubbed me the wrong way from day one. We were chalk and cheese. Mille-feuille and amethyst-charged açai power bowls. I wanted everyone to be nice to one another and she thrived on people's misfortune.

But I couldn't afford to make an enemy of anyone now that I was back in Azalea Bay and about to open a business. I needed to make connections here. I needed to rebuild myself in the community. And as much as I didn't love Starr's gossiping tendencies, she *was* someone in the know and well-versed in the business scene here.

Would it kill me to be on her good side? No.

Would I like it? Also no.

"You always seemed . . ." She waved a hand in the air as if trying to pluck the words from the ether. "Standoffish."

"I think you've done an amazing job with Sprout." That, at least, was true. She *had* done an incredible job with her café, even if it was categorically not my style. But I respected the Instagram haven for the smart business move it was.

"High praise coming from a Parisian pastry chef. I wanted to do something different here. Something healthier, because we can't all exist on butter and sugar, can we? It's a heart attack waiting to happen."

My instinct was to bristle, but I tamped it down. "Life is a heart attack waiting to happen, so we may as well enjoy ourselves."

Starr laughed. "True."

She went back to filling my box with the energy balls and bar that I'd ordered, and I tapped my credit card against the almost space-age-like terminal she had set up. It was very modern, sleek. I made note of the brand so I could check out something similar for the point-of-sale unit for my café.

"Why did you want to know what people were saying about the murder anyway? Like, are you planning to conduct your own investigation?" Starr asked, interest dancing in her eyes. "Oh! Can I help?"

I forced a laugh. "Sherlock I am not. I guess I want peace of mind that there's other people for the police to look at, besides my aunt. That's all."

"Fair enough." Starr nodded. "Rumor has it Detective Alvarez is *convinced* your aunt did it."

"How would anyone know that for certain?" Having met the detective, she struck me as overtly professional and not one to divulge something like that. I mean, we knew they were looking at Aunt Dawn, but surveilling and being "convinced" were two very different things, in my mind. But maybe my instincts were wrong.

"I know people in high places, babe." The nickname set my teeth on edge. "But I can't reveal my sources."

I thanked her for sharing the information and took my snacks away with me. Who knew whether I could believe a word out of Starr's mouth? The altercation between Brendan and his neighbor intrigued me, however. If the police weren't interested in hearing from Starr, then maybe they had no idea there was a conflict going on.

And poisoning someone's dog was certainly an act of aggression. An act which could provoke retaliation.

My mind flashed back to my altercation with Brendan.

*I'm set up now, got my own place and everything, right on Pine Wood Lane. Come on, Chloe. Let me take you out to dinner.*

Pine Wood Lane.

I guess I would have to take the Jellybean out for another ride.

# CHAPTER 12

Two evenings later, Grandma Rose and I were attending an Azalea Bay tradition—the Big Bay Potluck. Every year, right before the tourism season opened, there was a potluck event in the Azalea Bay Town Hall. Originally the event had started as a way for locals to get together before the craziness of late spring through summer, since so many of the businesses in town were tied to the massive influx of people who sought out our sandy shores and picturesque views.

Azalea Bay was a popular vacation destination in general, but it also boasted a large number of seasonal events that drew crowds to our small patch of the world. Each summer we hosted a huge surfing competition, which packed the streets for a week with guests from all around the world. There was also an annual ice cream festival where artisans showcased their unique, flavorful creations, and visitors indulged their taste buds while trying not to get brain freeze.

Azalea Bay had it all.

But the high season came with a lot of pressure. Businesses needed to cover the bulk of their earnings in those few months so they could sustain the quieter period after. Coming together right before people flooded into town was a way for locals to catch up and share plans. It was a night of great food, conversation and forging relationships with your neighbors.

I'd decided to keep my contribution cannabis-free, since the event was open to all ages. But I still had the opportunity to show off my skills in the kitchen by making bite-sized desserts that brought together my Parisian training and US heritage.

Macaron cake pops.

The thing about making food for a large potluck event was that it had to be easily consumed while standing. Where desserts were concerned, I preferred to go with something that could be eaten with one hand and wasn't likely to end up all over the person eating it—so nothing with flaky pastry or soft cream. Cake pops were a *perfect* solution since they came with a stick and had enough structural integrity that you could take a bite out of them without the whole thing falling apart.

I started with making two different types of cake—a simple vanilla cake with high-quality real vanilla and buttermilk, and a chocolate cake with a touch of cinnamon and nutmeg for a gentle spicy undertone.

While the cake was cooling, I prepared both the vanilla and chocolate buttercream frostings. Grandma Rose was a true kitchen pro and had *two* stand mixers with multiple bowls, which made life easier. Then after the cakes were cooled, I crumbled them into their matching bowls of frosting, ensuring there were no large clumps.

That's the real trick to cake pops—if you have large chunks of cake, the "pop" is more likely to fall apart when you eat it. Ensuring my ratios of frosting to cake were correct, I rolled tablespoon-sized portions into balls and placed them on a tray lined with parchment paper.

I chilled the balls for a few hours in the refrigerator to make sure they were nice and firm. Then I tempered the chocolate for the coating and worked a few balls at a time, dipping a lollipop stick into the chocolate and then inserting it halfway into the ball. The balls were then dipped into the chocolate—white chocolate with a touch of food coloring to create a beautiful pale pink for the vanilla pops and milk chocolate for the chocolate pops. The tops were dipped into an edible gold glitter for a glamorous touch and stuck into foam blocks to dry, so the wet chocolate wouldn't touch anything and ruin the perfect, round surface.

Rinse and repeat.

The previous day I'd also made dozens of mini macaron shells, about the size of a quarter, in shades of pink and a deep yellow. I frosted and sandwiched the macarons and then attached them to the tops of the cake pop with a little melted chocolate.

Voila! French–US fusion.

"These are adorable. Bellissima!" Luisa walked into the kitchen, her face sparkling with delight. "Such a clever girl you are."

The people who brought food to the potluck were required to follow local food safety laws, which meant most of the people generously providing food were working in the food and beverage industry. Or, at the very least, *had* worked in the industry at some point. Luisa fell into the latter category. Her mother had started an Italian restaurant back in the '60s and Luisa had done her time managing it until she retired and her daughter and two granddaughters took over. La Bella Cucina was a fantastic restaurant and I was really hoping they would bring some of their incredible mushroom risotto balls.

"Thanks, Luisa." I grinned. "I figured you can't go wrong with simple vanilla and chocolate."

"Nothing wrong with simple if it's done well," she said, patting my arm. "And you do it *so* well."

I beamed under her praise. "Thanks for agreeing to help us transport the pops. I thought you might have been giving the restaurant a hand."

"The girls have it under control." She waved a hand. "They don't need me meddling in their work."

I stifled a smile. Luisa might like to act like she was happy to let them take the lead, but I knew for a fact that she still surprised her family with visits to the restaurant to make sure they were running things to her standards.

"You should get changed," Luisa said, looking disapprovingly at my sweatpants, which were smeared with buttercream. My hair was slicked back into a greasy bun, since I hadn't had time to wash it yet, and I knew I probably had gold dust or chocolate on my face.

"What's wrong? I was planning to go like this," I said, deadpan.

Luisa looked horrified before realizing I was joking. "You gave old Luisa a heart attack."

"You're only as old as you feel."

"Or the *man* you feel." She wriggled her eyebrows. "I think I can fit one more marriage in before I die, what do you think?"

I snorted. Luisa's man-eater vibe was my favorite thing in the world. "And what would husband number three say about that, huh?"

"Giorgio? He's a pussy cat. He would not care." She flicked a hand back and forth. Her nails were painted a bright red, which matched the slash of vibrant lipstick on her mouth and the red buttons that accented her leopard-print top. "Now, go and shower before I drag you up there myself. Who knows, maybe you will find a husband tonight!"

"I'd rather stuff myself silly with great food." I kissed her cheek and headed to the bathroom to wash the hours of cooking from my skin.

As far as I was concerned, Luisa could have all the husbands she liked. For now, singledom seemed a whole lot safer to me.

Just over an hour later, the town hall was a hive buzzing with activity. Volunteers manned the long trestle tables, serving the eager attendees and making sure empty bowls and plates were cleared away. Each person who brought a dish to the potluck

was required to fill in a template with allergen information—
such as whether their food contained dairy, nuts, gluten, etc.—
and to give a little description of what it was and who made it.
That way if you ate something particularly delicious, you could
compliment the chef.

These days the event was run by a committee of volunteers
rather than the local government, because . . . well, legal liabil-
ity. Technically this event was like any other private party held
in the town hall. But it captured Azalea Bay's community spirit
like nothing else.

"Hmm." I almost groaned in delight as I forked a piece of
mushroom risotto ball into my mouth. "I was hoping La Bella
Cucina would bring these. They're *so* good."

Sabrina bobbed her head. "And the gyoza from Oishi are
divine."

"Oh, I got one of those, too."

Even though Japanese and French cuisine seemed very different on the surface, they had a lot in common when it came to
ethos. High quality ingredients, attention to detail, mastering
craft. And Sabrina was right, I thought as I tried some of the
gyoza, the Japanese dumpling was *incredible.* I made a mental
note to take Grandma Rose and Aunt Dawn there for dinner at
some point.

"Aww!" Sabrina gestured with her plastic fork. "Your grandma
looks so cute tonight."

Thankfully she'd been feeling better today, so she'd gotten
dolled up to attend the potluck. There was a cluster of tables
on one side of the room, reserved for the older town residents
and people with mobility needs so they had somewhere to sit
and eat, rather than standing. Grandma Rose was wearing a
pretty shell-pink top with vintage buttons and a pair of flowing
magenta pants with a floral print on them. She'd even asked for
my help with her makeup and I'd slicked some shimmery gold
eyeshadow on her lids to enhance her blue eyes.

"Doesn't she?"

"How's the treatment going?" Sabrina asked, her tone turning serious.

Our families were close and Sabrina had visited my grandmother many times while I was overseas, helping her with the tech questions Aunt Dawn couldn't answer and even setting up a good quality webcam so we had a better Skyping experience.

"The chemo is making her queasy and tired. I think she's losing hair, although not quite as much as she was worried about. Honestly, she's taking it like a champ." I shook my head. "I hope I'm half as brave as she is when I get to her age. She's the strongest woman I know."

"And is it my imagination or is she flirting up a storm with that suave gentleman sitting next to her?"

"That would be Lawrence St. James, retired mystery writer and absolute one-hundred-percent grandma-approved crush." I grinned. "She changed her outfit seven times before we came out tonight."

"Adorable!"

"Every time I ask her about it, she goes red like a beet and tells me to hush. But I think it's sweet. He's so attentive when they're together, and he seems like a really nice man."

"You're never too old to fall in love, huh?" Sabrina sighed.

"Girl, you have hearts in your eyes!" I nudged her with my elbow. "Who would have thought *you* would end up being the romantic and I would be the jaded cynic."

"You're jaded lite, at best. The second you're done licking your wounds over Pepé Le Pew, it'll be back to hearts and roses for you. I know it."

I wasn't so sure.

But I didn't have time to form a retort, because a woman walked up to us, a warm smile on her face. For a moment I didn't recognize her, but she sure seemed to know me. Then it clicked.

"Detective Alvarez." I blinked. "Hi."

"Hard to recognize me out of uniform?" She laughed. Her dark hair was long and loose around her shoulders, and she wore a simple outfit of blue jeans and an LA Dodgers T-shirt. Today she wore a pair of oversized tortoiseshell glasses that had a slight pink tint to them. Out of uniform, she looked much younger. "And it's Adriana when I'm off duty."

"This is a casual conversation then, not an interview?" I couldn't help the slight coolness in my tone. Off duty or not, if Starr was right and the detective was "convinced" of my aunt's guilt, then we were on opposing teams.

"Actually, I came over to compliment your dessert." She held up an empty lollipop stick. "They were so good I had to try both flavors."

Okay, now I felt horrible for being so frosty toward her. "Sorry, that was really rude of me to say that."

"If that's the worst you've got, then I'm sure we'll be fine," she said, graciously.

Sabrina was called away by her mother, leaving me alone with the detective. For a moment neither of us said anything, and we stood there awkwardly.

"Have you been in town long?" I asked, cursing my crappy small-talk skills.

"About a year. I got a transfer from downtown LA."

"Looking for a slower pace?"

"Something like that." She nodded, and I got the impression there was much more of a story to her move than she was letting on. "Your aunt said you've been living overseas for the last few years."

"That's right. I came back when my grandma got sick." A lump lodged in the back of my throat.

"She has cancer, right? Your aunt mentioned it. I'm so sorry." There seemed to be genuine concern and empathy in Detective Alvarez's voice. "The big C got my abuela when I was still in high school."

"It sucks."

"Yeah, it really does."

The conversation petered out for a moment, as we lost ourselves in thought. But then I turned to her, the need to say my piece like prickles under my skin. "My aunt didn't kill Brendan."

"Chloe—"

"Have you got fingerprints from the knife? DNA? Anything?"

"It might be hard to believe, but that stuff takes time. How they show it on *CSI* is *not* real life." Frustration created an edge in her voice. "Besides, I can't discuss the case with you, and as much as I admire your sense of loyalty, I've heard a lot of family members say that very thing about someone who turned out to be a killer. They never see it coming."

I bit down on my lip. "This is different. She didn't do it. In fact, there are other people you should be speaking to. Did you know about Erica Simms? She worked with Brendan and he got her fired by planting a stolen item in her bag at work!"

"You know this for a fact?"

"Yes." I paused. "Well, she told me it happened."

"Did anyone see Brendan plant the item?"

"I . . . I don't know."

The detective nodded. "Okay, so it's possible that she *did* steal the item and now she's blaming a man who can't contradict her."

"Technically she blamed him before he died." I rubbed my hand at the back of my neck. It didn't sound like much when the detective repeated it back to me. "But she was fired! And before that, she was winning a company competition."

"Then don't you think her boss would have believed her, if she was such a good employee?"

"That's what I thought. It sounds like something weird was going on between the boss and Brendan. Erica caught him sleeping at work and the boss didn't even reprimand him." It had sounded like a good lead in my head. But now that I'd said it aloud it didn't sound like much of anything at all. "Have you talked to anyone who worked with him?"

Detective Alvarez shot me a look. "Are you asking me if I followed the most basic of investigative principals by talking to the employer of a dead man to see if there were any conflicts at work?"

"I'm not trying to insult your work ethic, I promise," I said quietly. "I just thought . . ."

"Chloe." She held up her hand. "If you have some genuine, *factual* information to report then you can speak with either myself or Chief Gladwell while we're on duty. You have my business card, so you can call me or you can come by the station. I won't listen to gossip and hearsay, however."

"But it could be helpful. Don't you want to know everything?"

"I want to know the *right* things. Despite what people think, more information is not always better. I've seen plenty of investigations stall because of too many false leads." She sighed. "Part of being a detective is knowing how to filter information."

"But what about Brendan's future brother-in-law, Steve? Or his neighbor? Or the gym he went to? Have you looked at them?"

"I'm going to give you a piece of advice, okay?" Detective Alvarez said. "Let me do my job. I spent five years working homicide in LA and I closed more cases than people with triple the experience I had. I know what I'm doing. Please trust me."

I didn't. I couldn't. Not while she was looking at my aunt as a suspect.

Detective Alvarez struck me as a decent human. She seemed empathetic and intelligent. But people like that could still make mistakes. Nobody was infallible.

"Thanks for the great dessert. You're a talented chef," she said, motioning with the empty lollipop stick. Then she disappeared into the crowded hall, leaving me alone.

I looked down at my plate, which now had half a risotto ball, a small piece of crab toast and a lamb kofta going cold. Sighing, I stuffed the crab toast into my mouth and chewed. But not even the sweet, buttery crab could cheer me up. I had to find more information. *Then* I could report it to the detective or the chief and they would have to listen to me.

But where did I go from here?

I scanned the crowd, and almost dropped my plate when I saw a familiar face. It was Tate from the gym and he was hovering by one of the tables, alone. I took it as a sign to keep pushing ahead with my personal investigation and so I walked toward him, my eyes lingering on the food like I was any other hungry potluck guest.

Tate's gaze slid over me as I approached, and I immediately got slimeball vibes from him. Great. But at least it might help me to make conversation.

"Any recommendations from this table?" I asked, meeting his eye. We were standing in front of one of the dessert tables, where my cake pops were situated along with cookies and cupcakes from Sweet Tooth, a cheesecake I knew wouldn't be as good as my grandmother's, and an assortment of handmade chocolates and truffles.

"Oh, I don't eat anything with sugar," he replied, puffing out his chest. "Got to keep up my physique and all."

I fought the urge to roll my eyes. "Just admiring the visuals, then?"

"Anything to fight the boredom. Although I'm a little less bored now." He smiled at me and it made me immediately want to jump into a shower. It was a wonder how this guy and Brendan *weren't* friends, because they seemed cut from the same cloth. "What's your name?"

"Chloe." I fought the urge to run away and stuck out my hand. His palm was sweaty and his handshake was limper than week-old celery. "And you are?"

"Tate Duncan-Brooks."

Duncan-Brooks. DB.

I'd written off the connection between Tate and the knife based on his first name, but I hadn't even considered that he might have a double-barreled surname. "Nice to meet you, Tate. You, uh . . . you look familiar. Have we met before?"

"I'm pretty sure I'd remember meeting a lovely lady like yourself," he said, still making uncomfortably intense eye contact while holding my hand. I tugged it out of his grip and tried to smooth the action over with a girlish laugh. Ugh, I was *so* bad at this!

"I swear, your face is ringing a bell." I smiled sweetly. "You're not a member of the Iron Works gym, are you?"

"Yes, I am. That's probably why I don't remember you. I really get into the zone when I work out." He nodded. "A Victoria's Secret supermodel could walk right by me and I wouldn't even notice, let alone a normal person."

This guy was a certified douche canoe.

"I was thinking about joining," I said, desperate to see what information I could get out of him so I could get away as quickly as possible. "But I've heard . . . well, I heard some not-so-great things about the place."

"Oh, like what? I know *all* the gossip there." He moved closer and my body tensed up in response. "I'm kind of a big deal at the gym."

Oh boy. This guy's ego was something else.

"Well, I heard there was some bullying going on and then suddenly one of their regulars turns up dead."

I watched his face intently to see if there was anything that might indicate guilt or anger or deception. But Tate simply snorted. "And you think that's connected to the gym? No way. Brendan was a cool dude. I would say behind me, he was one of the other most popular guys at the gym."

*Give me a bucket.*

"You knew him?" I asked.

"Are you kidding?" He puffed his chest out. "We were practically best friends."

I wanted to scream, *but he almost killed you!*

"Such a tragedy that he's gone," Tate continued, shaking his head. "But you know what they say—the higher you climb the more people remember you when you fall."

*That is definitely not how that saying goes.*

Still, Tate's response fit with Jay's comment about him seeming desperate for Brendan's approval. Now that he was dead, Tate could make out like they'd been best buds and that he was in with the "popular" guys. Barf.

Truthfully, I didn't sense any malice in Tate. So, unless he had Oscar-worthy acting skills, I was having a hard time buying that he did it. Only, the guy's initials *did* match the knife and that couldn't be ignored.

Frustratingly, I felt like I somehow knew more *and* less after speaking to Tate.

"You should join Iron Works," Tate advised, nodding his head sagely like he was bestowing the world's greatest wisdom on me. "It's a good gym."

"Thanks for the advice. Enjoy the rest of your evening," I said, waving and turning on my heel before he had a chance to respond.

I mentally put an asterisk next to Tate's name. He *could* be a suspect, but my gut was telling me that he wouldn't kill a guy he idolized . . . even if Brendan could very well have killed him.

# CHAPTER 13

"You look like someone kicked your puppy."

I'd made my way deeper into the crowd to avoid Tate and turned to find Jake standing next to me, looking as roguishly handsome as usual. Now *that* was a man I was happy to see. He wore a rumpled white shirt with the sleeves rolled up, light blue jeans and a pair of black-and-white sneakers. An expensive-looking silver watch sat on one wrist, like a remnant of his time on Wall Street.

"That would require me owning a puppy, which sadly I do not." I eyed his plate. It was piled precariously high with a good selection of the potluck offerings. "Maybe I should get one."

"A puppy? Why not?"

Why not? His breezy response made me laugh, because naturally I would overthink such a decision. Maybe I needed a little more "why not?" energy in my life.

"It's a big decision."

"Do you *want* a dog?" he asked, taking a toothpick and stabbing at a small meatball covered in sauce, before popping it into his mouth.

"I've always wanted a dog, actually. My aunt has a border collie, Moxie. She's so smart and funny. But I see myself with something a little more . . . fun sized." I nodded. "Maybe like a Chihuahua or a little terrier of some kind. Something I can easily pick up if it's being naughty."

Jake chuckled. "Hello control issues."

I flushed. "Maybe a little."

"So why are you looking sad when you're here, surrounded by amazing food and lovely people?" he asked, seeming genuinely interested.

"I'm worried that the police are going to arrest my aunt for Brendan's murder." The words tumbled out of my mouth in a rush, like I had some deep-seated desire to share the burden of my worry with another person. The right person.

And in that moment, Jake felt like the right person.

"Okay." He nodded, his expression turning somber and his brows drawing together. There were fairy lights strung across the ceiling of the town hall and the glow reflected in the warm tones of his dark hair. "No wonder you're worried. Is there anything I can do to help?"

"Want to come and question suspects with me?" I joked.

Well, I was more *half* joking because I wasn't sure exactly how he would react. Most people would probably look at me like I was nuttier than a fruitcake for suggesting such a thing.

"Suspects?" He narrowed his eyes. "You have suspects?"

"I guess they're not considered suspects until the police deem them so, but let's just say there are people who could have motive. And maybe they had the opportunity. I simply want to gather some information and take it to the police to help them with their investigation."

"You're serious?" He blinked. "Wow."

"Ridiculous, huh?"

"I don't think so. If someone I cared about was in your aunt's position, I'd be doing everything in my power to help them. It shows what kind of a person you are."

"Oh." I was taken aback by the kind words, fully having

expected him to extricate himself from the conversation and avoid me until the end of time for being a freak. "Well, thank you. I *do* care about my aunt . . . a lot. She's like my big sister, and my grandma is like my mother. They're my whole world."

An expression flickered across his face—one of deep resonance. For a moment, I felt utterly seen and understood.

"Who are your suspects and when are we going on a road trip?" he asked with a crooked smile.

I laughed. "Don't you have a job or something more important to do than go on a wild-goose chase with me?"

"One, yes I *do* have a job. I'm a virtual financial coach, but the hours are flexible so I can work when I want. And two, I think trying to prevent your aunt from being arrested for a crime she didn't commit is pretty darn important." His hazel eyes searched my face, although for what I wasn't sure. I felt like he wanted to say something, so I held my breath, not daring to do a thing that might spook him. "My brother actually got done for a crime he didn't commit."

"No," I gasped. "What happened?"

"He was in with a bad crowd and they did terrible stuff—breaking and entering, theft. They broke into a shop once, thinking it was empty and it wasn't. He fled and someone else beat the poor shop owner to a pulp. The guy lived, thankfully. But the cops pinned the assault on my brother and he got sent off to juvie."

"Oh my goodness." I shook my head. "Did he get out?"

"Yeah, they eventually caught the real perpetrator out in a lie. But he'd been in there almost a year at that point. It changed him." Jake looked at the ground. "It was my whole drive to be perfect after that. I strived to get the best grades and win all my track-and-field meets and never make a mistake."

"Oh, Jake. I don't know what to say." It was such a heartbreaking story and I could see the impact it had on him. "I'm so sorry."

"It's all in the past," he said with a sigh. "And being a perfectionist to the point of self-sabotage isn't the way to correct things. Not caring at all and caring too much can have the same outcome."

"Mm-hmm." I nodded. "That is *so* true."

"I'm a good law-abiding citizen and I respect how difficult police work is. But I also know they get it wrong on occasion and it can ruin people's lives." He looked at me with an intensity that warmed me up inside. "So, if I can help prevent that happening to your family, then I would like to. Even if it's just another set of ears, anything. It seems like you could use a friend."

"I *could* use a friend, actually."

I had Sabrina, of course, but I knew she would try to warn me off getting too involved. Besides, if there did turn out to be a connection to Erica, then I didn't want to put her in the middle of things. But beyond that . . . I was only starting to rebuild my relationships here.

Not to mention that Jake was neutral ground because he was new to town. He didn't have the messy entanglements and connections us lifers did. He could look at this place with fresh, unbiased eyes. His perspective would keep me in check and stop me from seeing things that weren't there.

"Fancy taking a drive tomorrow afternoon?" I asked.

"Name the time and I'll be there."

Jake and I met the following day around four p.m. The plan was to head to Pine Wood Lane and see if we could find Brendan's house and, therefore, his neighbor's house. Instead of sleeping last night, I'd lain awake in bed with ideas swirling in my head. If we *did* happen to come across Darius, we needed a viable excuse as to why we were there, and an excuse to speak with him. If he was as reclusive as Starr claimed, then he may not take too kindly to a couple of strangers poking around.

Then it hit me.

Real estate in Azalea Bay wasn't always easy to come by. With the increasing number of people from the cities looking to acquire seaside property—not to mention the boom in Airbnbs—house prices were going up and the market had become more competitive. Azalea Bay was a desirable place to live because we weren't as small as other towns (even I, a lifer, didn't know everyone here) yet we still had that close-knit community feel. Life moved at a slower pace, yet we still had a good employment market. Plus, with the increase in remote working there were loads of people who would otherwise have needed to be closer to the city looking to live in a quieter, prettier place because they only had to commute on occasion as opposed to every day.

Jake was doing exactly that. So long as he had a computer and internet connection, he could work anywhere.

"We're going to pretend you're interested in buying Brendan's house and say that you're scoping out the area?" Jake clarified.

"That's right. It will give me an excuse to ask Darius about the street and make out like I want to connect with my potential neighbors." I pulled down the visor inside Jake's car and checked my makeup. I'd tried to present myself as well put-together, yet approachable. I hoped my white denim dress, light gray cardigan and brown leather sandals exuded an air of responsibility, like I could afford to buy a house . . . even though I certainly could not.

I might have been saving for a wedding, but property was a whole other financial ballgame.

Jake drove and I looked out the window, watching as Azalea Bay shifted. There were three different sections of my hometown: the wealthy side with its beautiful beachfront houses and fancy cars in the driveway, the "average Joe" section where Grandma Rose and I lived . . . and the area around Pine Wood Lane, which had the oldest houses. A number of properties here had temporary construction fences around them, with signs indicating they were going to be torn down.

Music blared as we turned onto Brendan and Darius's street

and I heard a dog barking in the distance. A group of young men in their twenties hung around in the yard of one of the houses, leaning against a car with all the doors open and the stereo cranked. We drove slowly, looking for a sign of which house might belong to Brendan. The street was longer than I'd thought, having looked it up on Google Maps earlier, and I worried we wouldn't be able to tell which one was his.

But then I saw it—a house with yellow tape across the door. "That must be it," I said, pointing. "The police are probably keeping it sealed in case they need to go back in and check through any of his things."

Jake pulled the car over to the side of the road and we got out. The house looked uncared for, and not only because it was closed up. The grass was overgrown and brown in patches, and a long-dead plant sat next to the front door. Spiderwebs decorated the corners of the windows, and flyers and other papers sat in a slumped pile by the door—more than what would have accumulated in the week or so since Brendan's death. Paint peeled away from the boards, desperate for TLC.

"He didn't take care of this place," Jake said, as if reading my mind.

"I don't think he took care of many things," I replied, frowning. "Now, I wonder which side belongs to Darius."

The houses in this street all resembled one another in style, made unique only by the color of the clapboards or stucco, and the plants they grew. The houses on either side looked better maintained than Brendan's, though not overly manicured. The one to the left had a tricycle in the front yard, bright pink and decorated with purple and yellow streamers on the handles.

"I don't remember Starr saying anything about him having a kid," I mused. "So, my guess would be that he lives on the other side."

Jake nodded. "Shall we knock?"

I glanced down the street. Aside from the guys blasting music from their car, it was mostly empty. Being a weekday morning, most people would be at work. I figured that Darius might work for himself, *if* he worked at all, considering Starr had made a comment that nobody knew what he did. If he was employed by a local business, people would know. So there was a chance he was home.

"Let's try." I nodded.

We walked over and knocked on the door. Nothing. There were no sounds inside, no sign of movement or life. We waited a moment before trying again. Still nothing. For the sake of being thorough, we also tried the house with the child's tricycle. Nothing there, either.

Feeling slightly defeated, I turned to Jake. "We could sit in the car and wait a bit."

"Fine by me."

As we headed back to the car, however, I noticed something odd when I looked toward Brendan's house. A large piece of what appeared to be flattened cardboard was draped with a dusty blue blanket and propped against one of the windows on the side of the house. It seemed an odd place to put it, especially when there was ample space on the wall beside it. Why would someone purposefully block the light coming in . . . unless it was hiding something?

"Hang on a second," I said to Jake. "I want to check something out."

I darted across Brendan's front yard. There was no gate sealing off the side or back part of the property, so I could get to the window easily. It was indeed a flattened box with a somewhat dusty blanket draped over the top—like the kind a removal company might use to protect items during transportation. I peeled the blanket back and confirmed that the cardboard underneath must have been used for a move, because it had the words "kitchen utensils, cookbooks & trays" written in black marker.

I moved the cardboard and blanket to one side. One of the window's panes had been smashed and glittering shards littered the inside of Brendan's house, making it clear the glass had been broken from the outside. As the morning light streamed in through the hole, I saw the slight mark of a shoe print on one of the larger pieces of glass.

Someone had broken into Brendan's house, probably *after* it was sealed by the police.

It would be a tight squeeze to get through the single pane and avoid the jagged edges, but someone my size could fit if they really tried. What could they have been looking for? Was it simply an opportunist wanting to loot the place, knowing it would be empty? Did Brendan own anything of value?

The side window looked into a room with a simple bed, side table, a near-empty bookshelf and a desk. Maybe there had been a computer there, although I figured the police had probably taken that for the investigation. A drawer was open at the desk, and a few papers were littered on the floor like oversized snowflakes. A photo frame sat on the desk, but the glass was cracked and the photo removed.

"Uhh, Chloe." Jake bounced on the spot next to me, his voice tight. "There's someone looking."

I jumped up from my crouched position and quickly slid the cardboard back into place over the window. A figure was striding toward us, a stern expression on his face. I recognized him instantly.

"Steve Boyd!" I shook my head and laughed like I hadn't been caught peering into his fiancée's brother's house. "Long time."

Steve, who was easily six-foot-four, faltered. He was as handsome as I remembered—bright green eyes, strong jaw, and a lanky but muscular frame perfectly suited to playing basketball. He wore a black hoodie and jeans, with a black baseball cap on his head.

"Chloe?" He blinked. "What the hell are you doing here?"

"Oh well, it's *such* a long story. But I went off to France to study and then I became a pastry chef—"

"I mean, *here* here. What are you doing at Brendan's house?" His eyes flicked to Jake, who moved closer to my side as if wanting to protect me. Steve looked wound up. He had dark circles under his eyes and he cracked his knuckles anxiously while waiting for my answer.

"I don't have to tell you how out-of-control the property market has gotten here." I laughed nervously. "I know Brendan's house isn't on the market yet, of course. But I figured it couldn't hurt to have a little look, right? Do some research on the street, see if the frontage is good."

*See if the frontage is good? Is that even a thing?*

I had no idea. Like for many millennials, home ownership was a stretch goal. I'd barely finished paying off my student loans, but Steve didn't have to know that.

"We haven't even had the funeral yet." Steve shook his head. "And you're already sniffing around his house?"

I gulped. Now was *not* the time to crumble—I had a duty to my aunt to find out whatever I could. So, I put on my best don't-mess-with-me smile. "What are *you* doing here?"

"That's none of your business," he said sharply, shifting from one foot to another and looking over his shoulder. "I could call the police and have you arrested for trespassing."

There was definitely something up with Steve. I got the distinct impression that he wanted to get rid of us as quickly as possible. He yanked his cap off his head and raked a hand through his dark hair, his hairline sitting a little further back than it had in high school. He had a nasty cut on his hand.

"Ouch. You should put something on that cut." I pointed. "It looks inflamed. Wouldn't want to get it infected."

He narrowed his eyes at me menacingly. "Get. Off. The. Property. Now."

"Come on, Chloe." Jake grabbed my arm and tugged me toward him. "Let's go."

As I headed toward Jake's car, my heart pounding, I kept an eye on Steve. He watched us leave, without moving from his spot, arms folded across his chest. As we drove away, I noticed a car in the street that I hadn't seen before—a dark blue SUV with a custom license plate that said D3F3NCE. Still hanging on to his basketball glory days, huh?

I felt his eyes follow us all the way to the end of the street and I shivered. Would he really be so pissed about a nosy property hunter? Or was there something more sinister going on with Steve Boyd?

# CHAPTER 14

By the time we made it home, my heart rate had finally slowed down. "Well, that was . . . somehow both eventful and un-eventful."

"I wouldn't want to get on the wrong side of that guy," Jake said, shaking his head. Not that he was small by any stretch, but Steve was bigger than most and there was a menacing air about him. "He looked like a bit of a loose cannon if you ask me."

"And that cut on his hand was *super* suspicious considering there was a broken window." I tapped a finger against my chin. "What could he have been looking for?"

"It's possible that it was a coincidence. Did you notice any blood on the broken glass or the window frame?"

"No," I admitted. "But what other reason could he have to be at the property? It's supposed to be sealed."

"Maybe he was collecting the mail? There *was* a bunch of it on the porch."

"Good point." I rolled the scenario through in my head. "And I guess it's possible he was angry simply because he thought we were being disrespectful snooping around before they've even said goodbye to Brendan."

I wasn't sure how to feel. Now I understood what Detective Alvarez meant when she said being a good investigator was about knowing how to filter information. Something could be a clue, or it could be nothing. And it was easy to follow the wrong piece of information down a rabbit hole and make a suspect out of an innocent person.

That realization, however, did not make me feel better about my aunt's position as top suspect.

"Hey," I said suddenly. "Do you still have access to the security camera footage that you gave the police?"

Jake nodded. "Yeah. I copied the files for them, but I keep the originals on a hard drive."

"Would you mind if I looked at it? I don't know if it will tell me anything, but . . . you never know, right?" I knotted my hands in my lap, hoping that I wasn't imposing. "I don't have to stay at your computer if you're busy, I can copy the files to a USB and check them out at home."

"Or we could order a pizza." He killed the engine and glanced over at me. "And look over it together."

Suddenly my heart was beating a little faster again. "I'd like that."

I took twenty minutes to check on Grandma Rose and change into something comfier before I headed over to Jake's. For all the teasing about my grandmother changing her outfit half a dozen times before the potluck event, I did *exactly* the same thing. Jeans and a T-shirt or leggings and a sweater? What about a cute little flowing dress . . . or did that look like I was trying too hard?

*Ugh!*

Knowing how to act around guys was *not* my strong suit. Never had been. That's why there were dozens of angsty teenage diary entries about my unrequited crush on Frankie Stewart—not because he wasn't interested in me, necessarily, but because I'd always been too chicken to do anything about it. I was even worse at reading signs. I couldn't tell if Jake was interested in helping me out because A, he was a decent human with a strong community spirit; or B, because of his brother's experience with false incrimination; or C, because he liked me.

Worse still, I didn't know which of those options I hoped was true. Maybe all three.

*You shouldn't want all three.*

Deciding that I wouldn't be able to solve this conundrum right away, I opted for a pair of worn-in jeans and a fluffy but lightweight pink sweater that was cute and casual. I brushed my hair out, added a slick of pink-tinted gloss to my lips, and gave myself a spritz of light perfume. I held the weighty fluted glass bottle in my hand, admiring the gauzy pink ribbon tied around the neck and fancy, scalloped gold cap. I'd bought it on a whim as a birthday gift to myself when I was feeling homesick my first year in Paris. The perfume was called Rosy Dawn, which had felt like a sign, and ever since then the smell had become a comfort to me when I was feeling confused or uncertain.

Like I did right now.

"Heading out again?" Grandma Rose asked, poking her head into my room. She hesitated by the door.

"You can come in," I said, laughing. "I promise I've shed my teenage need for absolute privacy."

She stepped over the threshold. "Where are you headed?"

Hmm. I couldn't very well dodge the question now that I'd declared I didn't care about privacy anymore. "To Jake's house."

"Oh!" Grandma Rose's face lit up. "Is it a date?"

"No, it's not. I asked to look over his security camera footage." I shot her a look. "I promise we're not getting up to no good."

"I wouldn't mind you getting up to no good. Might give me a great-grandchild to cuddle!"

I rolled my eyes. "I distinctly remember you being paranoid about me getting pregnant as a teenager because I wore lipstick to school one time. Now you want me to get knocked up?"

"Big difference between being a teenager and being almost thirty," she said sagely.

"I'm twenty-eight, that's *ages* before I turn thirty." I winked. "Plenty of time to make babies in the future."

She waggled a finger at me. "Time is fleeting, Chloe. The distance between plenty of time and a missed opportunity is shorter than you think."

I leaned over and kissed her head. "Don't worry, I won't forget about my uterus."

"And why are you looking at the security camera footage, anyway?" She looked up at me, a crinkle forming between her brows. "What are you hoping to find?"

"Anything." I sighed. "I don't know what exactly, but I feel like there's an important piece of information the police are missing, and I'm determined to find it. There has to be *something* that will clear Dawn's name."

"She won't even talk to me about it," my grandmother admitted, leaning against me. I slipped my arm around her shoulders, trying not to notice how she felt smaller than I remembered. "What was she doing in the park that night? I know with all my heart that she's not a killer, but . . . why won't she admit what she was doing and clear her name? Stubborn child."

"She's got your genes for sure."

Grandma Rose sighed. "My mother once told me that having two daughters as willful as your mother and aunt was punishment for being a difficult child myself."

"That's not very nice."

"Maybe not, but it's true. My daughters have the best and worst of me." She gave me a squeeze. "And luckily you got mostly the good bits."

I smiled. "Mostly."

"Well, nobody's perfect, dear." She released me. "I feel like I should tell you not to meddle in the police's work but . . ."

"They're looking in the wrong direction."

"Yes, I think they are. But promise me you will stay out of trouble, okay? If you find something, give the information to the police and let them handle it. I don't want you doing anything dangerous."

It was probably for the best that I didn't mention my encounter with Steve Boyd, then. "Of course. It's information gathering and nothing more."

"Well, have a good time at Jake's house and if you feel the need to get up to no good, just make sure you keep the blinds closed so the neighbors can't see."

"Grandma!" I said, scandalized.

"What? Sex is a natural part of life." She shrugged. "No point being embarrassed about it."

Tell that to my cheeks which were now fifty shades of crimson. "Can we *not* talk about the birds and the bees right now? Please?"

"Prude," she muttered under her breath as she shuffled out of my bedroom, her slippers making *whoosh whoosh* sounds against the carpet.

Shaking my head, I grabbed my purse and avoided looking in the mirror on my way out. The last thing I needed was her filling my head with things I was already confused about. And asking Jake about the footage *wasn't* a ruse to spend more time with him—it was a genuine request. I needed to focus my energy there.

I walked over to Jake's front door and knocked. A second later, it opened and the sound of The Strokes' *Is This It* floated out.

"Come on in." He stepped back and held the door.

"I *love* this album."

"Me, too. I got it on vinyl a few years ago and it's . . . chef's kiss." He grinned.

"I get the sense that you enjoy old things—the vinyls, fixing up your grandfather's car . . ." I glanced around the room, which was sparsely furnished in that typical bachelor-pad way. But the items he owned had personality—I spotted a cool mid-century chair in a deep forest-green velvet and a cut-crystal decanter containing some amber liquid sitting on a sideboard. "Vintage décor."

"The decanter is another inherited item from my grandfather. He liked his scotch," Jake replied. "A little too much, admittedly. I buy the same kind and barely drink it, but it smells smoky and it reminds me of him."

I darn near melted on the spot. "That's lovely."

"Tastes like an ashtray, though." He chuckled. "I never developed the taste for it. I'm more of a beer guy, myself. Speaking of which, can I get you a drink?"

"Tempting as that offer is, I want to be sharp while we're looking through the footage. But I'll take a soda if you have some?"

"Sure. I was thinking we could grab a pizza from La Bella Cucina? They do those awesome woodfire ones with the nice toppings."

"Great idea. We're friends with the family who run that restaurant, so I'm always happy to support good local businesses while stuffing my face with prosciutto." I laughed.

Jake motioned for me to follow him toward the open-plan kitchen and he grabbed two cans of Coke out of the fridge. This area was also sparse. I figured some of that was owing to the fact that he hadn't moved here all that long ago. An artistic black-and-white photo hung on one wall. It showed a man standing on the beach, wearing some rather short bathing shorts and holding a surfboard, and looked like it might have been taken in the '50s or '60s.

"I connected my laptop to the television, so we can watch the footage there. Might make it a bit easier to see, although the resolution isn't perfect." We headed over to his couch, which was a basic dark gray but had a cozy-looking blanket in gray and white checks thrown over the back. "I've got the mouse here, so we can skip ahead or go back as needed. Where did you want to start?"

"The day of the murder, in the afternoon?" I settled onto the couch and popped the ring-pull on my soda. "I don't know whether I want to kiss or shake Mr. Avagyan for setting up this camera."

Jake navigated to the folders where the backup files were contained, organized by month, and double-clicked the file for the day of the murder.

"We can set it to superspeed," he said.

"Is that the technical term?" I sipped my drink and he shot an amused glance in my direction. "I'm only teasing. I really appreciate that you've gone so out of your way with all this. I hope it hasn't dredged up any painful memories with your brother."

Jake looked away and shook his head. "I shouldn't have said that."

"Please don't worry about it." I reached over and placed my hand on his arm. "My lips are sealed, I promise."

It looked like he wanted to say more, but then he changed his mind. Instead he moved his mouse against the coffee table, dragging the curser until the clock read 4:00 p.m. On "superspeed" mode, the people in the video bustled by like ants, and cars zoomed down the street. The camera was angled, clearly aimed to capture the place where the roses had been planted by Mrs. Avagyan. You could see Jake's driveway and mailbox, about three quarters of the sidewalk in front of his house, part of the road and the edge of the park.

"Who knew so many people walked up and down this street?"

Parents pushed strollers, people walked dogs, and there were joggers and groups of schoolkids and more. Nothing at all looked out of the ordinary. Things became a little harder to see as it got dark outside, but the light above Jake's door came on and cast a glow across the driveway and yard. Around the time I went off with Chief Gladwell I saw Aunt Dawn's car roll past and disappear off the side of the screen, presumably as she parked in front of our house.

As the minutes ticked by quickly on the video's clock, my eyes were glued to the screen. At a few minutes past nine p.m. a figure hovered in front of Jake's house, a long skirt dusting the ground.

"Can we go back a bit and slow it down, please?" I said, leaning forward.

Jake moved the slider back and set the video to play in real time. Clear as day, my aunt appeared on the screen, her signature maxi-length skirt and boho-style handbag with leather fringe making it impossible to miss her. The footage was in color, but because of the low light it was difficult to make much out beyond the fact that there were big red flowers on her skirt.

The same skirt she'd been wearing when she confronted Brendan in front of the chief.

My throat tightened. What was she doing?

The video showed my aunt pacing back and forth, like she was trying to make up her mind about something. Her hands were knotted in front of her—something she only ever did when she was anxious. After a few minutes of deliberation, she turned sharply toward the park and walked into the street without even checking to see if any cars were coming. Then she disappeared out of vision.

"What on earth . . . ?" I shook my head. "Can we play it again?"

Jake dragged the video back and we watched the scene several more times, but I couldn't glean anything more. My aunt was clearly weighing up whether she should go into the park, and her body language suggested she was upset or nervous. It was so odd. I almost felt like I was watching a stranger.

I sat back against the couch and frowned, trying to make sense of things.

"Let's try once more," I said, unsure what more I could possibly glean. "Then I'll give up."

Jake nodded and restarted the video from earlier in the afternoon. I watched numbly, wondering whether there was anything that could save my aunt. For a moment, an awful prickling sensation crawled over my skin.

What if she did it?

I shoved the thought to one side. No way. But there *must* be an explanation for her being in the park, because it sure as heck didn't look like she was simply going for a walk.

*Why is she lying to you?*

I watched the footage again, feeling my eyes go blurry from the sameness of it all. There was the woman with the big white dog, followed by the two teenage girls on their way home from school. The thickening of traffic at the end of the workday as people came home. Soon we'd see the woman walking three little dogs who strayed all over the place and got their leads tangled.

Same. Same. Same.

I waited for the big truck to roll past, not long before my aunt was due to come out of the house. I'd memorized the exact moment. Ah, there it was. Truck time. Then . . .

"Wait." I pushed forward, squinting at the screen. "Go back a little and play it in real time. I want to see that truck again."

"Sure." Jake reached for the mouse.

The video played again. There was the woman with the three dogs and their tangled leads. She paused, bending down to free the paw of a little white terrier and give it a scratch behind the ear. Then she stood and continued walking, the dogs disappearing off the side of the screen as a truck came past. It was painted plain white with no logos. A scuff marked the front side panel, as if it had swiped against something and there was paint transfer.

It struck me as familiar.

*Maybe because you've watched this thing so many times you could recite it frame for frame in your sleep?*

"What are you looking at?" Jake asked.

"I don't even know," I replied with a sigh. "Something about the truck seems familiar, but I think I'm giving myself déjà vu."

I scrubbed my hands over my face as the video rolled on and we watched my aunt come into frame and stand on the sidewalk, pacing back and forth. I watched her again, hoping something might catch or spark. But nothing did. Disappointment was bitter on the back of my tongue and I was about to call it a night, when I caught something at the very edge of the screen.

"Pause it!" I jumped off the edge of the couch and walked right up to the TV screen, pointing. "Can you see that?"

"Uhh . . . no?"

At the very edge of the screen the nose of a white vehicle peeked into view. A white vehicle that looked like it might have a paint swipe on the front side panel. It was hard to tell, because it was barely in frame. There was no way to see the license plate or anything else distinguishing about it. But the swipe appeared to be in the exact same spot.

"I think this truck went past earlier. It looks like it has a mark right here." I pointed. "A paint swipe or a scuff or something like that."

"Okay." Jake nodded. "And that's suspicious because . . . ?"

"I don't know." I groaned. "I'm clutching at straws. But I don't think anyone on this block owns a white truck."

Other than Jake, all the houses within a block on either side of Grandma Rose had been owned by the same people ever since I was in high school. After returning, I'd seen many of them while going out for a walk or running errands, stopping to chat or answer questions about where I'd been and why I was back. I'd never seen a white truck parked in the street before with any frequency to indicate that someone who lived here owned it.

"I have to admit, I haven't seen many trucks around here, either. It's four-door sedans as far as the eye can see." He rubbed a hand along his chin. "Let's keep watching."

The last few times we'd watched the video, our focus had been on trying to see when Aunt Dawn reappeared from the park. She didn't—at least not on camera—so she likely crossed the road outside the field of view. We'd also been looking for any sight of other possible suspects or Brendan himself.

We *hadn't*, however, been keeping much of an eye on the vehicles.

Yet sure enough, when we continued watching the video, the truck that had been parked on the street around the time my aunt went into the park, eventually moved. We couldn't see anyone get in or out, because the doors weren't in frame. But at 9:27 p.m., the truck rolled past the screen with a paint smudge in the exact same position as it had been earlier, though the video quality and lighting weren't good enough to show us the driver.

"It's the same truck!" I gasped. "I wonder how many times it went past."

We watched the video over again, this time paying attention to the vehicle. It was on camera three times in total. At 8:45 p.m. it rolled past without slowing. At 8:58 it came past again. And at 9:04, it parked at the edge of the screen, remaining there until 9:27.

Twenty-three minutes. Was that enough time to walk into a park and stab a man to death? Quite possibly.

All I knew for certain was that I had to find out who owned that truck.

# CHAPTER 15

I spent the following day getting sweaty and working out my muscles in the shop I hoped would soon become the home for Baked by Chloe. It was already looking infinitely better with the cleanup job Aunt Dawn and I had done, which included washing the walls and painting them with a stark white primer. Not exactly the most elegant color—truthfully, it was more hospital basic than Parisienne chic—but it was *way* better than the orange paint that existed before. Once we had a proper go-ahead, I'd paint the walls a softer shade.

Today I was working on the kitchen, scrubbing the inside of the commercial oven and cooktops until they gleamed. I wiped down the countertops, shelving and cabinets, ridding them of a gritty layer of grime and sawdust particles. I swept and mopped the floor, cleaned the refrigerators and tested all the appliances. After, my arms aching from effort and brow dampened with sweat, I stood in the middle of it all, hopeful for progress and anxious to have a place where I could establish myself and get my life back on track.

Something about the space filled me with good energy. I could see myself here, dressed in traditional chef whites, doing what I did best—creating dishes and feeding people, helping them expand their taste buds. Beyond that, I could help to break down the stigma about cannabis use and help people like my grandmother find relief *and* indulge their senses. Knowing that my brownies had been a hit at the oncology clinic gave me the warm and fuzzies. And the more people who seemed excited about the idea, the less I worried about being run out of town.

Sure, there would always be people like Bertram Bottom who thought I was bringing the town into disrepute. But now I suspected they would be in the minority.

I knew in my heart that this is what I wanted. It might not have been the plan I'd started out with, but as the idea for Baked by Chloe had grown in my mind, I knew this was the right way forward.

A pounding at the front door startled me out of my thoughts. I dropped my rubber gloves into the sink and pushed the bucket filled with dirty mop water to one side so I wouldn't accidentally trip over it later. Then I went to see who was knocking.

My aunt stood on the other side of the door, purple hair like a violet cloud around her head as she waved a piece of paper at me through the window. My heart leaped into my throat. I unlocked the door and yanked it open.

"We're approved!" She let out a squeal so high-pitched I was sure every dog in the neighborhood was going to come running.

"Wait . . . for what? Which approval?"

"The bank." She threw her arms around me and I stumbled back, momentarily dazed from having the wind knocked out of me. Her rose patchouli perfume filled my nostrils. "We have a business loan!"

"Oh my gosh." I pulled away and snatched the paper from her hands. My eyes scanned over it and sure enough, Baked by Chloe was officially funded. "I almost can't believe it."

"That's one big item ticked off, with one more to go. But I have a good feeling." Dawn grinned and there was a tiny smudge of burgundy lipstick on her teeth. "That business plan you put together was wonderful."

"Thanks to Claude's input," I said. My old boss was a treasure trove of industry information. "He pointed out *so* many things that I would have overlooked."

"Well, you owe him a bottle of champagne. Because the bank manager told me it was one of the most impressive business plans they'd seen in a long time. You should be proud."

"Let's get our license first and then I'll be proud," I said, trying to temper my excitement. I couldn't put the cart before the horse. Or, in this case, the special brownies before the cannabis license. "One step at a time."

"You're always so cautious," she said, laughing.

"And you're always so throw-caution-to-the-wind." I folded my arms across my chest. Despite the excitement of clearing a big hurdle between myself and my business dreams, I still couldn't forget what I'd seen on the footage last night. "Have you spoken with the detective or the chief again?"

"No."

I could practically see the walls closing in around her. I loved my aunt, truly. But there *was* something she shared with my mother—an ability to shut herself away. I remembered seeing that exact same look when I sought my mother out as a child, finding her hiding away in her bedroom with the door closed. I used to nudge the door open and watch her while she listened to music, dancing around like a free spirit, with flowing hair and eyes like fire. So full of passion and life.

But the second she spotted me, all that passion would evaporate like smoke from a snuffed-out candle. It was like I reminded her of the things she hated about her life, and those walls would shoot up around her, forever locking me out.

"I saw the security footage," I said, dropping my eyes to the floor and focusing on a scratch there. "The one of you crossing the road and going into the park."

"And?" Her voice revealed nothing.

"What were you doing there?" When I looked up, she'd turned away from me to face the window. It was cooler today, with heavy clouds. She wore jeans and a floaty blouse with long, gauzy sleeves in swirling shades of turquoise, sapphire and aquamarine. The sneakers on her feet told me she had a busy day planned.

"Do you trust me, Chloe?" she asked, turning back to me. Her lips were pressed into a flat line and the air around her was charged with emotion.

"Of course I trust you."

"Do you think I did it?"

"No!" I shook my head vehemently. "Just because you were in the park, doesn't mean you killed him."

"Then let me handle it, okay? I don't want you getting involved and putting yourself on the line—either with your safety *or* your reputation."

I waited for her to make a joke about me spending time with Jake, but she didn't.

"Would you sit quietly by if this was happening to me?" I asked, and I hoped she would answer me honestly.

"No, I wouldn't. But you're a grown woman and I would trust you to make the right decisions for yourself. I hope you'll offer me the same courtesy," she said, sternly. "Now, if you're done poking around in my business, I have something to ask you."

"What?" I asked warily. I was annoyed that she was keeping things from me, but I didn't really have much recourse on it.

"This weekend Moxie and I are competing in a local canine freestyle meet. It's not part of the major competition circuit, but I'm doing a few of these smaller events for extra practice. It would be great to have some friendly faces in the audience."

I softened. My aunt might be infuriating sometimes, but she was still kooky and adorable, and I loved her more than anything. "I will *absolutely* be there."

"Bring friends," she said, fluffing out her hair in a dramatic way. "I want to have the biggest applause out of everyone competing."

"Sure thing," I said. "I'll see if I can rally a crowd."

The canine freestyle meet was next level. Growing up, one of my close friends was into cheerleading, and while glitter hairspray, bows and being tossed in the air were *not* my thing, we would always go to the games she cheered at, and we even traveled to one of her competitions in San Jose. I got a similar vibe from the canine freestyle culture. There was glitter, bright colors, and hairspray galore.

But instead of tossing tiny, flexible humans into the air, the tricks were *all* about the dogs.

"This is . . ." Sabrina shook her head as we walked into the high school gymnasium where the competition was being held, a few towns outside Azalea Bay. "I don't even know how to describe it. Let's just say your aunt doesn't stand out in this crowd, and that's *not* a criticism about her."

I snorted. "I know exactly what you mean."

It seemed most of the competitors were women, although I spotted a man in a fabulously sequined blazer in a brilliant shade of royal blue and gold. The costumes ranged from simple to extravagant, including one woman who was dressed like a fairy with a shimmering pink dress, ballet shoes and small wings made of wire and mesh. A panel of judges sat along a table that flanked what I assumed was usually a basketball court, which had been covered for the day's events.

"Oh look, there's Erica, Matt and Ben." Sabrina held up her hand and waved when she spotted part of the D&D crew in the bleachers. We made our way over. "Cal was *so* bummed he couldn't come today. Archie, too. He's on kid duty."

"It's all right. My aunt appreciates the thought."

"Cal was disappointed for himself, more than anything." She

chuckled. "As soon as I told him about it, he looked it up on YouTube and was fascinated!"

"It's a unique skill. Aunt Dawn has been training Moxie to do all kinds of things ever since she was a puppy." I still remembered the day that my aunt brought the little bundle of black-and-white fluff home. Even as a pup, Moxie had been sharp minded and goal oriented, always needing to be amused lest she destroy whatever was within paw's reach. "There's a few border collies here."

There were also several rough collies, poodles, golden retrievers and Australian shepherds, as well as smaller dogs, including one fabulous pup with long hair on its big ears and skinny tail.

"Thank you all for coming," I said as I slid in next to Erica. Matt and Ben were on the other side of her.

"It is our pleasure, seriously." Ben leaned forward and smiled, looking genuinely excited. He was wearing a Princeton sweatshirt and jeans, yet still looked neat and polished like the first time I'd met him. "I didn't even know this was a thing, but I'm *obsessed*."

"Ben wants to get a dog and start training it." Matt laughed and shook his head. He wore a casual, all-black outfit with a studded cuff on one wrist and scuffed combat boots. His blond hair was scruffily tied back into a man bun. He must have been the only guy I'd ever seen make that hairstyle look good. "Seriously, anything that has a competition element and this bloke is all in."

Ben shrugged in a "sorry not sorry" manner. "What can I say? I like to win."

"So your aunt is competing with her dog?" Erica asked. Her short pixie-cut hair was spiked up and she wore a faded Metallica band T-shirt over jeans and Doc Martens. "This is so cool!"

"That's right. They're in the novice category."

I glanced at the program printed on a piece of paper I'd been handed when we walked in. There were *way* more categories than I'd realized, including some that involved multiple dogs in one routine.

Ten minutes later, all five of us were sitting with our mouths hanging open as we watched dogs perform all kinds of tricks. There was leaping, running backwards, dogs picking items up, jumping over things, standing on their owners' backs, hiding in boxes. There was even a routine where a dog pretended to type on a typewriter!

"I hope Moxie had her Weet-Bix this morning," Matt said, after one routine. "That was bloody awesome."

I had no idea what a Weet-Bix was, but I sure hoped Moxie had had it, too. I found my foot tapping against the bleacher in anticipation, as the next routine started. The competition looked fierce. The music varied from classical music pieces like "Greensleeves," to modern pop songs from Katy Perry and Taylor Swift, '70s glam rock and Broadway hits from *Hamilton*.

"Hey, is that . . ." Erica leaned and pointed. "Oh my God, it's Maisey Brent."

"Maisey Brent . . . as in your old boss?" Ben raised an eyebrow.

"The one and only."

"Which one is she?" I asked, following her line of sight toward the area where entrants waited their turn before being called to the floor for their performance slot.

"See the woman in the sparkly red dress and with the feather in her hair?" Erica looked at me and I nodded. The woman had curly blond hair and a medium sized tricolor dog at her feet, which looked like a shepherd of some kind.

"I had no idea she was into dog dancing. That's so . . ." Erica wrinkled her nose and it gave her a very Tinkerbell-like appearance. "Not something I expected her to do."

"Why's that?"

"She didn't have much to do with us worker bees, since she

only ever came in for managerial meetings and wasn't really part of the day-to-day business. Ross was more involved with the business than she was. But the few times I talked with her she seemed stuffy and uptight. Definitely not the sort of person I'd imagine choreographing dance routines and wearing glittery dresses in front of a crowd." Erica shook her head. "Wait until I tell Archie about this!"

"And now, our next freestyle music competitors in the novice singles category . . ." The MC's voice rang through the gymnasium, aided by a microphone and speakers. "Maisey and Annabel."

The crowd applauded as Maisey and her dog took the stage. There seemed to be a '20s vibe about her outfit, including the flapper-style dress, elbow-length black gloves and a long necklace of black beads around her neck. Sure enough, when the music started, I recognized it as a track from *The Great Gatsby* soundtrack—the Baz Luhrmann one with Leonardo DiCaprio.

The routine was . . . okay. Annabel was a cute little dog—white with patches of tan and medium brown, skinny legs and a fluffy tail—but she seemed to want to do her own thing. There were a few times when it was clear she didn't want to take instruction and Maisey had to correct course. But when she *did* follow the instructions, Annabel was charming and funny. She wove through Maisey's legs effortlessly, her tail wagging with glee.

But right at the end, when it looked like the duo had finally managed to get on the same page, disaster struck. Maisey was down on one knee, leaning forward with her arms spread. She motioned to the dog with her hand, but Annabel skittered back and forth, nervous. Maisey motioned again. Even from this distance I could see the smiling facade cracking, her cheeks turning pink with embarrassment and her face beginning to glow with sweat.

"The secondhand embarrassment is too real." Ben covered his face with both hands, but Erica leaned forward and watched with unfiltered glee.

"That's live performance for you." Matt shook his head. "Some days you're golden and other days it's a dog's breakfast."

Maisey tried to signal Annabel again, as their song was dangerously close to finishing and they weren't in their final pose. Mercifully—or so I thought in the moment—Annabel backed up a little to get a run up. She raced forward, leaping up onto Maisey's back. But the poor little dog misjudged, or perhaps Maisey was cramping from being in such a low crouch, and had slightly changed her position. Whatever it was, the little dog did *not* stick the landing. Instead she bounced off the side of her owner's body, hit the floor and rolled to an awkward stop.

Maisey hung her head as the music finished, a terrified hush settling over the crowd. The little dog stood, shook herself off—thankfully, she appeared not to be hurt at all—and decided to exit the stage without waiting for her owner to guide her. Maisey rushed after the dog, head bowed, her feather drooping precariously to one side.

Erica cackled and clapped her hands together.

"Oh. My. God. That was hilarious! I mean, I'm glad the dog isn't hurt, of course. I'm not a monster. But still, the high-and-mighty Maisey Brent made a fool of herself in front of what . . ." She leaned forward and scanned the crowd, as if trying to work out how many people were here. "There's got to be a hundred people here? Maybe more?"

The MC hurriedly called the next act to the stage, hoping to distract the crowed from the unfortunate routine they'd just watched. But the woman and her dog were taking their time, slowly walking into the center of the room while the woman waved as the crowd applauded politely.

"You're bad, Erica," Ben said, shaking his head but laughing at the same time. "No wonder your D&D characters always have a chaotic alignment."

"Chaotic *neutral*. At least I don't play them evil." She grinned, completely unabashed. It made me smile. I got the impression Erica said whatever was on her mind and didn't worry too much about what people thought of her. I could see how she would have gotten on the wrong side of Brendan, because he wasn't a man who liked to hear anything that contradicted his view of the world. "And call me a terrible person if you must, but I worked for that family for almost ten years and they threw me out on my ass based on a lie from a guy that they *knew* was untrustworthy. So . . . karma?"

Matt snorted and Ben stuck an elbow into his ribs. "Don't encourage her. It's a good thing Archie isn't here."

I looked at Sabrina for context and she nodded in agreement. "Archie doesn't like it when people aren't getting along. He's one of those rare people who genuinely sees the good in everyone."

"To his detriment sometimes," Ben added with a serious nod.

"He gets upset when we speak ill of someone who isn't around to defend themselves," Sabrina continued. "It's a good thing. Every group needs a moral compass."

"And every group needs someone to keep it real," Erica said. "Because you can sit around your trust circle and drink the Kool-Aid all you want, but I'm going to tell it like it is."

The group's attention was drawn back to the day's events as the music started for the next routine. This one appeared to be smooth sailing, thankfully, and the rough collie pranced gloriously around the stage, her mane gleaming under the light.

"Your aunt is up next." Sabrina nudged me and pointed. "She looks fabulous. And is Moxie wearing a matching outfit? I can't even! That's so freaking cute."

I nodded, but my attention was elsewhere. I spotted Maisey and Annabel slinking out of the stadium and into the building's main area, where the registration desk was set up and where you could access the restrooms.

"I, uh . . . I have to go to the bathroom." I stood suddenly and went to squeeze past Sabrina.

"Are you serious? You're going to miss your aunt's routine." She grabbed my arm. "Just hold it, girl."

"I can't." I shot her a look that told her not to argue with me, and I shuffled my way to the end of the row and jogged down the stairs.

I don't know what possessed me. Aunt Dawn would be hurt that I bailed on watching her performance, but something in my gut told me I needed to follow Maisey. I walked quickly into the stadium's foyer area and saw a few clusters of people standing around and talking. Out of the corner of my eye, I caught a flash of red sparkle as Maisey disappeared right out the front door.

She was leaving.

I brought my phone up to my ear, pretending like I was taking a call as I ducked outside after her. There wasn't much out front, only the parking lot, and I couldn't follow her too closely or that would look suspicious. But I tried to keep within range as much as possible.

"I can't believe it," she said to the dog. "You did that trick perfect all week. We're going to have to work even harder next time."

She marched through the parking lot, with the dog trotting happily in front of her, seemingly oblivious to the failure they'd both encountered. As they slowed, I ducked behind a minivan to watch. I don't know what I was hoping to see—maybe a glimpse of her husband if he'd come to pick them up, so I knew what he looked like. But when she pulled a set of keys from her purse it became clear that wasn't going to happen.

I cursed myself for missing my aunt's performance when it was clearly all for nothing. Frustrated, I scrubbed a hand over my face. Maisey raised her keys and I heard the beep of a car remote unlocking a vehicle. When she pulled open the door to a white truck, my heart leaped into my throat.

The white truck featured a distinctive—and familiar—paint mark on the front side panel.

# CHAPTER 16

The following evening Sabrina convinced me to come along to her yoga class. I'd spent the entire day stewing on what to do with the information about the truck, which included the license plate number I'd recorded and a blurry picture I'd snapped on my cell phone.

This was concrete evidence that a truck owned by the Brent family was in the vicinity of the crime. I could hand over the license plate number to the police and tell them what I'd seen in the footage, along with the photo I'd taken. But would that be enough to clear my aunt's name?

*What else do you think you're going to find? A hand-written confession note from the killer?*

"What's going on with you?" Sabrina asked as we pulled into the parking lot behind the yoga studio. The space was shared by a few businesses—including a hair salon, physiotherapy clinic and a wine-making supply store. The other side of the lot backed onto the park near my house.

I'd offered to walk over and meet Sabrina, to save her driving out of her way to pick me up. But she was concerned about me going through the park at night on my own. Especially now that it was the scene of a murder.

*Better safe than sorry*, she'd said. I tended to agree.

Which made me sad, honestly. I'd never seen the park as dangerous before. Heck, I'd never seen *anything* in this town as dangerous before. But Brendan's murder had shaken the townsfolk's collective confidence in the place we called home and now we were looking at it through a different lens.

"Nothing's going on with me," I said. "I'm just tired. I spent the day researching and testing some new infusion methods for making cannabis butter, oil and honey."

"Honey?" Sabrina's eyes shot up. "I didn't know that was a thing."

"Me, either. I'm learning so much." I grinned. One of the things I loved most about baking was that you could continually learn new skills and refine old ones. I never got bored. "I had the idea to hold a 'dosed dinner party' to test out some of the recipes and get feedback before the café opens. Well, provided the licensing comes through."

"It will," Sabrina said, encouragingly. "And I think that's a great idea. Who do I have to suck up to for an invite, huh?"

I laughed as we got out of the car. "You know you'll always be at the top of my guest list."

We retrieved our yoga mats from the back of the car. Mine was on loan from Aunt Dawn. Sabrina had promised the class was slow-moving and relaxing, with a good meditation period at the end, which sounded like heaven. And bonus! It looked like my Lululemon leggings would *finally* make it to a yoga class after all.

The studio, adorably named Go With The Flow, was easy to spot, as there were a few women gathered outside, carrying mats in a variety of shades. The studio had been called something else when I was home last, but apparently the previous owner had retired and sold the business.

I spotted a familiar face, beyond the cluster of women. Andrea. She was standing with her fiancé, Steve, and they appeared to be in a heated discussion. She, too, had a yoga mat under her arm. Dressed in leggings and a fitted sweatshirt with the words *Strike a Pose* written on the front, I suddenly noticed how slight she was in build. Much more than I remembered from high school.

"Is Andrea sick?" I asked Sabrina as we stood outside, near the other people waiting for the studio's current class to finish. There was a small waiting area inside, but it didn't look like it would fit many people and no one seemed in a hurry to enter.

"Sick?" Sabrina cocked her head.

"She looks . . . frail."

I hadn't noticed it when I ran into her at the beach because she'd been wearing a baggy sweater and loose pants. Her face had seemed drawn, but I'd put it down to the stress of Brendan's death. But now, with the fitted exercise outfit, it was easier to see that she had lost a significant amount of weight since high school. And that was a significant amount of weight on a frame that was slim to begin with.

"I don't know for sure," Sabrina said, frowning. "But I heard she was being treated for an eating disorder."

My heart ached for her. I was grateful to have grown up with women who were very body positive and had never made me feel self-conscious about the weight fluctuations that happened during puberty and beyond. But I knew not everyone was so lucky and that made me sad. We all deserved to love ourselves.

"I remember that Brendan used to make horrible comments about her appearance in gym class," I said.

"Yeah, he did." Sabrina made a sound of disgust. "I know we're not supposed to speak ill of the dead, but he was an awful person. I still remember that time he tripped me while we were playing soccer and I ended up on crutches. All because our team captain picked me before she picked him."

"He was vindictive. After I said I didn't want to go to prom with him, he left nasty notes in my mailbox and I had to go outside every day to get them, because I didn't want Grandma Rose to see them."

"Maybe you should have let her see. Someone should have put him in his place a long time ago."

"Well, that someone decided now was the right time for it."

We fell into silence and I watched Andrea and Steve. It seemed like he wanted her to leave, rather than go into the class. Then he looked right at me and I swear there was fire burning in his eyes. Andrea put her palm up to his face and turned his head back to her, saying something that made him sigh. When he looked at her, all the tension left him, and whatever she said, it must have worked, because he leaned down to kiss her and then he turned away from the group, striding up the street and disappearing around a corner.

To my surprise, Andrea came straight over. "I heard you and Steve had a little encounter at Brendan's house."

Beside me, Sabrina's eyebrows almost shot off the top of her head. "Excuse me?"

"Oh yeah, that." I smoothed a hand over my head, laughing nervously. "I'm sorry if I upset him. It was . . . I shouldn't have gone."

"It's fine. The property market is cutthroat these days." She nodded, her voice a little strained, like she was trying not to cry. "But we're not selling the house yet. Not until everything is . . . resolved."

"Of course, I totally understand." My face felt hot. I must have seemed completely heartless. "I'm so sorry for crossing that line. I wasn't thinking and I should have apologized to Steve."

"Don't worry about Steve. The last couple of weeks have been rough on our family and he's been taking the brunt of it." She white knuckled her yoga mat. "The police . . ."

"Have they been questioning him?" I asked.

"Relentlessly. They've been sniffing around since day one,

but that Detective Alvarez has no idea what she's saying." She practically spat the words out. "Steve wouldn't hurt a fly. Just because he's strong enough to do something, doesn't mean he has the *will* to do it."

I wasn't sure I agreed. I'd witnessed how quickly his temper could heat up the day he caught me at Brendan's house. And he might not be bad by nature, but that didn't mean he wouldn't snap under the right circumstances.

"If only he had an alibi." Her eyes filled with tears. "I should never have come to yoga class that night. But they were hosting a special meditation workshop, and I was so stressed from all the wedding planning. He convinced me to come. But I should have been home, because then the police wouldn't be hounding him right now."

"Oh my goodness, that is *not* your fault." I shook my head.

But I couldn't help fixating on the information that Steve didn't have an alibi *and* that the police were looking at someone beside my aunt. That gave me some relief.

The door to the yoga studio opened and people from the previous class trickled out. Once the doorway was clear we headed inside. Andrea found a friend and walked on ahead, while Sabrina and I hung back, bringing up the rear.

As we walked into the studio, I noticed a security camera overhead. Wow. Between the security cameras and my aunt locking her gate and an unsolved murder, maybe Azalea Bay wasn't quite the safe haven I'd once thought it to be. When had that changed?

"You went to his house?" Sabrina hissed, pulling me out of my thoughts. "What were you thinking?"

"It's long story," I said under my breath. "I'll tell you later."

"You'd better, girl. Because I don't want you getting tossed into jail for obstruction of justice."

"I wasn't obstructing anything. Now come on, we're here to relax."

\* \* \*

An hour later my limbs felt like jelly in the best way possible. I was sure that, at least for a few seconds, I had dozed off during the meditation at the end of class. The studio had a chill vibe, with lots of white wood, fluffy rugs and cool wall-hangings, and touches of purple silk with pieces draped in neat folds from the ceiling.

"That was *just* what I needed," I said as we walked into the evening air. "I feel so relaxed."

"That says a lot given your extensive house hunting," Sabrina replied drily.

"Not really that extensive," I mumbled. "I only looked at one."

"Don't lie to me, Chloe. I know you're not in the market to buy a house." She planted her hands on her hips. "What were you doing there? Snooping?"

"Snooping makes it sound so . . ." I waved a hand in the air, channeling some of my aunt's self-assured energy. "Juvenile."

"Oh, and it's *not* juvenile?"

"No, it's not." I felt my defenses going up.

I loved Sabrina like a sister, but I'd known she wouldn't like the idea of me getting involved. Her grandfather had been a police officer back in the day and she had great respect for the profession. And I did, too, but I also knew they would be under pressure to close the case quickly, because the residents of Azalea Bay didn't want an unsolved murder hanging over them. Me included.

We walked down the street and around the corner into the parking lot. It was emptying out now, as most of the other businesses were closed for the evening and the yoga participants were getting into their cars. As I reached Sabrina's car, I waited for her to hit the unlock button on her remote.

But she didn't.

"We need to talk about this," she said, folding her arms across her chest. "Why did you go to Brendan's house?"

I had an instinct to tell her to mind her own business. She

might not agree, but I was doing what was best for my family and wasn't, despite what she said, obstructing justice. I was simply gathering information with the plan to hand it over to the police so that they *could* do their job, with all the facts in hand.

"I was there to talk to his neighbor, actually." I met her stare with one of my own.

"Why?"

"Because I heard about a dispute that he and Brendan had, and I wanted to find out more in case the detective hadn't spoken with him. Apparently, Brendan poisoned his dog."

"And what did you find out?"

"Nothing. The guy wasn't home."

"But Steve was there?"

I nodded. "It looked like Brendan's house had been broken into and his home office had been ransacked. I was looking through a window when Steve showed up."

Sabrina cringed. "Yikes."

"He was furious. I know Andrea said that he wouldn't hurt a fly but . . ." I remembered back to how he'd looked at me that day. "Let's just say I'm glad I wasn't there alone."

She frowned. "Who was with you?"

"Jake." I anticipated the next question that was coming, so I held up my hand to stave it off. "The reason I didn't ask you to come was because I knew you wouldn't agree with what I was doing and frankly, as much as I love you . . . you can be a little judgy."

Her mouth popped open, but then she snapped it shut and tilted her head to the side. "I can see how my concern might come across judgmental. But it's only because I'm worried about you."

"I appreciate that, but I don't need you to be worried about me. I need you to trust that I'm doing the right thing." I sucked in a breath. "We've already had a note on our shop's front door with the word *murderer* written on it in red ink."

Sabrina gasped. "You're kidding."

"I wish I was. If this case doesn't get solved soon then I'm worried about what it will mean for my aunt's reputation *and* what it will mean for our business. Or worse, if the police are pressured into closing the case and she's the most likely suspect then that could mean a lengthy trial. Our family name will be dragged through the mud. We'll have to move and . . ."

My imagination was spinning out of control.

"Chloe, stop." Sabrina pulled me in for a hug and her dark curls brushed against my cheek. "We're not going to let that happen."

"We?"

"You might think Jake is a better partner in crime than me, but I'm happy to prove you wrong."

"I want a partner in *solving* crime, not committing it," I joked. "But thank you."

"Can you promise me one thing, though?" she asked, looking at me imploringly. "Don't do anything without letting someone know where you are. Because if something happens . . ."

"Point taken." I nodded. "From now on, I'll be honest about what I'm up to."

"With your grandma and aunt, too. Promise me." She held out her pinkie finger like she used to when we were kids. I hesitated a moment, because pinkie promises were not to be broken under any circumstances. "Promise me, Chloe."

"Fine." I hooked my little finger around hers. "I promise."

Sabrina and I took the scenic route home, driving down the road that ran along the beach because the way the moonlight reflected on the rippling waves always put me at ease. I told her everything—about what I'd seen in Jake's security footage, and about Maisey Brent owning the truck with the paint smudge, and my trip to the Iron Works gym. To her credit, Sabrina listened and chimed in encouragingly, leaving all judgment back in the parking lot.

It felt good to unburden myself with her.

But after a while of us cruising around town, we noticed something.

"Is someone . . . following us? Or am I just being paranoid?" I glanced in the rearview mirror as a set of headlights bobbed behind us.

"It *does* seem a little odd that we've had a car behind us for a while at this time of night, especially since we're not really going in any one direction." She leaned forward and turned the radio off. An uneasy tension settled in the car and we glanced at one another. "I won't drop you off yet. Let's see how long it stays behind us."

"Thanks for not making me feel crazy," I said, knotting my hands in my lap. "I'm sure it's nothing."

Sabrina flicked her turn signal on and we eased around a corner, not picking up speed or doing anything to draw attention to ourselves. A few seconds later, the headlights appeared behind us. We turned again, and so did the car.

Sabrina glanced in the rearview mirror. "Okay, now I'm worried."

"I wonder if it's the police. Aunt Dawn said she'd seen a black car around a number of times and was sure it was the detective or one of her minions." I chewed on the inside of my cheek. "But why would they be following me? I'm not a suspect."

"Let me try something." Sabrina sped up and the headlights faded into the distance behind us, but only for a few moments. Soon, the car behind was back to maintaining the same distance as before, matching the increase in speed. "I don't like this, Chloe."

"Me either." I drummed my fingertips on my thigh. "Head to Grandma Rose's and don't go too fast. We'll pull up in front of the house and see what they do. If it's the detective, maybe she just wants to talk."

Sabrina did as I asked and we ended up at my grandmother's house a few minutes later, with the car still behind us. We pulled over and I quickly got out of the car, hoping to catch the driver unaware. But the sedan zoomed past, and I could barely see anything through the tinted windows. I didn't catch the license plate number, either. Only that it appeared to be a standard, local plate.

Why on earth would the police be tailing me? And, more worryingly, what if it wasn't them?

# CHAPTER 17

I promised Sabrina that I would go to the police to: A, tell them what I'd found out; and B, about the cars we'd noticed following us. So the next morning, I dug out my most respectable outfit—blue jeans with no distressing and a silky white blouse that was one of the fanciest things in my closet, along with some faux pearl earrings I'd bought at a boutique in Paris. I spritzed a little light perfume and brushed out my hair.

Perhaps it was excessive to dress up for a visit to the police station, but I wanted them to take me seriously. And, as Grandma Rose had drummed into me since I was a little girl, personal presentation made a big difference in how people perceived you.

Now that the Jellybean was back to working condition, I could drive to the station and save myself from getting sweaty on the walk over. As I headed out of the house, I sucked in a breath of fresh air.

*Everything will be okay. You're doing the right thing.*

I sat in the waiting area of the Azalea Bay police station for a good twenty minutes before Detective Alvarez came to get me. She looked frazzled. Her dark hair was usually slicked back into a neat bun or ponytail, but now she had some flyaway hairs around her face. Her glasses—which seemed to change every time I saw her and today were a cool minty green—had slipped down her nose.

"Ms. Barnes, come with me." She turned on her heel and didn't even wait for me to respond, so I had to scramble to follow her down a hallway and into an interview room. "Take a seat."

The room was sparse—a simple table with four chairs, one of them not matching the others. On the wall was a map of Azalea Bay and in one corner stood a portable whiteboard, which had been erased but not very well, as there were dirty streaks across the surface. I guess the police didn't have time to thoroughly clean their whiteboards, what with a murderer on the loose.

"You said you had information for me?" She folded herself into one of the chairs across from me, her tablet out and a stylus poised. The piece of tech seemed out of place in the otherwise run-down, analogue room.

"I did." I sucked in a breath, not quite sure how this meeting would go down. I decided to start with one of the simpler items. "Firstly, there appears to have been a break-in at Brendan's house."

Her eyebrows shot up, but she recovered quickly. "How did you find out about it?"

"I was there."

"During the break-in?"

"No." I shook my head. "I was at his house and I noticed one of the windows was covered with a piece of cardboard, so I . . . went to have a look. The window had been smashed, and a room was ransacked."

"Did you touch anything?" she asked with a tired sigh. "With your bare hands?"

"I moved the cardboard." I scratched my head, trying to remember if I'd been smart enough not to leave fingerprints behind. Then I remembered, "Oh, there was a blanket over the cardboard. Yes, I touched it, but I didn't go inside the house or do anything else, I promise."

Detective Alvarez took her glasses off and pinched the bridge of her nose. Uh-oh. That wasn't a good sign.

"And what were you doing at Brendan's house?" she asked.

"I was there to talk with his neighbor. I'd heard about a dispute between them involving his dog being ill and Brendan being suspected of poisoning it. Someone saw them fighting in the street." I held my breath.

"His neighbor, Darius Jackson?"

"I didn't know the surname, but yes his name is Darius."

"And why were you hoping to speak with Mr. Jackson?"

"Well, you said that you didn't want to hear any rumors or gossip," I replied. "So I figured if I went to speak with him in person then maybe I could find some concrete evidence to bring you."

"Chloe." She sighed. It felt a lot like how my mom used to say my name whenever I wanted to spend time with her. For some reason, it struck me hard in the chest. "I understand you're concerned about the investigation, but it is not your job to go around questioning people. Frankly, you're as subtle as a hammer and besides, this work can be dangerous. You don't want to put yourself in the firing line."

"Is Darius a suspect?" Clearly, I was going to push my luck as far as I could take it. "Did you know about the dog thing?"

"Yes, we knew about the dog thing because he reported it to us when it happened, so everything is on record. *And* we were able to confirm within the first twenty-four hours of the investigation that Darius wasn't even in town when the murder happened."

"Oh." My shoulders sagged.

"This is not my first rodeo." Her lips pressed into a thin line. "So if you're here to tell me about the dispute between Brendan and Darius, then I can save you some time and let you go now."

"It's not just that," I said, shaking my head.

The detective slipped her glasses back on and her dark eyes pierced me through the lenses. "What else?"

"I saw Steve Boyd there. He had a cut on his hand and he *really* didn't want me to be there. He was quite aggressive."

"Maybe because his fiancée's brother just died and you were poking around his house?"

I ignored the pointed look she gave me. "Also, there's a truck that appears multiple times in the security footage from Jake's house. It has a paint swipe on it and it's parked outside the park right around the time of the murder! And I found who owns it."

For a moment, the detective said nothing. I couldn't work out if she was ready to wring my neck for interfering or if she was shocked I'd given her something she didn't already know. There was a clock on the wall and it ticked so loudly, I almost jumped every time the hand moved.

"I should ask how you got access to that footage but I'm going to overlook it for the moment," she said. Would I get Jake in trouble by bringing this to the police? He knew I was gathering evidence for them when I asked to view it, so surely he knew I would follow through.

Unease settled into my stomach.

"What do you know about the vehicle?" she asked.

I told her everything—from what I saw in the video, to seeing it in person at the canine freestyle event, to what I'd heard about Brendan's strange relationship with his boss and how he'd gotten Erica fired. The detective made a few notes, but didn't question anything I told her. Nor did she probe deeper.

"There's also a guy at Iron Works," I said in a small voice. "His name is Tate Duncan-Brooks. I honestly don't think he killed Brendan, but his initials match the knife . . ."

Hmm, was I supposed to know about that? Crap.

"When I said you could bring me information I meant if you *came across* it, not that you should go digging yourself." The detective closed the cover on her tablet and put her stylus down on the table. "I can't express seriously enough that you're play-ing with fire, okay? I've seen people get hurt for poking around where they shouldn't, and I don't want that to happen to you."

"It's not like I don't think you can do a good job or anything, but if you've got people tailing my aunt then . . . heck, you've got people tailing me! What gives with that?"

The way the detective stilled as she sat across from me turned the uneasiness in my stomach to outright fear. "You're being tailed?"

"My aunt mentioned that a black car was following her around and she assumed it was you or one of the people work-ing with you. Then last night, after I went to yoga class, I no-ticed there was a car following me. We made a few extra turns to be sure, and they were definitely following us."

"We don't have anyone tailing you or your aunt."

My stomach dropped.

"Then who is it?" I scanned my memory thinking back to last night. "I didn't get the plate because they drove off quickly when I tried to look."

"This is why you need to be careful," she said, shaking her head. "Tell me everything you saw. What kind of car was it? Any distinguishing details?"

"It was a black sedan and I think either the windows were tinted or I just couldn't see because it was low light." I scrubbed a hand over my face.

"Make, model?"

"I don't remember. Maybe a Toyota? Or it could have been a Honda. Or a Nissan."

"So a Japanese brand, then?"

"I'm not certain about that." I shook my head.

"A black sedan of indeterminate model and brand, possibly with tinted windows." She made a note on her tablet.

"That's not much to go on, I know."

"No, it's not," she admitted. "If you see the car again, I want you to report it to me immediately."

"I will."

"And no more DIY investigating, okay? You're not Miss Marple and this is not a Lifetime movie." She folded her arms across her chest. "You could get seriously hurt."

"Azalea Bay isn't supposed to be that kind of town," I replied with a sigh. "I lived here my whole life before I went to college and the worst thing we've ever had was a single shark attack."

"It's different when you're a kid," she said matter-of-factly. "The world has a rose-tinted lens over it and you think you'll always be safe. But the things I've seen would make your head spin. No town is immune to crime, not even a beautiful place like this."

Our conversation was interrupted by a knock on the door and Chief Gladwell poked his head inside. "Mind if I have a word with Miss Barnes?"

"Of course." Detective Alvarez stood and gathered her tablet, but before she left she looked right at me. "Be safe, okay?"

Chief Gladwell took her place at the table and waited for the detective to leave. Unlike her, who'd been dressed in civilian clothes, the chief was in full uniform. His shirt was tucked into his pants and a black belt dug into his slightly protruding belly. Age had softened him physically. His personality, however, remained as sharp and focused as ever.

"I know the detective probably already told you this, but in case it hasn't sunk in yet I'm going to reinforce her message." He leaned forward against the table. "You need to keep your nose out of things, Chloe. I mean it."

"So you can interrogate my aunt and tar our family name? No thanks." Perhaps it wasn't best to defy the chief of police, but Theodore Gladwell had known me since I was a kid. He knew I wasn't a troublemaker. Usually.

"I'm going to be straight with you. Based on what we have, I could arrest your aunt right now. She was at the scene of the crime, she doesn't have an alibi, she has a ton of motive, and there's a connection to the murder weapon."

He wasn't telling me anything I didn't already know. But I also knew he was bluffing slightly, based on what Andrea had told me. They could just as easily arrest Steve, so I knew the chief was throwing his weight around to get me to comply.

"Then why don't you?" I asked smartly.

"Because we do things right around here. I investigate *all* the angles before I make a decision about how to proceed, but you getting involved doesn't do anything to make her look more innocent." He shook his head. "In fact, all you're doing is drawing more attention to yourself. And given you're wanting to open a business soon, I'd say that's not a very wise move."

Frustration bubbled up inside me. "Then solve this case. Because when you do, you'll know my aunt didn't do a thing and we can move on with our lives free of people scrutinizing us."

"I don't do this job to be liked, I do it because it needs to be done. And that means I won't be swayed by what people want." The man was as immovable as a brick wall, stubborn and sure of himself. I guessed those were good qualities for a man in his position, as much as they grated on me in the moment. "While your aunt is a suspect, I will need to interview her and ask questions. That's simply how it is."

"You're wasting time."

The chief's jaw twitched, but he didn't bite. "And you trust too easily."

I frowned. "What's that supposed to mean?"

"Exactly as it sounds. Maybe Paris filled your head with romance, but it's time for you to grow up. The world isn't sunshine and roses, and people are not always what they seem on the outside. You need to be careful."

"If you want to give me a warning, then don't put it in riddles." I shoved my chair back and stood. "Because otherwise it means nothing."

The chief watched me but didn't respond. Perhaps he was trying to get into my head as payback for me sticking my nose into his business. Whatever the reason, if he wasn't going to tell me anything concrete then I would take the advice with a grain of salt.

The fact was, Paris *hadn't* filled me with romance. Quite the opposite. I knew that people couldn't always be trusted and that promises were easily broken and that words meant nothing. It was also that experience which taught me not to sit by and watch things happen. I was in control of my life, not the other way around.

And I wouldn't sit idly by while the police were looking in the wrong direction.

# CHAPTER 18

The following week went by without much action. A few times I got the sense I was being followed, but I never caught anyone. Likely, it was a classic case of paranoia. I kept seeing black cars everywhere but that was more due to the popularity of black cars than anything sinister. After I found out it wasn't the police following us, I called Aunt Dawn to ask her to keep a lookout in the hopes that one of us might be able to spot a license plate or something useful.

But otherwise, there was nothing else I could do.

Planning for my "Dosed and Delighted Dinner Party" kept me busy. Between figuring out how to dose and balance a cannabis-filled three-course meal and testing the actual recipes, I fell into a tired slumber each night. But now that the event was almost upon us, I was jittery with excitement. Since our license to sell edibles hadn't yet come through, we would host the party at my aunt's house, i.e., on private property. We'd have appetizers, entrées and dessert, plus a little goodie bag for people to take home, which would include some information about what we hoped to achieve with the café and our business.

The latter had been Sabrina's idea, business whiz that she was, and Baked by Chloe was going to have its official welcome into the world, at least on a small scale.

I'd thrown myself into dosing research the past week, including taking another trip to Greener Pastures for supplies and to talk with Cindy about the best cannabis strains for the experience I wanted for my guests. There was a balance to be struck; I wanted them to feel something, but without sending them deep into a couch and killing the mood. She helped me select a sativa strain, which was most associated with a head high—helping people to feel energetic and uplifted, rather than sluggish.

I'd designed a menu based around micro-dosing, which would deliver the THC slowly over multiple courses, almost treating it like a spice or herb. For dessert, I'd decided to lower the THC dose even further and add CBD to create a relaxed feeling at the end of the night. As part of the conditions of invitation, people attending the dinner party were required to organize transportation home, whether it was a lift from a loved one, calling a cab or ordering an Uber, so we knew they would get home safely. I'd also contacted a private car company about having one or two vehicles on standby, should we need them.

I was excited to see what everyone thought of my creations. For appetizers, I would serve a feta and watermelon salad, with an infused lime and mint dressing. On the side, there would also be non-infused items, like roasted pistachios and freshly baked herb rolls. For the main, I wanted something rich but also appropriate for the mild weather. Seafood pasta it was—rigatoni with clams, white fish, capers, spinach and chili pepper, all tossed in a buttery cannabis-infused sauce. Then for dessert, I had been drowning in options. Macarons, eclairs, brownies, or something else?

Pots de crème was my choice. Rich chocolate custard with fresh whipped cream, grated chocolate and candied hazelnuts, along with a CBD chai latte.

In less than forty-eight hours I'd be serving this all up, and I had plenty of prep to do.

After doing a grocery shop, I'd headed out for some fresh air and to grab a coffee. Before any big event, I liked to visualize the cooking process. It might sound silly, but it was almost like how an athlete mentally prepared for a big game or competition. I couldn't lose my cool in the kitchen and this was part of my process.

At Bean and Gone, I ordered a latte and found a quiet spot in the corner where I could sip and think. The atmosphere of the café was great—warm and inviting, the air filled with scents of roasted coffee beans, steamed milk and caramel syrup. Warming my hands around my mug, I sat back and stared into space, my mind moving around the kitchen as I choreographed the meal service.

I don't know how long I'd been sitting there when a flash of movement near my table startled me and I jumped, sloshing some of the coffee over the edge of my mug.

"Hey!" It was Archie from the Dungeons and Dragons group.

He stood at the edge of the table, dressed in a pair of black slacks and a blue and white checked shirt. His gold wire-rimmed glasses were perched on his nose and his hair was neatly styled, like he'd made a little effort but not too much. He must have come from work.

"Hi there." I placed my coffee down, grabbing a napkin to wipe up the dribble down the side of the cup.

"Sorry. Didn't meant to startle you," he said.

"It's fine. When I zone out, I *really* zone out."

"Do you mind having a table guest?" He smiled. "I was hoping to chill with my lunch for a bit, but it's rammed."

He wasn't joking. In the time I'd been there, Bean and Gone had filled out to maximum capacity and there was a line out the door. It made me happy to see one of my favorite businesses flourishing and I hoped it was a sign that my café could be full like this in the future, too.

"Sure." I motioned to the chair on the other side of the table. "Be my guest."

"You're a lifesaver." Archie placed his pastry and coffee down—which was in a takeout cup almost bigger than my head—and took a seat. "I was desperate to get out of the office today. The thought of having to go back there before my break is over was killing me."

I frowned. "That's no good."

"You wouldn't know what that's like," he teased, taking a sip of his drink and letting out a happy *ahh* sound. Then he took a bite of the pastry and brushed the errant flakes from his shirt. "Being that you're not a cubicle rat like myself."

"Cubicle rat? That's funny."

"It's my personal favorite, followed closely by desk farmer and office plankton." He chuckled. "I swear . . . I love my job, I love my job, I love my job."

The way he said it reminded me of the opening credits of *The Simpsons*, where Bart was writing phrases on the school blackboard as punishment for being naughty.

I pulled an *eek* face. "That bad, huh?"

"Human resources is a thankless career. I thought I would be helping people and putting together best practices for company culture and talent retention. Stuff that would make employees feel happy and satisfied in their work." He sighed. "Turns out HR is more about firing people and covering the backsides of those higher up the food chain."

"It must have been rough when you had to fire Erica," I sympathized. I sipped my coffee and it was lukewarm, but I wasn't in a hurry to head home.

"It was honestly the worst day of my working life." He shook his head and looked genuinely stricken. "I consider Erica a friend but, more than that, I know she would never have stolen something from a customer. No way, not ever. But orders are orders, and of course the boss didn't want to do the dirty work himself, so . . ."

"That leaves it up to you." I frowned. "Why do you think

your boss believed Brendan over Erica? I mean, if she was such a great employee it seems odd that he would fire her without giving a warning or something first, even if he *did* believe the accusation."

Archie shrugged. "Who knows why people behave the way they do?"

It seemed an evasive response. Archie didn't strike me as a closed book, but Sabrina *had* made the comment about him not liking to talk about people who couldn't defend themselves. Still, if Erica was his friend then surely he felt strongly about her getting fired for something she didn't do.

"Do you think Brendan's murder had anything to do with his work?" I asked.

Archie's demeanor changed slightly, and I sensed a cool guardedness in him. "Why would you think that?"

"I don't think it. Just musing aloud." I smiled blandly, trying not to give him more reason to get his defenses up. "But there's something about having an unsolved murder in town that's giving me the heebie-jeebies, you know?"

His shoulders lowered and he reached for his pastry again. "I definitely understand that. This place is supposed to be one of those safe havens where nothing bad ever happens, right? My mother-in-law was telling me they never locked their doors here when she was growing up."

"My aunt has said the same thing." I nodded emphatically. "I guess I'm pissed off on Erica's behalf, too. It riles me up when good people get screwed and bad people get away with everything. Murder included."

I hoped the statement might appeal to Archie's sense of fairness and it seemed to work—he was back to looking relaxed again. "I totally agree."

"So, what's it like working for the Brent family?" I asked.

He raised an eyebrow. "You know them?"

Hmm, to lie or not to lie. I preferred to keep on the right side of the moral highway, but maybe fudging things a little might help him open up some more. For some reason, I felt like Archie might be able to shed light on the situation at his place of work. Didn't the people in human resources always know the behind-the-scenes dirt?

I decided to take a detour from the moral highway, down White Lie Lane.

"She and my aunt know each other through a mutual hobby. I saw Maisey on the weekend, in fact." Maybe dropping the first name might make it sound like I'd done more than stalk the woman to her car and snap her license plate with my phone. "It was at a canine freestyle dancing meet."

"Oh that." Archie snapped his fingers. "I was so sad I couldn't make it. Erica called me when she got home and regaled me with the uh . . . mishaps."

"It was an unfortunate outing for poor Maisey." I cringed, and I didn't have to fake much secondhand embarrassment there. For someone who could never watch those purposefully awkward comedies, like *The Office* or *Arrested Development*, seeing Maisey's routine had made me want to crawl under a rock. "I imagine she's rather different at work than all dressed up in sparkles for a dog dancing competition."

Archie let out a dry laugh. "You're not wrong there. Honestly, I don't have a huge amount to do with Maisey directly. She seems almost . . . disinterested in the company. I know it was her grandfather and father's pride and joy, but I get the impression she was roped into being part of the business even though it wasn't what she wanted to do with her life."

"That's a shame. Although I guess one can't make a career out of canine freestyle dancing." I shrugged. "It was a shame Ross wasn't there to support her."

Archie didn't look surprised by this information. "Figures."

"Why do you say that?"

Archie looked genuinely sympathetic. "She and Ross . . .

they don't seem in love, you know. When I come home after a day at the office, seeing my wife and kids is the best feeling ever. If she was competing in something, you best believe I would be there cheering her on."

I pressed a hand to my chest. "That's so sweet."

"It's how my parents and my in-laws are—still totally in love after all these years. We had great role models." Archie nodded. "But some days I wonder if Ross married Maisey because he wanted the business for himself."

"What makes you say that?" The question popped out of me and I cursed myself internally. Archie didn't respond too well to probing questions that might seem like gossip, so I had to make sure I positioned myself as a concerned friend. "Maisey has always seemed so . . ."

Hmm, this was risky. Because I didn't know what her personality was like, only that Erica had said she basically ignored all the worker bees.

"Well, you know she can be a little reserved," I said, hoping that I sounded like I knew what I was talking about. "But when she warms up, you can tell she's a good person."

"I say that all the time to people when they complain she's an ice queen and whatnot." Archie nodded and I breathed an internal sigh of relief. "I honestly think people at work don't like her because they haven't got to know her. Yes, that's partially her own fault. But I don't think we should judge someone until we know them, right?"

"Totally agree. I haven't ever met Ross, though."

Archie blew out a long breath and immediately I sensed he didn't like the man, though he probably wouldn't come right out and say it. "Ross is . . . slippery."

"Slippery?"

"Yeah. One of those people where he says one thing and then turns around and does the exact opposite. I don't like to speak ill of people, but I find him a hard man to trust." Archie took another bite of his pastry and chewed, his eyes drifting over my head like he was remembering something. I didn't dare say a word, in case he clammed up. "He told me at first that he wasn't going to fire Erica because he believed her side of the story."

"What made him change his mind?"

"I'm not exactly sure. But I saw him and Brendan having an argument in his office after work that night. Ross was all red in the face and he wasn't saying much at all, Brendan was doing most of the talking. I'd never seen my boss look so mad. But then he sent Brendan out of the room and called me in. That's when he told me that I had to fire Erica the next day."

For a moment Archie didn't say anything further, but his neck was tinted with red and he white-knuckled his coffee cup so hard I was surprised the lid didn't fly off. His usually calm and approachable demeanor turned sour. Angry.

"I don't know what Brendan said to him . . ." He shook his head. "But he wanted Erica out of a job. That much I know."

"Has she been able to find other work?" I asked, genuinely concerned.

"At first Ross wouldn't give her any references because of the whole stealing thing. I wrote her a letter of service on company header, in the hopes it might help but . . . this is a small town. People wanted to know why Ross wouldn't back her. Then she told me yesterday that he called and asked if she wanted her old job back."

"What?" I blinked. "That makes no sense at all."

"Tell me about it."

"Did she accept?"

"She's thinking about it. I know part of her wants to tell him to shove it, since she's still angry. But she *did* like working there and all the staff—barring Brendan—really respected her."

I leaned back in my seat. "That's super weird."

"I don't want to speculate on what it means." Archie shook his head. "Frankly, I want to bury my head in the sand and let them all figure it out amongst themselves. I just do the paper-work."

I felt for him, it must be rough being stuck between a friend and his employer.

"You seem very interested in all this," Archie commented. "Why's that?"

"Like I said, heebie-jeebies and I guess I'm wired for certainty." I forced a laugh. "Cliffhangers are the *worst* thing in the world to me! It's why I didn't even bother watching *Game of Thrones* until the whole show was over. I couldn't stand being forced to wait a week between episodes because I have to have answers right now."

"I know that feeling. Be warned, Sabrina loves to close out a Dungeons and Dragons session on a cliffhanger sometimes."

"Really?" I groaned. "And I was so excited about playing."

Archie laughed. "Maybe she'll go easy your first few sessions. You really thinking about joining us?"

"I mean, I have no idea how to play and I don't want to disrupt a group who already has a good flow . . ."

"Pssh." He waved his hand. "Don't worry about that. The more the merrier!"

"Thanks."

I was about to excuse myself from the table so I could get on with my day, when a familiar figure walked into Bean and Gone. Of all the people . . .

Maisey Brent.

This was my first chance to see what she looked like in person, without the glitz and glamour of her canine freestyle costume. She was tall with light hair and high cheekbones. There was a severity to her—a rigidity that showed in the harsh slash of liner on her eyes and the tight way her hair was pulled back and in the long nails that were filed to a slight point.

Money. Most people thought you could tell if someone was rich by how many labels they flashed and the kind of car they drove. But living in Paris had taught me to look for the more subtle details—well manicured hands, expensive but dainty jewelry like the small glittering diamonds in Maisey's ears, and sharply tailored but not necessarily flashy clothes.

She had all those things.

Archie caught sight of her immediately and waved. "Hi, Maisey."

Oh no. He was going to make a comment about how my aunt and I knew her, and then it would come out that I'd been lying, and I'd never be able to join the Dungeons and Dragons group out of shame.

"Archie, nice to see you." She smiled as she walked over, but the expression was guarded. Remote. Not unkind or unfriendly, but like the kind of smile you give when you're used to keeping a barrier between yourself and the world.

"Chloe and I were talking about how you were a mutual acquaintance," he said, smiling. I got the impression that Archie was used to being a social lubricant.

Maisey looked at me, a faint crease forming between her brows. Crap. I'd better steer this ship or else this conversation was going to sail into a metaphorical iceberg.

"I'm Chloe, Dawn Barnes's niece. I was at the canine freestyle event this past weekend." I smiled brightly and recognition flashed across her face.

But then she went as white as a sheet. The only other time I'd seen the blood drain from a person's face like that was when I confronted Jules about his affair. Was she ashamed about how badly her routine had gone? It seemed like an extreme reaction, but perhaps she was one of those people who was terrified of failure.

*Welcome to the club.*

"Chloe." She said my name almost like it was choking her. "Of course, of course."

Hmm, so she wasn't going to blow my cover. Interesting.

"I am *so* sorry," she said, looking at her watch. It had a gold bracelet-style band and diamonds dotting the edges of the face. "I realize I left my wallet back in the office. I'll catch you later, Archie. Nice to see you, Chloe."

And with that, she hurried away from the table and out the café like someone had lit a fire under her feet. I looked at Archie, but he seemed oblivious to the speedy exit. Instead, he was happily munching away on his pastry.

"I have to go as well," I said, gathering my things quickly. I wanted to get outside ASAP and see if I could tail her. "Table's all yours."

"Thanks." He smiled and reached for his phone. "I hope we see you at the next D&D session."

"Sure thing!"

I hightailed it out of Bean and Gone, hoping that I could see where Maisey Brent was headed.

# CHAPTER 19

Outside the café, I caught sight of Maisey hurrying down the street, her cell phone pressed to her ear. She was going in the opposite direction of the furniture removal company. I dug a hand into my bag and pulled out my sunglasses as I walked, keeping an eye on her. Thankfully, I'd gone through an Audrey Hepburn phase a while back, and purchased an oversized pair that obscured most of my face. I also stripped off my sweater and stuffed it into my bag and then pulled my hair back with a spare hair tie, hoping that if she happened to glance over her shoulder, she wouldn't immediately recognize me.

I walked as fast as I could without drawing attention to myself. More "career girl on her way to a meeting" than "amateur sleuth stalking suspect," if you know what I mean. Thankfully there were enough people around, that I could blend in with other residents running errands and grabbing lunch.

Up ahead, Maisey turned off the main strip and down a smaller street, which made it harder to follow inconspicuously. I created insurance by sticking my AirPods into my ears, so if she happened to turn around I could pretend to be bopping along to music or listening to a podcast. This street had a few businesses—including a dry cleaner, a tattoo parlor, a shop that sold espresso machines and other coffee-making tools, and a secondhand bookstore.

She slowed as she got to the bookstore and slipped inside. Again Books was gloriously dusty and crammed; a real bookworm's dream. I adored this shop—probably because my grandmother was such an avid reader and when I was young, we'd spent countless weekends searching through teetering piles of pre-loved tomes and come home after every trip with a big stack of literary bounty. There was something about the cracked spines and coffee-stained pages and notes in the margin that I adored.

I waited a moment before walking into the store, hoping that Maisey had slipped down one of the aisles rather than stand at the front, where she would immediately catch me. The store was dimly lit, with books filling every inch of the place. An elderly man was perched at the desk out front, sitting with his head tipped forward to show a shiny bald spot, glasses perched precariously on the end of his nose. Mr. Page—yes, that was his real name—was ninety-something and could often be found napping at his post.

Creeping as quietly as I could, I followed the sound of Maisey's hushed voice. She was in the romance aisle, so I picked the one next to it—nonfiction. I spied my target through a gap between the books.

"The way she looked at me, it was like she *knew*." Maisey pulled a book off the shelf and admired the cover. There was a pause and I could hear the soft mumblings on the other end of the line, though I couldn't work out what they were saying or even if it was a man or woman speaking. "I trust you. I know you wouldn't have told anyone."

She replaced the book on the shelf and I heard the soft mumblings on the other end of the line again.

"No one else was there. It's precisely why I suggested we meet at the park. I had to be sure no one would catch me."

My heart almost stopped. The park.

I knew Maisey's vehicle was at the park the night of the murder and now she'd admitted to being there with another person. Was it Brendan? Or someone else? If Maisey was unhappy in her marriage, like I'd heard, was it possible she and Brendan were having an affair?

I couldn't think of two more unlikely people.

"My whole life would be ruined." Her voice shook. "My father. God, he'd never forgive me . . ."

There was more mumbling on the other end of the line.

"They won't see it like that. They wouldn't understand."

She walked further into the bowels of the bookstore and I followed along in my own aisle. But I was too busy trying to listen to what she was saying instead of looking where I was going, and my toe clipped a stack of books that had been piled on the floor. They toppled over, sliding to the carpeted floor in a dull *thud*.

The voice in the other aisle went deadly quiet. For a moment, all I could hear was the thudding of my heart.

"Hello?" Maisey asked. "Who's there?"

Without taking time to weigh the consequences, I ran down the aisle toward the door where I'd entered. The ruckus roused Mr. Page from his sleep, and he was shoving his glasses up his nose, squinting at me as I bolted out of the door.

"Chloe, is that you?" I heard him say as I made it outside. "Wait. Where did you go?"

Crap. Now Maisey would definitely know it was me in there.

My heart was still pounding by the time I made it to my shop, and I unlocked the door with shaking hands. Letting myself inside, I closed the door and sighed back against it, taking a moment to collect myself.

"Subtle as a freaking sledgehammer," I said, shaking my head. The detective was right about me. "Why didn't you sound an airhorn to announce your presence instead?"

How could I have been so clumsy?

I wasn't cut out for this! I was a pastry chef, not a detective. My senses were made for detecting nuances in flavors— for knowing the difference between Madagascar and Tahitian vanillas—not for knowing whether someone was a murderer.

I closed my eyes for a moment. Six months ago my life was perfectly on track, perfectly *normal*. I was planning a wedding, deeply in love, confident in my dreams, sure of what the future held. It was like finding out about the affair had created a ripple effect that was still going.

"You know food," I said to myself. "You know taste and texture and flavor."

It's what I always came back to. Whenever the world felt unsteady beneath my feet, I baked. Since the dinner party was in two days' time and I had so much to do anyway, losing myself in the kitchen was a grand idea. Stewing on what I'd learned about Maisey could wait, because I knew that Detective Alvarez and Chief Gladwell wouldn't want to hear about it.

Gossip, they would say. Not real evidence. And then they'd chastise me for getting involved. But the connection between the Brent family and Brendan's murder kept coming; I just didn't know how all the pieces fit together yet.

Shaking myself off, I locked the door behind me and headed into the kitchen. Everything was working and even though we couldn't yet sell anything from the shop, I could still use the kitchen. I set the oven to 240 degrees Fahrenheit, threw an apron over my clothes and retrieved the cannabis buds from the container I'd brought with me.

*Wait! First things first*, I thought to myself. *The most important ingredient in any kitchen: music.*

I grabbed my phone and opened my music app, selecting a late 2000s playlist and hit the randomizer button. Beyoncé's "Single Ladies" blasted out of the tinny speakers.

"You know me so well, phone."

It was time to get to work.

I needed about forty minutes to turn the cannabis's THCA into THC through the decarboxylating process, which would help to make the buds psychoactive and ready to be infused. I already had a batch of cannabutter prepared, so today I was infusing the oil I planned to use in the dressing for my watermelon and feta salad.

While the cannabis decarbed in the oven, I set up the required system for infusing the oil. There were *so* many different methods that could be used—including a sous vide, which seemed very clever, although I didn't have a vacuum sealer, unfortunately. I made a note to add one to my list of things to purchase for the business if our license came through.

*When the license comes through*, I corrected in my head. *Think positive.*

Instead I was going to use a good old-fashioned double boiler method. After I got everything ready, I consulted the notebook I'd been scribbling in while I planned the dinner party. It had all the calculations required to get the correct dosing per dish. This involved dividing the total milligrams of cannabis used in the recipe by the percentage of THC in the strain, divided again by the number of portions.

It was important to get this correct: A, because I took my responsibility as host seriously; and B, I believed that people deserved to know what they were putting into their bodies.

Once the buds were done, I slipped on an oven mitt and pulled them out of the oven. I added them to the jars, along with the oil, which needed to infuse for at least two hours. In that time I could prepare the pots de crème. I started by chopping up the high-quality semisweet dark chocolate, using my knife to split the dark block into smaller chunks. As I was doing this, my phone buzzed and a message appeared on screen. It was from Aunt Dawn.

**Where are you? We need to chat.**

Frowning, I wiped my hands down the front of my apron before touching my phone.

**I'm at the café. Come through the back, I'll leave the door unlocked.**

I unlatched the door so Dawn could get inside, since we hadn't gotten a second key cut yet and I hated to be interrupted in the middle of an important step. There was nothing more stressful for a chef than being pulled away from their work at a critical moment.

I fetched a saucepan from one of the shelves, which we'd filled with odds and ends from Grandma Rose and Aunt Dawn's extensive collection. Once we were full steam ahead, I'd be hitting up a kitchen supply store to get some fresh tools, but this would do for now. I'd made plenty of excellent dishes before with pots and pans that were older than me!

I poured heavy cream into the pot, which was sitting over a low-medium heat, and then I added the chocolate, stirring to get everything going and singing along at the top of my lungs to the song blaring out of my phone. We'd had Lady Gaga, Beyoncé, Kings of Leon, Katy Perry, Black Eyed Peas. All the tunes from my school years.

While the chocolate was melting, I cracked the eggs and separated the yolks into the mixing bowl, putting the whites into another container to be used for something else. Maybe I'd make some meringues for dessert tonight.

As I was tossing out the eggshells, I heard a noise in the front of the shop. It sounded like someone was knocking on the door and they must have been knocking loudly for me to hear it over the music. It was probably Aunt Dawn, wondering why she couldn't get inside.

"I told you to come through the back," I muttered to myself, walking out of the kitchen and through to the front of the shop. Nobody was there and there was no sign of my aunt. "Strange."

I went to the door and flicked the lock. When I pulled the door open, a piece of paper fluttered to the ground. The breath stilled in my lungs. Was this going to be another note like the first one, accusing my aunt of something she didn't do? For a moment I simply stared at it, unsure if I wanted to know what message it contained.

"Don't be such a chicken," I chided myself. "Words can't hurt you."

The familiar opening of a Rihanna song floated in from the kitchen, where the music was still playing on my phone. Sucking in a breath, I leaned forward and picked up the note. Opening it up, I saw it was simply an advertisement for the local car wash.

"What the heck?" I screwed up my nose. Why would someone pound on my door for that? "Talk about an aggressive marketing campaign."

I wadded the paper into a ball and looked down the street but didn't see anything out of the ordinary. Shrugging, I pulled the door closed and was about to lock it again when I heard something behind me. I turned and almost walked straight into something.

Or rather, someone.

A figure dressed in black rushed me, holding up an item to obscure their face—a heavy-bottom skillet from the kitchen. I gasped, ready to let out a scream as the skillet swung in my direction. It connected with my skull and a white-hot flash of pain tore through my head, blinding me momentarily. I crumbled like wet tissue paper, clutching my head and clamping my eyes shut. The music played on from the kitchen.

"Chloe?" I heard my aunt calling out from the back of the shop.

I opened my mouth to respond, but a hard boot landed into my stomach, winding me. I gasped for air and tried to roll out of the way. Something heavy clattered to the floor and the figure jumped over my prone body. The front door slammed a second later.

I saw my aunt emerge from the kitchen, her eyes bulging. "Chloe? Oh my god!"

I lay on my side, doubled over. My head throbbed and my lungs ached as I tried to suck a breath in, adrenaline skittering through my body and making me tremble. I tried to push up into a sitting position, but the world spun and I slumped back down.

Aunt Dawn rushed over, dropping down to her knees by my side, her hands clutching my face. Relief flooded through me. If she was here, then I was safe. Her gaze was stuck on my head, where I assumed I had either a big bruise or a lump—or both—blooming.

"Your timing is impeccable once again," I croaked, my eyes fluttering shut.

That was twice now, since arriving home, that someone had attacked me.

# CHAPTER 20

Fifteen minutes later, Detective Alvarez was standing in the shop, frowning so hard I thought she might create a permanent indent between her eyebrows. Aunt Dawn had turned off the boiler for the cream, which had already started to stick and burn before I remembered I'd had it over the heat. I'd need to start the pots de crème all over again.

Thankfully, the oil infusion still had plenty of time to go, so that wasn't ruined.

"What happened?" the detective asked.

I was able to sit upright now, and my aunt had given me some water and a cool compress for my head, along with a few pain-killers. She'd wanted to take me to the emergency room, but the hospital was quite a drive and I didn't feel like sitting in the waiting room for three hours only for them to tell me to pop some Advil and monitor my symptoms. I felt battered and bruised, but nothing was seriously damaged, and I hadn't lost consciousness.

"I heard a knock at the front door and I thought it was my aunt," I said, holding the compress to my head. Thankfully the painkillers were starting to kick in. "But when I got to the door, no one was there. Someone had stuck a flyer for the car wash in the door. When I turned around, there was a person and they hit me with a skillet."

I pointed to the heavy-bottomed pan sitting on the floor.

"Does it belong to you?" Detective Alvarez asked and I nodded. "Did you see the person who hit you?"

I tried to remember, but it had all happened so fast that my memory was a blur. "They were dressed in black. Or, at least, they were wearing a black hoodie and the hood was pulled up."

"Hair color, eye color? Anything distinguishable?"

I shook my head. "They had the skillet up in front of their face, but uh . . . I think they were taller than me."

The detective looked me up and down, as if assessing my height. Or rather, lack thereof. "Tall or just taller than you?"

"I don't know. I was so startled that I didn't . . ." I squeezed my eyes shut, cursing myself for not taking better note of the details. "It all happened so quickly."

"It's okay." Detective Alvarez offered a tight smile. She was dressed in her usual practical tan slacks, black blazer, white shirt and tight braid. Today her glasses were chunky and black, which gave her an even more serious look than usual. "And they exited out the front door?"

"That's right."

"Did you see anything?" Detective Alvarez asked my aunt.

"No." My aunt toyed with her hair, worry deepening the lines around her brow and eyes. "I entered through the back, like Chloe asked me to. Music was playing, but she wasn't in the kitchen and I called out. Then I heard a bang and came running out here. Chloe was on the floor but the person who attacked her had already gone."

"We'll see if we can find anything in the CCTV footage from the businesses on the street." The detective looked back to me. "I don't suppose you have any cameras set up in here?"

"No, we don't."

"Did they say anything to you at all?"

"Not a thing. I don't even know what they wanted."

The detective had a look on her face that said she had an idea what the person wanted, but she kept her mouth shut. I knew what she was holding back . . . the very thing she'd said to me before.

*No more DIY investigation. You're not Miss Marple and this is not a Lifetime movie. You could get seriously hurt.*

And what had I done today? I'd followed a woman and listened in on her private conversation, and then I'd been stupid enough to get caught doing it. Could Maisey Brent have attacked me? Possibly. The shock of it had stunned me so much that I had no idea if the attacker was a man or a woman. If they were large or small, old or young. It didn't help that I was vertically challenged enough that most people felt taller than me.

*Except Erica.*

She was the only person I could think of who was shorter.

"Do you have the ad you found in the door?" the detective asked. I pointed to the wad of paper on the floor not far from me, and Detective Alvarez picked it up. "It's old, from three months ago."

"You think it was a distraction?" That hadn't even occurred to me.

"Possibly. Maybe they tried the front door and found it locked, and went around the back to see if they could get in that way. Or maybe they were always planning to come through the back and it was meant to be a diversion for them to get inside."

"No more being alone in the shop," Aunt Dawn said, her arms folded tightly across her chest. "And we're getting that second key cut today."

"Well, we don't need a second key if I'm going to be chaperoned," I muttered.

My aunt looked like she was going to open her mouth to chastise me, but when she glanced at the detective she thought better of it. No doubt that would be coming later. I may not have had a mother for most of my life, but I was never short on discipline.

"Can I have a word alone with Chloe?" the detective asked, smiling at my aunt like it was nothing at all. But the request immediately put my senses on high alert.

Anticipation prickled along my skin like beetles and my muscles bunched, hiking my shoulders up and tensing my hands. "Anything you have to say—"

"Sure." My aunt cut me off. "I'll start cleaning up the burned cream. Just yell if you need me."

I watched her disappear through the kitchen doorway and a second later the music came back on. My aunt was a better woman than I was, because I had been about to tell the detective to stick it, in the politest way possible.

Detective Alvarez looked at me intently through her thick-framed glasses. It gave her an almost owlish appearance and contrasted against her deep olive skin. "Has anything happened since we spoke last that might have provoked this attack? Have you had any encounters with anyone, which didn't sit right? Have you noticed anyone following you?"

"Other than the black cars I told you about, no." I shook my head. "And I haven't even noticed the cars the last few days."

"Mm-hmm." She waited for me to continue.

Silence stretched on as I tried to figure out whether I should tell her about the incident with Maisy Brent, but I knew what she would say. At best, I'd get a lecture for trying to play sleuth. At worst, I'd get a warning about interfering with the investigation.

There was no winning. I needed something concrete before I told the detective anything else.

"I haven't had any strange encounters," I lied, hoping she didn't see right through me.

"Are you sure?" She narrowed her eyes and it was like being scanned by a machine. I could practically feel a laser tracking over my skin, detecting flaws and weaknesses in my story.

"Totally sure," I squeaked.

Disappointment washed over her face. What did she know? I guess she trusted me as much as I trusted her.

"How long was the time between the assailant exiting the shop and your aunt coming through the back?" she asked.

My mouth popped open. "Do you *seriously* think my own aunt attacked me?"

"Answer the question, please."

I gritted my teeth, anger rushing up inside me so hot and so fast I was sure if I turned my wrist over that I would see the emotion bubbling in my veins.

"It was less than a minute," I gritted out. "An impossible amount of time for her to run out the front, get around the corner and come through the back. Oh, and also change her outfit at superhuman speed while she was doing that."

"That's all I needed to know," the detective said in a calm tone. "I have to ask these questions, Chloe. I need to cover all options, no matter how unpleasant."

"I don't know if it's Chief Gladwell's doing—he never liked my aunt—but whatever you have in your head about her, you're wrong. She's a good person." Tears of frustration pricked my eyes. I was sore, tired, emotionally drained and now I'd ruined the pots de crème and would have to start over.

I wanted the real murderer to be found so I could go back to worrying about normal things like if people would support my business and what I should wear the next time I saw Jake. Not whether my family member was going to be thrown into jail.

Detective Alvarez simply nodded and stood, taking a few notes on her tablet before closing the cover and tucking the stylus away. "If you remember anything else, give us a call. I'll ask around the businesses outside and see what we can find."

"You don't sound too confident," I commented.

"I don't feel like I'm working with all the information."

She knew I was keeping things from her. For someone who seemed so intelligent and perceptive, her focus on my aunt was a little baffling. But then again, what I'd said about the chief and my aunt was true. They'd been at loggerheads for *years.*

She'd called him uptight and a traditionalist, and he'd called her a weirdo hippie. Something told me they had beef going all the way back to high school. But that wasn't a reason to try and pin a murder on someone, was it?

"If I remember anything else, I'll let you know," I said, meeting the detective's eye.

"You do that, Chloe."

She walked back through the shop toward the kitchen, presumably to let my aunt know what the next steps were, since she was the one who'd put the call in. The music shut off and I heard muffled voices for a minute, before the closing of the back door. Aunt Dawn came back through to the main area of the shop.

"What do you make of her?" I asked, gingerly touching my head. Oh yeah, there was a lump all right.

"The detective?" My aunt sat down on the floor next to me. Her long skirt was tie-dyed with indigo and had metallic gold stars and moons on it, and she wore a pair of sandals that showed off her bright orange pedicure. Her jewelry jangled as she got into position and the sound soothed me. "I honestly don't know. I usually have a good read on people, but she's a tough nut to crack."

"She wanted to know how long between the attacker exiting the front and you coming through the back."

She made a *hmph* sound. "I appreciate her thinking I'm so athletic, but sadly I haven't run since I was on the track team in high school."

"*You* were on the track team?" I snorted.

"Don't laugh, girlie. I'm accomplished in a great many things." She winked at me. "It had nothing to do with the fact that the entire team came down with the stomach flu right before the race and they were desperate for fill-ins."

I laughed. "How did that go down?"

"Came dead last." She chuckled. "But it made me realize that I enjoyed competing. So I did calisthenics for a while and then I played tennis. And now, I do things with Moxie."

"I want to get a dog," I said with a nod. It was easier to talk about this than to think about what the heck else was going on in my world. "Something small. Do you think Grandma Rose would mind having a pet around the house?"

"You should ask her," my aunt encouraged. "So long as you take care of all the labor-intensive stuff, I'm sure she'd be happy to have the companionship. She adores Moxie."

"I *will* ask her." Suddenly, it seemed like a little ray of sunshine penetrated the day.

Aunt Dawn slipped her arm around my shoulder and leaned her head gently against mine, away from the side with the bump. I breathed in the scent of her perfume and closed my eyes for a moment.

"What did you want to talk about?" I asked, remembering the text she'd sent earlier.

"Nothing important." She patted my leg. "Everything will be okay, girlie. I promise."

"I promise, too."

Because I loved my aunt with all my heart, and I would never let anything bad happen to her.

Everything looked perfect.

It was the night of the Dosed and Delighted dinner party and my aunt's backyard had been transformed into the perfect venue. We'd created a long table for our eleven guests by pushing her regular outdoor table together with a trestle table we'd borrowed from her next-door neighbor. I'd covered them both with a crisp white tablecloth, to make it feel like one seamless surface, and had decorated the table with vases of flowers and greenery picked from both her and Grandma Rose's garden.

There were sprigs of lavender, rosemary, plush pink roses, and green fern fronds arranged in a mismatched set of vases that came from both houses.

We'd strung up fairy lights, set up a table for the little goodie bags we'd created and set up a drink station with big jugs of cucumber-infused water, fresh-pressed juice and a simple iced tea with lemon. I'd designed and printed place cards to ensure people mingled, and matching information sheets about the menu and dosing, to make sure everyone knew exactly what they were consuming. All the elements had a touch of pink and gold, because Aunt Dawn and I had settled on those to be the Baked by Chloe brand colors.

We'd even gone so far as to find a set of pink plates and some gold cutlery, which looked romantic and soft against the white tablecloth, and some cut faux-crystal water glasses, which added a glamorous touch.

"It looks incredible." Aunt Dawn threw an arm around my shoulders as we surveyed our hard work. "You have such a keen eye."

"You were the one who suggested the flowers, and it really finishes the table off. I was only going to do pink tea light candles."

"We make a good team."

My aunt had played sous chef, helping me prep ingredients and allowing me to focus on the actual cooking and creation. Then we'd stayed up late last night, bagging up the edibles I'd made for people to take home, which included pink-tinted white chocolate cannabis truffles and a sachet of my favorite brand of tea for them to enjoy together, and handwriting the thank-you cards.

The whole thing looked incredibly thoughtful and professional, and I could see our vision for the business coming to life right before my eyes.

"How's the head?" she asked, looking at me with concern in her eyes.

I reached up to gingerly touch the bump, which had developed a lovely—*not*—blue-green shadow to it. Thankfully I hadn't experienced any worrying symptoms, like nausea, vomiting or dizziness. But it certainly didn't look great.

"I'm fine," I said. "It looks worse than it feels."

"You should get changed," Aunt Dawn suggested, giving me a nudge. "People will be arriving soon and I don't want you to feel rushed."

"Good idea."

I headed inside and gathered my things from the spare bedroom, where I'd stashed them earlier. After a quick but steamy shower, I blow-dried my hair and attempted to give it a little shape and volume. Since coming home to California, I'd noticed that my natural medium blond shade had lightened from all the sun, and my skin had a slight warmth to it. Since I didn't want everyone looking at the egg on my head all night, I'd borrowed a vintage silk scarf from Grandma Rose and she'd shown me how to fold it into a cute twisted headband-style that would work double-duty to cover my bump and keep my hair out of my face.

I slicked on some mascara, a little bronzer to enhance the glow in my face, peach blush and a shimmery lip gloss. Then I changed into the outfit I'd brought with me—a sleeveless dress made of soft grass green linen with a wide band of a darker forest green at the bottom. I'd bought it in a boutique in the south of France during a girls' weekend away and it always conjured good memories, making me feel glamorous and special whenever I wore it.

By the time I made it back downstairs, Grandma Rose and her date—sorry, *not* her date as she kept telling me—Lawrence St. James had arrived.

"Don't you look lovely!" Grandma Rose enveloped me in a big hug. I noticed she was also wearing a pink silk scarf around her head. The hair loss was increasing.

But she looked happy and vibrant, dressed in her signature

rosy tones. Beside her, Lawrence looked dapper in a blue shirt and black slacks, his tie a shade of pink that matched my grandmother perfectly. They were in sync, which was completely adorable.

Not a date, my backside!

"Thanks, Grandma. You look lovely as well." I turned to Lawrence. "I see my grandmother is having an influence on your color palette."

"I am not," Grandma Rose said, flushing.

But Lawrence beamed. "I know pink is her favorite color so I picked this one out especially."

Bless. "I'm so glad you could both make it."

"I'm very happy to be here." Lawrence leaned forward and winked. "You know, back when I was a young man I did enjoy a little 'creative enhancement' for my writing. Helps to manage the stress and uncertainty of a career in the arts."

"Your career hardly seemed uncertain," I replied, surprised.

Lawrence was one of the most successful mystery authors in the game, or he *had* been before he retired. He'd sold millions of copies of his books, had them translated into dozens of languages, and I'd seen his office once, which was lined with multiple editions of the forty-plus books he'd written in his long and prosperous career.

"There were times when I wondered if I had another story in me. The words would dry up or my characters wouldn't behave, and I thought I was done." He nodded solemnly. "But we must pursue what we love, no matter how difficult it feels at times, for the satisfaction comes once the sun starts shining again."

"That's very wise." I smiled, catching my grandmother looking rather adoringly at her "not date."

At that moment, I heard more voices coming from the backyard as guests filtered in through the side gate—which my aunt had finally fixed and which bore a sign welcoming everyone. I spied Sabrina and Cal chatting with Jake, and my heart rate kicked up a notch. Then there were two of my aunt's good friends, plus Luisa and one of her granddaughters, and Matt and Ben.

For the first time since coming back to Azalea Bay I saw the kind of life I could have here. It was like a picture had been painted of a possible future, one filled with family and a strange but wonderful motley crew of friends, with good food and support and passion.

And maybe even love.

# CHAPTER 21

By the last course, I was finally able to relax. I had put aside some portions of food for myself that didn't contain any cannabis, because it was my responsibility to ensure everyone had a good time, was safe and that I had my wits about me in the kitchen. Satisfied that my guests had enjoyed a good meal, I finally let myself sit and chill out. Everyone was slowly enjoying dessert. The pots de crème had turned out beautifully, even with my frustration at having to start them over.

They were made without any cannabis, but were accompanied by CBD chai lattes, which turned out to be a surprise hit, thanks to the water-soluble CBD powder, which provided a calming effect. That combined with the milk and spices had my guests feeling mellow and happy, and I would *definitely* be serving this on the Baked by Chloe menu. After all the laughter during the dinner, the energy had been brought down a few notches now.

"I don't think I could eat another bite." Matt leaned back in his chair and rubbed at his washboard-flat stomach. Frankly, I was shocked he could fit three courses into his lean and wiry frame, but he'd attacked each one with gusto. Although, that was probably helped along by the appetite-boosting effects of the THC.

Ben reached over to give me a high five, his eyes a little unfocused. "That was incredible."

He'd been a little nervous about his first experience with cannabis, which was completely understandable. So, I'd coached him through the meal, showing him where he could reduce his consumption by adding a little less of the infused elements to his meal and he'd relaxed and opened up, telling stories about how he and Matt first met that had everyone in stitches.

I looked around the table, my heart full to bursting. Grandma Rose, Lawrence and Luisa were involved in an animated discussion about something at the other end of the table and my grandmother looked happier than she had in the last few weeks. My aunt was giggling with her friend Michelle, and Sabrina and Cal were regaling Jake and Luisa's granddaughter with stories about their adventures at comic conventions.

"You're onto a winner, here," Matt said with a nod. He raked a hand through his longish hair and looked around the table. "This was an absolute ripper."

"Ripper means excellent," Ben said, giggling. "I don't know why but I find that one so funny."

"Ben thinks he needs to be my translator," Matt said, rolling his eyes indulgently. Although his accent made the word sound more like *translate-ah*.

"Throw a shrimp on the barbie, mate." Ben did a terrible impression of Matt, moving his shoulders up and down. "The dingo got my baby!"

"You shouldn't joke about that," Matt said solemnly. "The dingo really did get her baby."

"Is Australia as dangerous as people say?" I leaned forward, feeling pretty darn mellow myself. Now that my work was done, I sipped on my chai latte along with everyone else. "Do you really find snakes in your toilets and stuff?"

"Not usually."

My eyes almost bugged out of my head. "Not usually, but sometimes?"

Ben pulled a face. "It's not the snakes I'm worried about. It's the spiders."

"It's not that bad. And you guys have some pretty dangerous stuff here, I might add. Remember that trip we took to Yellowstone and we saw a bear?" Matt grinned at Ben, who shuddered. "So cool."

Ben made a sound of disgust. "Only an Aussie would find that cool."

"Well, you'll get to meet even more Aussies in a few months' time," Matt said. "There's that big surfing competition coming to town."

"That's right!" I said.

Aunt Dawn and I had already talked about it, because we wanted to be up and running before the surfers flooded Azalea Bay. The surf competition brought a huge wave of tourism— pun totally intended—and it represented big business. I didn't want to miss out.

"I'll be able to introduce you all to my little bro." Matt beamed. "He's a right legend."

"Is he competing?" I asked.

"Yeah. Gonna put on a show, I reckon. He's been training hard and he's had some luck recently. This could be his year."

"I can't wait to meet him."

As the conversation lulled and I noticed everyone was done with their desserts, I stood and collected the plates. Jake immediately jumped up to help. I tried not to grin like a silly teenage girl, but there was something so appealing about a guy who was always ready to help out. Jules had never been like that.

In fact, whenever we'd thrown dinner parties in our small Parisian apartment, he'd all but kicked me out of the kitchen so he could do what he loved—cooking—and then he would leave a huge mess that had me scrubbing dishes until the wee hours of the morning. That should have been a red flag, but I'd put it down to his head-chef temperament. And he *was* a better chef than I was at everything besides dessert.

The difference between Jake and Jules was night and day.

"You did such a great job tonight," Jake said as he followed me into my aunt's kitchen. Normally, both my aunt and grandmother would be on their feet to help, but they were conspicuously absent this time. "And you look . . . amazing."

His eyes dropped for a moment, almost like he'd meant to think the words instead of saying them aloud.

"Thanks." I hated being the center of attention and yet there was something about the compliment that warmed me inside.

I placed my dishes into the sink and he followed my lead. I'd load the dishwasher later, after everyone had gone.

"I have a good feeling about your business, Chloe. You've got what it takes to create something spectacular."

I turned to him, having to crane my neck up thanks to him being a full head taller than me. Balmy evening air carried the scent of jasmine from my aunt's garden, and it mingled with the woodsy cologne he was wearing and the spices still lingering in the air from the chai lattes.

"I appreciate that," I said softly, feeling shy all of a sudden.

It was just the two of us in here, alone. I could hear the quiet chatter of the event coming to an end outside, along with the playful bark from Moxie, who'd finally been allowed to join the festivities. It made the kitchen seem all the more intimate. The air crackled between us, and my stomach fluttered as though a colony of butterflies had gathered there.

He looked so handsome in his white shirt, blue jeans and tan leather shoes, which matched the belt highlighting his trim waist. His dark hair was lightly styled and his hazel eyes were flecked with green and gold, the colors enhanced by the warm indoor lighting. My pulse picked up speed and it felt like there was champagne in my veins.

Was he going to kiss me?

My breath caught in the back of my throat, his eyes dropped down and then back up. His lips parted.

"There's something I want to say," he said, his voice husky.

"Yes?"

"I . . ." He rubbed a hand along his jaw, as if he was trying to figure out exactly how to word his message. Or maybe he was still feeling a little sluggish from the cannabis.

In that moment, I felt the air shift. The butterflies stilled and the champagne went flat. I don't know how I saw it coming, but I did. Déjà vu ripped through me like lightning. I'd been here before.

I'd been *hurt* like this before.

"I lied to you," he said. "About something really bad."

"He *what*?" Aunt Dawn gasped.

The conversation with Jake had happened in a blur and I'd been mute the entire time, one foot in the past and another in the present. Sure, this wasn't as bad as what happened with Jules, because Jake and I weren't in a relationship, but still . . .

He lied to me. Right to my face.

I'd been so shocked that I hadn't been able to do more than nod and mumble that I had to get back to my guests, leaving him in the kitchen with a face full of regret. I hadn't seen him after that. By the time I'd returned to the kitchen with more dishes, he was gone.

"He told me that it was his brother who'd gone to juvie, when it was actually *him*." I swallowed. "Turns out, he doesn't even *have* a brother."

I'd listened to Jake's explanation with numbness crawling through my body. The story about "his brother" falling in with a bad crowd and getting pegged for something he didn't do? Yeah, that was all him. A stint in juvie had forced him to look at the path he was taking in life, and so when he was freed, he cleaned up his act, ditched the bad crowd and stuck his nose in a book. Everything else was true—the Wall Street job in Manhattan, the crazy hours, his friend having a heart attack, him quitting the rat race.

"Why did he lie?" Grandma Rose asked. She was settled on my aunt's couch with a cup of peppermint tea and her feet up on a pouf. Her eyes were a little droopy and she looked comfy and content.

"Apparently, he really likes me and he was worried how I'd react if I found out . . . blah, blah, blah. Like lying makes it better." I tossed my hands in the air. I'd changed out of my green dress and into a pair of sweats and a T-shirt stolen from Aunt Dawn's wardrobe. "Am I destined to attract habitual liars?"

"You don't know it's habitual, dear," Grandma Rose said gently. "Perhaps he really *was* worried about how you'd take that information. You're rather a straight arrow."

I folded my arms across my chest. "I'm about to open a weed café! How is that being a straight arrow?"

My grandmother and my aunt exchanged glances, and Aunt Dawn lifted one shoulder into a shrug, stifling an amused smile. "There's nothing wrong with it, Chloe. It's a good thing that you have a strong moral center."

"A strong moral center and a shitty radar for liars," I grumbled. "Maybe I should give up on ever having a relationship. Because if he's lying about this now, then what *else* might he be lying about? Who knows, maybe he killed Brendan!"

"Well, now you're just being silly," Grandma Rose chastised me, letting her eyes shut as she sank back against the couch. "What reason would he have to do that?"

"None," I admitted. "And he has an alibi, as far as I know."

I didn't really think Jake had done it. And yes, on some level I understood why a lie might have slipped out in that moment. It wasn't an aspect of his past to be proud of, but straight arrow or not, I *wouldn't* have judged him for it. In fact, I found it quite an inspiring story.

But I was hurt. Jake had picked at a wound that I'd barely finished stitching up, which wasn't even *close* to being healed.

"Then why did he tell you now?" Aunt Dawn asked. "Why not keep it secret?"

"He said that he really liked me and that it was eating away at him that he'd lied, because he wants to ask me out but doesn't want to start anything with skeletons in his closet."

"People make mistakes, dear," Grandma Rose said, her eyes still closed. "The fact that he owned up to it on his own says a lot. He could easily have kept it quiet and hoped that you'd never find out. It takes a lot of courage to own up to something like that."

"I wonder if that's what the chief was talking about," I mused. "He said I was too trusting and that there were people around me who weren't being entirely truthful."

Aunt Dawn scoffed, her cheeks a little pink. "The chief is full of it."

I knew my aunt didn't think much of him, but maybe he *had* been genuinely trying to warn me. If they'd questioned Jake and run a background check, then they probably knew about his past. Or were those records sealed? Clearly, I was too much of a straight arrow to know about such things.

*Okay, enough with the pity party already.*

"What are you going to do about Jake?" Aunt Dawn asked.

"I don't know," I said honestly. "I understand the point about him coming clean of his own accord, but . . . I promised myself after Jules that I would never let someone lie to me ever again."

The chief was wrong about me—I *didn't* trust easily. I was cautious in new relationships—whether business, platonic or romantic—and slow to open up. My childhood fear of rejection and abandonment turned me into an adult with a lot of boundaries and trust hurdles. I didn't seek out being the life of the party or having a huge posse of friends, because I would much prefer having one person I could trust than ten whom I wasn't sure about.

"Don't make a decision right away," Grandma Rose advised,

her voice a little sleepy. "Have a think on it and see how you feel in a day or two."

"You just want me to shack up and start making babies," I said, burrowing deeper into the couch. "Both of you."

"We might joke about it, but we only ever want you to do what makes you happy," Dawn said. "And Mom isn't saying you categorically *should* forgive Jake, because that's your decision. But he does seem like a nice young man and perhaps you shouldn't cast him off for a simple mistake, especially when he made the effort to rectify it without being prompted."

"We'll see," I said noncommittally. I had bigger things to think about than romantic entanglements right now, anyway.

My dinner party had been a hit, and I was more anxious than ever for our license to come through, but the high of that wasn't enough to overshadow the fact that I had been attacked two days ago. There'd been no word from the police and I hadn't gone anywhere except to shuttle between Grandma Rose's house and Aunt Dawn's house.

Moxie trotted over to me and shoved her wet nose into my hand, as if sensing that something was amiss. I patted my thigh and she leaped up onto the couch with her signature agility and grace, then plopped down next to me, with her head in my lap. Two big brown eyes looked up at me adoringly as I scratched behind her ear. Thank goodness my aunt had a huge couch, because there was plenty of room for Grandma Rose, me *and* Moxie with space to spare.

"What do you think about getting a dog?" I asked my grandmother, realizing I had forgotten to bring the topic up after the attack at the store. "Something little and cute. I'll take it for walks and clean up the poop and make sure it's fed, I promise."

My grandmother's eyes snapped open and she looked at Aunt Dawn. "This is your doing, isn't it?"

"I didn't say a thing." Aunt Dawn put her hands in the air and winked at me.

"You're not supposed to wink! Now she knows we're in cahoots," I said with a laugh.

"Think of what great company it would be during the day, Mom." Aunt Dawn grinned. "You used to make me bring Moxie around your house three times a week before Chloe moved back home, because you hated the house being so quiet."

"That's true," my grandmother said with a nod.

"Also, I know someone who is looking to re-home a sweet little guy." My aunt pulled her phone out of one of the deep pockets in her maxi dress and brought up a photo of a small tricolor Chihuahua to show us. "Michelle mentioned it tonight."

I gasped. "He's beautiful!"

"His name is Antonio and he's three years old. He belongs to her mother, but she's moving into a retirement village soon and it's an allergen-free place, so they don't allow pets." My aunt held the photo up to Grandma Rose's face. "He's *really* cute. Michelle's devastated that she can't keep him herself, but Big Blue doesn't do well with other animals."

Big Blue was Michelle's cat, a Russian Blue that was more like a small dog than a cat. He had the disposition of a grumpy old man and *hated* any other animals being in his space. They'd found this out the hard way when Michelle invited Dawn and Moxie over one time and to say the meeting didn't go well was an understatement. Moxie ended up with a nasty slash on her nose and a fear of cats, and Big Blue got himself a reputation for being a jerk.

"Please, Grandma." I literally brought my hands up into a begging position and she rolled her eyes at me.

"You are not six years old anymore, Chloe. Begging is not cute." Grandma Rose huffed, but I could see she was trying to act more annoyed than she actually was. The fact was, Grandma Rose was a *huge* animal lover, although she hadn't owned a pet since our beloved Foggy the white Persian cat passed away when I was in high school. "But maybe we can arrange to meet

Antonio. I suppose Chihuahuas are small enough that they won't take up too much space."

I grinned. "We're getting a dog!"

"No promises." Grandma Rose waved a finger at me, but Aunt Dawn pumped her fist into the air. "It's just a meeting."

We were totally getting a dog.

# CHAPTER 22

Michelle and her mother, Phillis, were keen to meet as early as possible, because they still hadn't found the right home for Antonio and packing for the move had already begun. So we decided to head over the following day. On the drive there, I asked Dawn if any more black cars had been following her.

"I feel like that's all I see on the road now," she replied with a sigh. "I thought someone was watching me as I got out of my car the other night, but I think I'm being paranoid."

"I know that feeling," I muttered. "Why couldn't they have a lime-green SUV or something?"

Dawn chuckled as she slowed at a red light, glancing over her shoulder to where I was sitting in the back seat and shot me a wry smile. "Wouldn't be too smart to follow someone in a lime-green car, now would it?"

"You would think leaving the murder weapon in the victim's neck when it had someone's initials on it wasn't too smart either, but here we are." I folded my arms across my chest. "I've racked my brain to think of someone connected to Brendan whose name matches DB, but I'm coming up empty."

The more I'd thought about Tate, the less convinced I was he had any involvement at all. So I had done some digging on

Facebook. Jay had sent a friend request recently and when I accepted it this morning, I saw he was also friends with Tate. A quick glance at Tate's profile—which was public—confirmed that he was at a sales conference in Sacramento for the three-day period around the murder.

So I could officially cross him off my list.

"What have I said about letting the police do their job, Chloe?" Aunt Dawn shot me a look. "We've already seen how getting involved can be dangerous, or are you looking for a matching egg on the other side of your head?"

I frowned and self-consciously touched the brim of the baseball cap I'd put on to cover up the lump. "Hardy-har."

"We want you to be safe," Grandma Rose said firmly. "No more interfering."

She'd changed her tune since the attack, now siding with Aunt Dawn and telling me to stay out of things. Sighing, I looked out of the window at the scenery rolling past. I had no intention of stopping until I knew my aunt was no longer a suspect. I might be the kind of person who doubted herself on occasion and was apparently a "straight arrow," but when someone tried to hurt my family, I turned into a bear.

Okay, maybe not a bear. More like a honey badger.

"Here we are," Aunt Dawn announced as she rolled the car to a stop. "Can we *please* not mention the investigation while we're here? Michelle is worried enough as it is and I don't want Phillis knowing about it."

"Don't worry, I'll keep my trap shut," I promised.

Phillis lived in a small but well-kept split-level house. The inside was like a perfectly preserved time capsule of the 1960s—from the pistachio-green kitchen to the paisley wallpaper to the pristine white shag rug in the sunken living room.

Phillis herself looked immaculate—wearing a yellow dress that complemented her brown skin, and a deep bronze lipstick—despite the fact that she was in the middle of packing up her home. She had a reputation for always being impeccably dressed. Michelle, on the other hand, wore a much more practical moving outfit of a black tank top, paint-smudged jeans and her long, dark braids piled on top of her head. It looked like she'd been doing some repair work.

"Thanks for coming by," she said with a wide smile. "And I understand you're looking for a furry companion."

"I'm hoping they'll be more trustworthy than the human kind." Clearly I was still feeling a little bitter about finding out Jake had been lying to me.

Michelle snorted. "I'm divorced, girl. I understand that sentiment like you would not believe."

"Second time's a charm?"

"Second time's the same mistake you made once already." She winked. "Now come through the back. I'll introduce you to Antonio."

As we walked through the house, Phillis came up beside me. "Don't you listen to my daughter. Marriage is a gift. I had fifty-three wonderful years before my Richard passed, God rest his soul. Never a bad day between us."

The group filtered out into the back part of the house, where a lovely room, which looked like it had started as a porch but had been closed in at some point, opened up with views of the backyard. A beam of pure sunshine cut a line across the floor, and right in the middle of the warm patch was a little tricolor Chihuahua, curled up and sleeping.

"Antonio, wake up," Phillis called.

At the sound of his name, the little dog lifted his head sleepily, his tail thumping lightly against the floor.

"Oh my gosh, he's adorable!" My voice climbed higher with every word, which caused Antonio's satellite-dish ears to flick up. It looked like he could take flight with those things. "Grandma Rose, look! He's such a sweet little bean."

The dog got to his feet and trotted over to his owner, big luminous brown eyes full of love. My heart melted.

"His original owners called him Antonio because his markings look like a mask, see," Phillis pointed.

The dog was mostly black, though part of his chest, underbelly and three of his four paws were white. Tan patches ringed his snout and jaw and lined the top part of his legs, bridging the white paws and black body. The black markings around his eyes, which were circled with a touch of tan fur, really did make it look like he had a bandit mask on.

"Antonio . . . as in Antonio Banderas from the Zorro movie. That's cute." I grinned.

"I like Antonio Banderas." Phillis winked. "He's so handsome."

"Why don't we make an introduction?" Michelle motioned for me to come closer and crouch down beside her in front of the dog. "This is Chloe. She's a nice lady who's looking for a little pup to keep her company and we need to find you a new home, bud."

Above me, Phillis sniffled. "I've only had him a short while, about six months. We adopted him from a rescue place after he'd been brought in by a family. Their kids were too rough with him, I think, and he was sensitive to me touching his tail at first, but he's calmed down a lot."

"Awww, poor thing." I reached my hand out and let Antonio have a sniff before I attempted to pet him. "You've been bounced around a bit, huh?"

"It was a very hard decision to move into a retirement village, knowing I couldn't take him with me." Phillis sighed. "But he's so small and he kept getting under my feet. I'm worried I'm going to hurt him."

"Mom tripped on him a few times, because he's so quick and she's not as nimble as she used to be," Michelle added. "Then when she had the fall on the stairs into the living room, we knew it was time to make a move. There are too many stairs in this house, too many places to have a slip-up."

Antonio pressed his head into my palm, tail wagging harder,

so I took that as a sign he was ready for some affection. As I patted him, he came closer, and jumped up on my leg.

"He wants to be cuddled," Phillis said. "You can pick him up."

So I did. The little guy weighed no more than a bag of sugar and he immediately nuzzled into the crook of my arm. "He's so affectionate."

"That boy would be cuddled all day, every day, if he could," Michelle said with a laugh. "I know you're looking to start a business soon, so I guess that means long hours . . ."

"I'll be home during the day." Grandma Rose stepped forward to stroke his head. "He won't be alone."

I caught Aunt Dawn's eye and she winked at me. I knew it would only take one look at a cute dog for my grandmother to be won over.

"In fact, I would quite like someone to keep my lap warm while I watch my soaps," she added.

"I would be so happy knowing he was going to a good family like yours." Phillis clasped her hands together in front of her. "I really didn't want to take him back to the shelter in case they placed him with another family with young kids. He's so sweet and friendly, but he really doesn't like playing rough."

"We can give him plenty of love and cuddles. What do you say, Grandma Rose?" I stroked Antonio's face, drawing the tip of my finger up between his eyes in a way that made them flutter shut. A second later, I was pretty sure the Chihuahua was napping in my arms. "Do you think the Barnes residence has room for one more?"

"I'm not even sure he counts as one. A half, maybe. Or a quarter," my grandmother joked, looking utterly smitten. "And yes, I think we could see fit to make him part of our family."

Half an hour later, we were home with our newest family member. Phillis had no use for any of her pet paraphernalia either, so she'd been more than happy to give us Antonio's water bowl, harness and leash, dog bed, car seat, chew toys, and the near-fresh bag of dog food he liked. I found a home for all the items, including filling up his water bowl in the kitchen and finding the perfect spot for his bed right near the front window, which got tons of afternoon sun and would be optimal for napping.

Antonio sniffed around the house, checking out his new surroundings and, to my relief, didn't appear stressed by being in a new location. I supposed since he'd only been with Phillis for six months, then maybe he hadn't fully settled there, either.

"I can't believe you convinced me to get a dog," Grandma Rose said, shaking her head.

"Convinced you?" I scoffed. "Please, you took one look at that little guy and it was love at first sight."

"I'm a sucker." She laughed ruefully and shook her head, slipping an arm around my waist. "But it will be nice to have an animal around the house again. It's been too long."

"And don't worry, I *will* look after him. This isn't like when I was a kid and you had to convince me to do my chores, okay? I'm a responsible adult now."

"You were responsible back then, too," she said. "I swear, you were a mini adult from the age of four, always so serious and thoughtful. In fact, I found something that you will have quite a laugh over."

We settled onto the couch and Antonio continued his trail around the perimeter of the room, trotting happily and getting his nose into every nook and cranny. I hoped he wouldn't be too sad about leaving Phillis's home, but I knew Grandma Rose and I would shower him with so much love that he would never feel lonely.

Grandma Rose lifted a box onto the couch between us and pulled out a slim book. "I have your final yearbook."

"Oh my gosh." I grabbed for it, eager for a nostalgic trip

down memory lane. It had been ten years since I graduated, and it somehow felt like both yesterday *and* a lifetime ago.

Flipping through, I found a picture of Sabrina and me, arm in arm. We wore matching pink aprons while manning one of the many charity bake sales our high school liked to hold in support of issues around the community. I still remembered the epic layered triple chocolate cake I'd made for that particular bake sale, the slices of which sold out in less than half an hour. It had gotten me my first professional baking gig, making a birthday cake for my vice principal's husband.

They'd paid me fifty dollars, which had felt like a fortune back then.

"Oh god, the Voted Most Likely To section . . ." I scanned the page, which was filled with school portraits and captions, assigning catchy and sometimes nonsensical labels to people.

"There I am." I cringed at my crocheted cardigan and over-the-top dangly feather earrings. I graduated in the peak of my "boho" phase, where I'd regularly raided Aunt Dawn's closet since her style had finally made it back into fashion. "Most likely to get a Food Network TV show."

"One day," Grandma Rose said, "you might end up on TV yet!"

I found the smiling faces of other people I knew, old friends who'd since moved away and some I remembered only in snippets.

"Look, it's Brendan." I pointed to the picture of a leaner but no less intimidating face. Acne dotted his chin and a sad burgeoning moustache dusted his top lip. "Most likely to stay in Azalea Bay."

"That's . . . painfully fitting."

"They wanted to have him listed as 'most likely to end up in prison,' but the teacher overseeing the yearbook wouldn't allow it." I stared at the picture, wondering if he had any inkling that his life would be so short. "There's Andrea. Most likely to get a PhD."

"She was a smart cookie," Grandma Rose said with a nod. "I

know she went off to college for a bit, but I'm not sure about the PhD thing. It might have been put on hold by what happened when she came back."

I cocked my head and looked at my grandmother. "What do you mean?"

"She had an eating disorder, poor love." Grandma Rose shook her head. "She was very sick for a while there, lots of hospital visits and lots of stress. It was a hard time for the Chalmers family, Andrea most of all."

"How do you know all that?"

"Her aunt does my hair. I had an appointment one day and when I asked how the family was, as you do, she burst into tears. I sat with her outside while she got it all out. Andrea had been admitted to the hospital because she'd collapsed." My grandmother let out a heavy sigh. "I felt so sad for her. I know you young girls are exposed to so much pressure around your appearance, what with all those fashion magazines and the skinny people on television and all the airbrushing and whatnot."

I'd certainly felt that pressure myself over the years. Working in a restaurant kitchen had made it hard to live a balanced life—we slept late to compensate for working until the wee hours, and often couldn't be bothered to cook properly for ourselves when we spent our working day cooking for others. I'd eaten grab-and-go pastries for breakfast or lunch more times than I cared to admit, and I'd had to work hard not to compare my body to the slim French women I passed in the street.

"I wonder if it was brought on by the stress of moving away for college," I mused.

"I remember Collette telling me that she wished Andrea would leave Azalea Bay for good. I never understood that. Don't we all need family in those tough times?"

"Unless family is the source of the problem? Brendan did some horrible things to her, like bashing in her car window with a bat."

Was it a stretch to think he might be the source of the stress that caused her eating disorder? Perhaps not. Or it could simply be that such a thing had no concrete explanation and it was simply human nature to assign blame.

We fell into contemplative silence for a moment, before something more uplifting caught my attention.

"Look, there's Sabrina. I see she was going through the boho phase, too." I giggled at the ridiculous floppy hat she used to wear, always getting in trouble with the teachers because it would block the people sitting behind her in class. They must have let her keep it on for portrait day. "Most likely to become a millionaire."

Antonio trotted up to us, pink tongue poking out of his mouth and his tail wagging happily. I patted the couch and he leaped up with ease, settling next to my leg and nudging my hand. I stroked him while I looked at the yearbook page.

"She always had a sharp business mind, that one." Grandma Rose nodded. Then she grinned. "Look, there's Frankie Stewart."

I rolled my eyes. "You have one crush and people want to remind you of it forever."

"Most likely to win a Pulitzer. That's a high bar."

"We thought we could take over the world then." I laughed and shook my head. "It feels like so long ago and yet also like it was yesterday. I wonder how many people are where they thought they would end up."

"Are you?" my grandmother asked.

"Yes and no." Coming home had felt like a blow to my dreams at first. Like taking a sledgehammer to everything I thought I wanted.

But sitting here now, with a tiny Chihuahua snoozing by my side, my beloved grandmother next to me, a new goal on my horizon and memories of a glorious dinner with friends still fresh in my head . . .

*You're home. This is where you're meant to be.*

"I'm glad I'm here," I said, after stewing on things for a moment. "It feels . . . right. Even after everything that happened. Not that I'm one to be fatalistic about things, but there's part of me that's beginning to wonder if I was always meant to come back here. That because I would never have made the decision to leave on my own, circumstances had to push me in that direction."

"Sounds like you've been having some of those crystal-charged whatnots that Dawn likes from Sprout," Grandma Rose teased.

Of *course* my aunt loved the crystal-charged smoothie bowls.

"I don't believe in all that mumbo jumbo, but . . ." She looked at me long and hard. "What people see as fate I see as intuition. You read the situation in front of you and make the best decision that you can. You *could* have stayed in Paris, Chloe. You could have stayed and moved on from your relationship. You could have made another dessert that would blow the socks off that critic. You could have supported me dealing with my problems via Skypeface."

I giggled. Grandma Rose could never keep the names of all the technology platforms separate in her head.

"You could have done all those things, but your intuition told you to come home and you listened. It's not fate, because that would make you passive. It's all you."

"That's very wise, Grandma Rose."

"If you get to my age and you haven't picked up a pearl of wisdom or two then you're in trouble," she quipped.

I looked down at Antonio and stroked his little head, a contented sigh making his rib cage rise and fall. His fur was soft and silky, and his ears felt like velvet.

"You're right, I could have stayed. But I didn't want to."

It felt vulnerable to admit that out loud. Because it was taking ownership of walking away, rather than acting like I was pushed into it. Taking ownership was scary, because if it was the wrong decision then *I* was the one who'd messed up. It was all on my shoulders and I could only look into the mirror for someone to blame.

"You're a bright young woman, Chloe. You'll figure things out."

We sat for a while longer, laughing over the silly categories in the "most likely to" pages of the yearbook, like Most Likely to Win a Hot-Dog-Eating Contest and Most Likely to Become a C-List Celebrity. I flipped the page to where all Azalea Bay's star athletes were listed and spotted Steve Boyd immediately.

"Steve 'Big D' Boyd, Most Likely to Make It to the NBA."

"Big D?" Grandma Rose wrinkled her nose. "What does that mean?"

"D as in Defense. He was the center for the high school basketball team and known for making these epic blocks at the rim." Not that I had been a huge basketball fan, but my high school crush—the frequently aforementioned Frankie Stewart—had been the sports reporter for our school newspaper, so I always made an appearance. "I'm pretty sure no one even called him Steve in the final two years of high school. He was just Big D."

There was another reason people called him Big D, but I figured my grandmother probably didn't want to hear about that.

"He's still using the personalized number plate that spells out defense, which he got when he graduated. Trying to keep the glory years alive, I guess," I said. "Big D Boyd lives on."

I looked at the photo and something churned in my brain. Big D Boyd . . . DB. Holy crap.

I doubted anyone actually called Steve "Big D" anymore, since it sounded like he'd never even made it close to the NBA and had been living in Azalea Bay for years. Frankly, until I saw the nickname written in the yearbook, I'd forgotten all about it. Chief Gladwell probably wouldn't be aware of it, either. His two kids would have been in college by the time Steve, Andrea, Brendan and I started at the high school, so the chance of him following the high school basketball team at that time was slim.

It was even less likely that Detective Alvarez knew about it, since she was a recent addition to our town.

My mind whirred with yet another possible connection between Steve and the murder. A few days ago I had been sure it was the Brents, but now I was back to thinking about Steve. Andrea had let slip that he didn't have an alibi for the night of the murder, and now it was possible that he owned the knife used to kill Brendan. Plus, if Brendan's bullying *had* contributed to Andrea's eating disorder, then maybe Steve wanted to protect his future wife from relapsing.

Opportunity. Means. Motive.

Steve Boyd ticked all the boxes.

# CHAPTER 23

The following day, after letting Antonio get comfortable in his new home, I decided to take him to the dog park Phillis had been taking him to, because apparently he had friends there. When I looked up the address, I noticed it was only a street over from Brendan's house.

So, I bundled Antonio into the Jellybean, where it took a good ten minutes to figure out how to secure the doggy car seat into the back. Then Antonio was in his harness and secured in the back seat, his leash ready to be clipped on at the other end, *and* I'd filled up a water bottle to bring with us in case he got thirsty. I'd debated shaking a few kibbles into a ziplock bag in case he was hungry, but he'd already had a little breakfast that morning and only ate twice a day, according to Phillis.

A Chihuahua felt like the right level of responsibility—twice-daily feeding, cuddles and a warm spot to nap. I could handle that. Phillis had described him as "a handsome little man with very good manners and a deep affinity for sleep."

*My kind of dog.*

"Ready to go?" I looked at him in the rearview mirror and he was peering out the window, paws braced at the edge of the doggy car seat and his giant ears pointed skyward. "I'll take that as a yes."

An hour later, Antonio had run himself out of energy playing with a friend at the dog park, and I'd gotten to know some of the other owners who frequented the place. It was a fun outing. After, I bundled Antonio back into the car to head home. But on the road, I took a left when I should have taken a right.

And I kept going instead of turning around.

"Just a quick detour," I said to Antonio as we paused at a red light. But he was already fast asleep in the car seat, his body folded into a kidney shape and his tail wrapped around himself. "You won't even notice."

I turned onto Brendan's street and drove slowly. Outside his house were two parked cars: a black sedan and a familiar white truck with a paint smudge. Two men were on the lawn, talking. As I got closer, I confirmed that one was Steve Boyd. The other, I assumed, was likely Ross Brent. He was tall and stocky, with reddish hair and an unkempt beard. A cigarette dangled from one hand as he gestured toward the house with his other, using a jabbing motion. Steve glared, arms folded across his chest.

They didn't notice me as I drove by, consumed by whatever they were talking about.

I rounded a corner into a small dead-end street and pulled my car over. For a moment I sat there, unsure what to do. Were Steve and the Brents in it together? Or was Steve simply negotiating with Ross to have Brendan's furniture removed so they could sell the house?

It could be something. Or it could be nothing.

As much as I didn't always appreciate Detective Alvarez and Chief Gladwell's methods, I respected the challenges of their job. How easy it would be to miss something by not being in the right place at the right time. Or to misinterpret something as a clue when it wasn't.

I glanced back at where Antonio was snoozing and bit down on my lip. I didn't want to leave him in the car because I was pretty sure that was rule number one of responsible dog ownership. Maybe I could park closer and roll my window down to see what I could catch.

I turned the car back around and eased back into the street, driving along at a slower pace until I spotted the truck. I slipped in behind it and kept the engine running. The truck was so chunky that it obscured the view of Brendan's front yard, and I couldn't see either Steve or Ross directly, which hopefully meant my tiny little Fiat would be somewhat hidden.

I rolled the windows down and voices floated on the air. It was hard to hear exactly what they were saying, though, and only snatches made it to my ears.

"I don't want . . . not getting . . . problem." The voice sounded unfamiliar.

"I know . . . he told me . . . nothing you . . ." That was Steve. "I won't . . ."

Ugh. This wasn't going to tell me anything! But what else could I do? At the very least, I should try to get the license plate of the black vehicle in case it was the one following me. All I could tell was that it wasn't the same car with the D3F3NCE license plate, because that had been an SUV.

But then the voices got louder, as if the pair were walking closer. They were probably getting ready to leave.

"I suggest you stay out of my business." The gruffer of the two voices, the one not belonging to Steve, suddenly sounded clear as a bell. They must be standing right in front of where the cars were parked.

Uh-oh. I had to hope that neither of them decided to look behind the truck before they got into their respective vehicles.

"I don't want any trouble, Ross. You know that." Steve sounded like he was trying to keep the peace. "I would prefer to keep this information to myself."

I sucked in a breath. This definitely wasn't a conversation about moving some furniture.

"You can't prove a thing." Ross, again.

"I know Brendan kept a record of what he found. I don't have it yet, but I'll find it. Do you want the nosy gossips in this town knowing you were stealing money from your wife's company? She made you sign a prenup, right? Maisey ain't stupid."

"You really think that dodo was smart enough to read financial statements, let alone uncover a theft? Please." Ross scoffed. "He was dumb as a post. Couldn't even fill out a client charge sheet properly. I was always cleaning up his mess."

"Why?" Steve asked, and I thought it was a very good question. "Why have a useless employee on your payroll when you could hire someone better? Because he was blackmailing you."

There was a sudden and all-encompassing silence as the two men stopped talking. It was like someone had yanked the cord from a pair of headphones out of the socket. What had distracted them? My heart thundered in my rib cage and my palms grew damp against the steering wheel.

Then I heard it, the sound of footsteps coming closer.

"Time to go," I said to Antonio.

I pulled the car into the street and hit the accelerator, causing the Jellybean to lurch forward. The old gal wasn't used to being driven like that. As I took off, I glanced in the rearview mirror. Steve was standing in the middle of the street, arms folded over his chest.

I swear, he was looking right into my soul.

I went immediately to the police station. It didn't matter what Detective Alvarez or Chief Gladwell thought of me anymore. They could scold me all they wanted. But I couldn't sit on this information. Unwilling to leave Antonio in the car, I picked him up and cradled him against my chest as I marched into the station. Just as I got to the front door, I turned and saw a black car driving down the street. A chill ran through me.

Was it the same car I'd seen just now outside Brendan's house? I didn't know.

In my panic to get away, I didn't take note of the car's make, model or license number. *Again.* It was a rookie error. I *should* have gotten that information. But as the adrenaline had pumped through my system, only one thing had mattered in that moment: getting away from those two men.

One of them was a killer, I was sure of it.

It was up to the police to figure out which of them did it and all I could do now was hand over what I had.

I headed inside and asked to speak with either the detective or the chief. I was left with the big guns, it turned out. Chief Gladwell came into the waiting area with a stormy look on his face.

"I was hoping I wouldn't see you in here again," he said, frowning.

"Give me five minutes, and then tell me if you're happy I came." I tilted my chin up to him. I wasn't about to let the man intimidate me or make me feel like a silly girl. "But I have important information about the murder of Brendan Chalmers."

# CHAPTER 24

By the time I got home, all the adrenaline had left my system and it felt like I'd run a mile. Or two miles. Or however many miles was considered a lot to people who knew about running.

I let Antonio out of his harness when we got inside and he immediately made a beeline for his bed, curling into a ball and going straight back to the land of nod.

"I know how you feel, bud."

The house was oddly quiet. I hung the leash and harness in the cupboard by the front door and poked my head into the kitchen. There was a Post-it note on the table indicating that Grandma Rose wasn't feeling one hundred percent and had gone to take a nap. I pottered around the house, tidying up, putting a load of washing on, and taking out the trash. Then I sat on the couch with a blanket, having every intention of reading another chapter of the Lawrence St. James book I borrowed from her shelf, but after only a page I drifted off to sleep.

I woke with a start sometime later to shrill ringing. Blinking with bleary eyes, I tried to figure out where the sound was coming from, mistaking it for a doorbell in my grogginess before realizing that it was a phone. Gosh, I hadn't lived in a place with a landline for years.

I groped for the portable receiver. "Hello?"

"Chloe?"

"Yes." For a moment after my response, there was a faint crackling on the line, like white noise. Then nothing. "Hello?"

"You've stepped over a line." The voice had been altered digitally. It sounded squeaky and high-pitched, like I was being threatened by a cartoon baby. It might not sound as menacing as if it had that low robotic tone they liked to use in movies, but it sent a chill down my spine nonetheless.

"Who is this?" I demanded.

"I thought you knew everything."

"I don't." My heart pounded and I looked at the phone's small square screen, but there was no number displayed.

"Then why don't you shut your big mouth and stop following people around? I thought hitting you over the head would scare you into seeing sense. It was meant to be a warning. Why didn't you listen?"

The person who attacked me had our phone number. They likely knew where I lived. This was the downside of small towns; personal information was *way* too easy to find.

"You're going to get caught eventually," I said, my voice trembling. "Whoever you are."

"I don't want to hurt you, Chloe. Stay out of this." For a moment I thought they were going to hang up, but they remained on the line. In the background, a musical chime sounded. "I suggest you don't leave your house in case you have an accident on the road."

The line went dead. I stared at the phone receiver in my hand as my breath came hard and fast. The person who'd attacked me had now threatened to run me off the road. Or worse.

But something stuck in my brain from the call. The chime! "Another One Bites the Dust." The person had been calling from the convenience store, I was sure of it. Probably using a pay phone so if the police got involved they wouldn't be able to trace the call to a cell phone.

Grandma Rose appeared in the doorway. She blinked owl-ishly at me. "Who was that?"

"Sorry, Grandma, I should have taken the phone off the hook. I forgot about the landline." I put a smile on my face. "It was a wrong number."

I hated lying but I didn't want to tell her that I'd gotten a threatening phone call within hours of going to the police station to report the two men I thought could have killed Brendan. She had enough to worry about right now.

"Seemed a long call for a wrong number?" Her brow wrinkled.

"They were insistent they had the right number, but they didn't." I walked over and steered her back to her bedroom. "Why don't you go back to bed?"

"Okay." My grandmother nodded and she shuffled back into her room.

The first thing I did was find the phone receiver and push the button so that no one would be able to ring through. If there was an emergency, both Grandma Rose and I had cell phones and those numbers were harder to find than looking in a phone book.

As soon as Grandma Rose was back in her bedroom, I grabbed my purse and raced out of the house. Threat or no threat, I had to get to the convenience store.

My heart pounded like a bass drum the entire time I hustled to the convenience store. I decided not to drive, since I figured I was probably safer on the sidewalk. The chance of someone running down a pedestrian in broad daylight felt slim.

Twelve minutes later, I almost skidded through the front door of the convenience store, sweat dripping down my back. Glancing around, I didn't recognize anyone who was currently shopping there. I jumped in line behind a group of teenagers buying candy and sodas.

"Hi, Mr. Collins," I said when I reached the front.

"Chloe." The older man smiled. "How can I help you today?"

"This is probably a weird question, but has anyone used the pay phone today?" I asked.

"You know, it's funny. I was thinking about getting rid of it recently because it hardly ever gets used anymore." He shook his head. "I wondered if it was too old-fashioned. But now I see I might be wrong."

"Someone used it then?" I prodded, trying not to let my impatience show.

"Yes, a woman." He nodded. "She was acting very strange. Wiped down everything with one of those sanitary wipes before *and* after her call. I mean, I know hygiene is important but—"

"What did she look like?"

"Oh, well, she was wearing a baseball cap and sunglasses. Very odd."

I had to fight the urge to shake the older man. "Was she tall, short? Fat, thin? Old, young? Anything?"

Mr. Collins scrubbed a hand across his face, squinting. "I don't usually take much notice of people's appearance, you know. Especially not since my eyesight is so bad. I really need to get that checked out. My wife is always on my back to go and see the doctor because she thinks there's something wrong. But I'm healthy as a—"

"Mr. Collins, please. This is really important," I pleaded. "Someone called me from here, but I don't know who it was."

"I wish I could help, but I was serving customers and she came straight to the pay phone without speaking to me. Actually, now that I think about it, there was something funny about her voice. It sounded really high-pitched."

If he could hear the way her voice sounded, then likely she was using an app on her phone to disguise her voice. Was it Andrea? Maisey Brent? Heck, maybe it was even Erica or someone else that I hadn't even thought of!

"And you're sure it was a woman?" I asked.

"I think so," he said. "But then again, I swore I saw a cat in the backyard last night but my wife said it was only a bird. Maybe I *should* get my eyes checked out."

"I don't suppose you have security footage."

He chuckled and rubbed a hand across his head. "Speaking of things that need to get checked out. The camera started turning itself off and on last week and I was getting so annoyed that I turned it off for good. I really need to call the technician to come and look at it."

I wanted to scream in frustration.

"Thanks anyway," I said, my shoulders slumping in defeat. "It's really important, so if you remember anything at all, could you please text me?"

It was a long shot, but I wrote my phone number down on a piece of paper and slid it across the counter.

"My granddaughter taught me to text," Mr. Collins said, grinning. "Now I send her messages and I even use those small picture things. What are they called? Mochis?"

"Emojis." I mustered a smile. It wasn't Mr. Collins's fault I was in a panic, he was a sweet old man and he couldn't have known what was going on. And it really did sound like he should get his eyes checked. "Please, if you remember anything at all. It would really help."

"I will think very hard," he declared.

I walked outside into the sunshine, my T-shirt damp from the sweat of hurrying over here. I looked around, trying to see if anyone was watching me. Or if there were any shadows lurking. But Azalea Bay looked as beautiful as ever. Everyone went about their business—people laughed, children skipped, dogs tugged on leads, and seagulls scavenged for food.

It was just another day.

About half-way through my journey back home, my phone rang. It was Sabrina. "Hey, what's up?"

"Have you heard?" She sounded breathless. "They arrested Steve Boyd."

I almost dropped the phone. "What?"

"For Brendan's murder."

"Thanks, Sabrina, I figured it was for that and not a parking violation," I said sarcastically. "How did you find out?"

"The police pulled up in front of his house, lights blazing. He lives a few doors down from Mom, and she was in the garden when it happened."

"Oh my god. It *was* him." I shook my head. "Wait, when did this happen?"

"About ten minutes ago. Mom called me right away as they were cuffing him. He just got home and they didn't even let him go in the house." She blew out a breath. "I can't believe we not only went to school with a murder victim but now a murderer, as well."

My shoulders sagged and I felt like a balloon deflating the day after a child's birthday party. All the tension seeped out of my limbs. It was over.

"Poor Andrea." I sighed. "Does she know?"

"I'm not sure. She's been working at the sports rehabilitation clinic outside town, so I guess it depends if she's on shift or not. That would *not* be good news to come home to."

"Certainly not."

"We still on for yoga?" Sabrina asked hopefully. "I'll be leaving in half an hour. I can pick you up if you like?"

"That's okay," I said, having completely forgotten that we'd planned to meet tonight. I needed to change into my yoga gear and grab my mat. Plus, I should probably let Grandma Rose know what I was doing. "I'll meet you there."

My head whirled with the news as I finished the walk home, at a slower pace this time. Steve Boyd was a killer. I had suspected him for a while, but part of me still couldn't believe that someone I knew would be able to commit such a heinous crime. In truth, I didn't feel like going to yoga at all, but I knew the class—and time with my best friend—would make me glad I went.

I was impossibly distracted in the yoga class. Multiple times Sabrina had to say *psst* to get my attention so I would change pose or face the correct way. I couldn't seem to shake this awful feeling that something was wrong. I wanted to know *who* had called me from the pay phone—was it Steve, and Mr. Collins was just *really* short-sighted? Or was something else going on?

About halfway through the class I couldn't take it anymore, so I slipped out under the guise of needing a bathroom break. The rest of the studio was quiet, and soft, relaxing music played through unseen speakers. I walked down the hallway that ran behind the two rooms where classes were held, looking for the restrooms. There were two, the kind with the toilet and basin in one area. But something at the end of the hallway caught my eye.

A *huge* canvas painting leaned against a wall. It was taller than me and featured a lotus flower, painted in beautiful shades of white, pink and yellow. But it wasn't the painting that caught my eye. It was the fact that there was something behind it.

I crept closer, looking over my shoulder to make sure no one was watching, and when I was sure the coast was clear, I nudged the canvas to one side. Behind it was a door. It was marked DO NOT ENTER and a small bolt was secured with a padlock. I could tell from the damp draft coming through that it led outside rather than into another room.

At that moment, my phone buzzed again, and I pulled it out of the side pocket on my leggings. I wasn't supposed to have my phone on me in class, but I'd forgotten to stash it in my bag before we started. There was a text from an unknown number.

**Hello Chloe.**

My heart leaped into my throat as the three dots blinked on my screen.

**This is Mr. Collins from the store. I remembered something. After the person used the pay phone they got a phone call on their cell phone. Why were they even using the pay phone if they have a cell phone? I don't understand people today with all their phones and computers and gizmos.**

I resisted the urge to write back, watching with my heart in my throat as the three dots indicated he was still typing.

**My eyesight is terrible, but I can hear like a fox. It sounded like someone was in trouble with the police. They said 'don't say anything, Steve. I'll be right there.' I'm pretty sure it was a woman. I hope this helps.**

A string of unrelated emojis followed the message, creating a chaotic and colorful tail to the words that had ice filling my veins.

"Oh my god. It was Andrea."

I looked at the door in front of me and rattled the handle, but it wouldn't budge with the padlock. Her alibi had been based on the yoga class. The police would likely have confirmed it with the staff here, possibly through security footage from the cameras I'd noticed the first time I came here. I looked up and around. The hallway was dimly lit and I couldn't see any cameras secured to the roof, like they were in the main area.

I walked quickly back down the hallway and came out into the reception area. A young woman I vaguely remembered as being a few years below me in school sat at the front desk, twirling the end of her long brown ponytail while she scrolled on her phone with her other hand.

"Excuse me," I said sweetly. She looked up, confusion pinching her brow. "I'm sorry to interrupt you and I know this might be an odd question, but do you have security cameras in here?"

She nodded. "Yes, we do."

"Where?"

The frown deepened. "Why do you want to know that?"

Hmm, I probably should have taken a moment to come up with an excuse. "Uhh . . . I saw a documentary a while ago about a gym that was filming its female patrons and it stuck with me, you know. The violation of privacy. Even the thought of being filmed in class, while I have my backside in the air, is very disconcerting."

"Oh, of course." The young woman nodded, mollified by my explanation. "That's a totally valid concern."

"Can't be too careful, right?"

"Absolutely. We have cameras that cover the foyer area only, because we have our cash register here for the merchandise sales." She gestured to the wall where a few branded clothing items hung, along with some beaded bracelets and yoga equipment like blocks and bands. "But the studios themselves aren't filmed."

"And the back hallway near the restrooms?" I probed.

"Nothing there either. You can come and go from the restroom in complete privacy." She smiled. "We have no need to film that area."

"What about the back door?" I was aware that I was pushing my luck, but right now I didn't care. The information I had given to the police could have resulted in the wrong person being arrested.

"The back door?" The frown returned.

"Behind the big canvas."

"Oh that." She shook her head. "It's locked and we don't use it. Like I said, there are no cameras back there."

"Is it always locked?"

"It's supposed to be. One of the girls here is, like, *so* lazy and she unlocks it to take the trash out instead of walking around the corner to the dumpster like we're supposed to do. We got broken into a while back, so the owner doesn't like us to use that door because she's paranoid about it being left open."

At that moment, my phone started to buzz. Jake's name flashed across the screen, but I stashed my phone away without answering. I didn't have time or energy to deal with him right now.

"So it *has* been open in the past?" I asked. "Where does it go? Out to the parking lot?"

"Yes, but you can't use it to get to your car. You have to come in and out of the front entrance. Studio policy."

The parking lot backed onto the park near my grandmother's house. The park where Brendan had been murdered.

She looked at me closely. "Is everything okay? You look pale and a little sweaty."

I touched my brow. Sure enough, it was damp. But it wasn't physical exertion that was making me sweat. It was all the puzzle pieces clicking into place. The fact that Andrea's alibi wasn't solid—she could have slipped out in the middle of class like I had done now and gotten out the back door if it had been left unlocked. Then she could have cut through the parking lot and into the park, murdered her brother with Steve's knife and made it back into class via the same door, then been filmed leaving through the front.

My heart was pounding in my chest. And then one thought exploded into my mind. Andrea knew about Steve's arrest. What if she'd gone to the house to make good on her threats?

Grandma Rose was there all alone.

# CHAPTER 25

I ran through the parking lot behind the yoga studio, my brain whirring. It was pouring with rain now, the air thick with humidity, and my feet slipped on the pavement. Thank goodness Sabrina and I had driven separately tonight, because I didn't have the time to explain what was going on. I'd simply rushed back into the studio to grab my shoes and my purse, and then I'd taken off into the night.

I got into the Jellybean and yanked the door shut, the rain drumming on the roof. Jamming the key into the ignition and cranking the engine, I turned to look over my shoulder as I reversed out of the spot and peeled out of the parking lot as quickly as I could.

"Hey Siri," I said to my phone. "Call Grandma."

"Okay," replied the robotic voice. "Calling Grandma."

The phone dialed Grandma Rose's cell phone, but it went straight to voicemail. Crap. I knew there was no point trying the house either, because I'd made sure no calls would go through and I'd forgotten to fix that before I left for yoga.

"Everything will be okay. You're overreacting," I said to myself as I drove, leaning forward to squint through the rain as the Jellybean's windshield wipers struggled to keep the glass clear.

"Grandma Rose is probably still napping and you're going to feel like a fool when you get home."

Still, better safe than sorry in my book.

I spotted the turnoff for my street up ahead and slowed down for the corner where water had gathered in a blocked gutter. The rain was teeming down and didn't show any signs of letting up. I turned into the street that ran along the side of the park and pulled into my driveway. I didn't see any strange cars parked close by, although it was hard to see more than a house or two in either direction with how bad the weather was.

Getting out of the car, I raced up the driveway, before realizing I'd forgotten to turn off the car's headlights. I'd come back for that in a minute. Fumbling for my keys, rainwater ran down my face and my neck, quickly saturating my hair and clothes.

"Come on," I said, cursing under my breath as my shaking hands struggled to get the key into the lock. Finally, I made connection and the lock clicked.

I pushed the door open and stumbled inside, dripping water all over the tiles in the entryway. The house was dark and I didn't detect any movement inside. She must still be sleeping. The breath whooshed out of me and I shook my head. Sabrina would think I was ridiculous when I told her about this later.

Everything would be okay. I'd check on Grandma Rose and then I would call Detective Alvarez to tell her what I'd found out and then I was *never* getting involved in anything like this ever again. My nerves couldn't take it.

*Don't forget about the headlights.*

I flicked on the lights in the entryway and toed off my shoes. Scanning the living room, I couldn't see Antonio anywhere. I headed toward the hallway where the bedrooms were, when I heard a noise. It was small. Quick. The sound of metal scraping against something. But it made all the hairs on my body stand on end.

Something was wrong.

I could feel it in my bones. The sound had come from the

kitchen, so I did a one-eighty and moved toward the archway that led there. Groping for the light switch, I gasped when the fixture overhead illuminated the room.

Grandma Rose was sitting at the dining table, a piece of duct tape covering her mouth. Standing beside her and holding a knife to her throat, was Andrea Chalmers.

"You didn't listen, Chloe." Her face was contorted with anger, making her almost indistinguishable from the woman I thought I knew.

Her dark hair was yanked back tight and she wore light makeup and a pistachio-green blouse. The professional outfit seemed completely at odds with the wildness in her eyes. My gaze dropped to the knife at my grandmother's throat. Grandma Rose's blue eyes were red-rimmed and they pleaded with me to not screw this up.

At least, that's how it felt.

"Aren't you going to say something?" Andrea asked, her voice ringing with frustration. "You've had plenty to say to the police ever since my brother was killed, and now suddenly the cat's got your tongue?"

"You mean, since *you* killed him."

She didn't deny it.

"Why are you here?" I took a step forward and Andrea's hand pulled the knife closer to my grandmother's neck. Grandma Rose made a muffled cry against the duct tape and Andrea winced, regret flashing in her eyes for a moment before she blinked it away—resolute and refocused on her goal.

The Andrea I knew was in there, somewhere. But desperation made people do extreme things, so I had to tread carefully. I couldn't do anything that might push her over the edge, but how the heck was I supposed to get us out of this situation? God, why didn't I call the police on the way over? I'd been so worried about rushing to Grandma Rose's side that in my panic I didn't think of anything else.

*Stupid, stupid, stupid.*

As if she was reading my thoughts, Andrea said, "Put your cell phone on the table. Keys too. Then step back."

I did as she said. The phone's screen lit up with a text message. It was from Sabrina and the preview showed a bunch of question marks.

"Does she know where you are?" Andrea asked, and I shook my head. "Don't lie to me."

"She's at yoga," I said. "I was supposed to meet her there, but I was running late."

I hoped she bought my story. More than that, I hoped Sabrina didn't try to interfere, because the last thing I wanted was anyone else I loved getting drawn into this mess. Andrea looked at my outfit, as if trying to determine whether I was lying. I was wearing black leggings and a baggy T-shirt, both of which were soaked. It would be difficult to tell what I'd been up to in such a generic outfit.

"Why are you doing this?" I asked.

"Because of *you*," she spat. "Couldn't keep your nose out of my business, could you? I had everything worked out and it was all going fine, but you had to lead the police right to Steve. You had to point the finger at *my* fiancé, one of the kindest and most loving men on the planet! You had to ruin everything."

Her voice cracked and tears filled her eyes. She looked wild and out of control, her features twisted in pain. This wasn't a master villain. She was a woman hurting on a soul-deep level. I don't know if that made things better or worse, because she *had* killed. And she was unpredictable.

"Andrea, please." I kept my hands in the air so she wouldn't see me as a threat. "We can work this out. I'll retract everything I said to the detective—"

"What if it's too late?" she asked, a tear tracking down her cheek. "They know the knife is his. There's no getting out of this now."

"Was it self-defense? Brendan treated you badly all these

years, Andrea. The police will understand." I had no idea if any of that was true, but I had to calm her down. Maybe if I could take the emotions down a notch, I might be able to convince her that hurting Grandma Rose wouldn't help things. I didn't even know what she wanted from us now. Frankly, I didn't think she knew herself. She was simply lashing out, not thinking straight. "If you tell them that he threatened you—"

"He did." Her lip curled and another tear traced the same line down her cheek. Then another. They were flowing more freely now. "That night he . . ."

The air in the room was so thick you could carve it up. My grandmother looked terrified and sat still as a statue, not daring to move a muscle.

"He stole that knife from my house because he knew it meant the world to Steve. It was a graduation present from his basketball coach. Then my idiot brother decided to text me a photo showing him holding the knife, just to taunt me. He was always doing stuff like that—breaking things, stealing things, anything to get a rise out of us." She let out a sob. "He was a demon from the moment he was born, determined to spread hate and pain."

"He hurt you badly," I said, keeping my voice slow and even. My eyes darted around the room while I tried to think of anything I could grab to disarm her. But Andrea had positioned herself well. And my grandmother's fastidiousness in keeping her house clean, meant nothing was in easy reach.

"He used to taunt me in high school. Fat Andrea, he called me. I weighed one hundred and three pounds." She gritted the words out. "He systematically broke me down year after year, making me believe I was ugly and worthless and unlovable."

I didn't want to empathize with her, because she was a murderer and she was threatening my family. But in so many ways, she was a victim, too. I had to push that empathy to one side, however, because right now she was dangerous and I had to protect my grandmother.

Andrea had been pushed to the edge of her emotions. That was bad news, because what if she decided there was no way out? Then there'd be nothing for her to lose. Nothing to keep her in check.

"Steve loves you," I said.

"Steve is about to find out that I murdered my own brother. Do you think he'll love me then?" She swiped the back of her free hand across her face. "He's going to think I'm a monster."

At that moment, my phone rang. Jake's name flashed up on the screen and Andrea's gaze flew to me.

"Leave it," she said.

I swallowed as I watched the phone jittering about on the table, spinning slightly from the vibrations. Then it went to voicemail and the house was silent again. My heart was thumping so loudly I was sure everyone could hear it.

This was going south, quick.

*Think, Chloe. If you don't figure this out, then things are going to end very, very badly.*

"You're not a monster," I said, trying to get her talking again. I wondered if she got lost in the story if I could reach the broom sitting inside the walk-in pantry.

It was risky. But I might be able to knock the knife out of her hand and give Grandma Rose a chance to escape.

"He pushed you too far."

"I didn't plan it, you know. I'm not a violent person." She hung her head for a moment. I could see she was grappling with how she'd gotten to this place. To this moment. "I'd just walked into my yoga class when he sent me the picture of him holding the knife. I was furious."

"Why the park?" I prodded.

"He was always hanging out at that damn park, drinking and smoking like a teenager. He never wanted to grow up. He told me to come to the park and get the knife if I wanted it back. I slipped out the back of the studio because I was crying and I didn't want anyone to see . . ." She gulped in a breath. I inched closer to the pantry and she didn't seem to notice. "I couldn't take the shame of it. I was sick of being weak."

"What happened at the park?"

"I wanted to scare him, you know? Make him feel even an ounce of the fear he'd poured into me our whole lives. But he laughed when I turned the knife on him, telling me I was too weak to ever do anything. When I stabbed him, he stumbled back and fell. The knife was sticking out of him and there was blood. So much blood. I froze. Then I heard voices close by. I should have grabbed the knife, but I got scared and I ran . . . I knew I had to sneak back into the yoga studio so I'd have an alibi."

To the very end, Brendan had been a jerk. It had been his undoing. His downfall.

I took another small sidestep toward the pantry and Andrea froze, her eyes locked onto mine. "Don't even think about it."

"What are you going to do?" I asked, my voice trembling. I was so out of my depth. I couldn't call for help. Couldn't even come up with a plan.

"Does it even matter? My life is over." She sniffled. "Steve will leave me, my parents will hate me, this town will make me a pariah."

"Please," I begged. "Don't think like that."

"If I'm going to go out, then I may as well do it in a blaze, right?" Her voice had taken on this disembodied quality that I didn't like at all. "I might as well give them even more reason to hate me."

At that moment, I sensed movement behind Andrea. She had her back to the door that led out to the garden. It was dark outside, but a shadow shifted. Someone was there. Jake! I tried not to look directly at him because I didn't want to alert Andrea to the fact that there was someone outside.

Then I heard it—the wail of police sirens.

Andrea's face hardened. "Did you call them before you came here?"

"No, I promise. It could be anything—fire, ambulance."

"You're lying." Desperation vibrated in the air around her.

"I'm not. I didn't call them." My eyes flicked to the door and she caught me, glancing over her shoulder.

At that moment, Jake burst through the door and I lunged for the pantry, my hand slapping against the wall as I groped for the broom. Got it! A scream rose into the air as Jake grabbed Andrea and the knife slashed, catching Grandma Rose's cheek. She yelped and everything tuned to chaos. For a woman with a slight build, Andrea fought back hard. Clearly all the yoga had made her strong and she struggled against Jake, her strength catching him off guard as she swiped the blade at him. He ducked back, releasing her. As she went to grab Grandma Rose again, I swung the broom hard, hitting Andrea's arm and sending the knife clattering to the floor. Jake kicked it away with his foot and then lunged for her, both hands clutching Andrea's wrists. She struggled against him, but this time he was prepared and he hung on to her.

"This wasn't supposed to happen!" she cried, a rage-filled scream shattering the air. But Jake held strong. "None of this was supposed to happen."

"Grandma Rose, go!" I held the broom in front of me like a weapon and my grandmother scrambled to safety as best she could. I could see her wrists were also bound with duct tape. We could deal with that soon.

"I called the police," Jake said, breathless as he struggled to keep hold of Andrea. "They'll be here soon."

Emotions tangled inside me—fury that someone had tried to hurt my family, relief that Grandma Rose was out of harm's way, empathy that Andrea had been pushed to the edge of reason by her brother. It would take time to untangle it all.

For now, I chose to focus on the positive. Grandma Rose was safe. That was all that mattered.

"No!" Andrea tried to break free, but I hit her in the back of the knees with the broom, forcing her to buckle. "No."

Tears streamed down her face and when heavy fists pounded on the front door, followed by a cry of "Police, open up!" she slumped in defeat.

It was over.

Grandma Rose sat on the couch, free of the duct tape and with a bandage over the scratch on her face. I sat beside her, clutching her hand and using my other to cradle a snoozing Antonio. Once the police had secured the scene here, I'd gone looking for the little dog and found him huddled under my bed, trembling. Poor little man. A guard dog he was not.

I would make up for the fright by giving him as many cuddles as he needed, so he knew it was safe here.

Jake stood a few feet away, hazel eyes brimming with concern as Chief Gladwell and Detective Alvarez threw question after question at us. Andrea had been led away by one of the uniformed officers, handcuffed and silent. There was no fight left in her.

"How did you know something was wrong?" the detective asked Jake.

"I'd tried to call a few times this evening." He raked a hand through his dark hair, his eyes darting to mine before pulling away. "The phone was off the hook for hours."

"How did you have a phone number for this place?"

"When I moved into my house, the previous owners had given it to me." He cleared his throat. "They said the woman next door was older and that they checked in on her from time to time, and that it would be kind of me if I did the same."

I had a feeling that was true, although it wasn't necessarily the reason Jake had been calling on this particular day.

"And when you noticed the line had been busy for several hours, you automatically called the police?" Detective Alvarez looked as though she'd come straight from home, not from a shift. She wore blue jeans and a gray sweatshirt, her dark hair haphazardly pulled back into a loose ponytail and a pair of clear plastic glasses perched on her nose.

"No. I tried Chloe's cell a few times, but she didn't answer." Jake shook his head. "I decided to knock on the front door. However, when I walked up the driveway, I noticed that Chloe's car was there, and the headlights were still on. The driver's door was ajar, which seemed odd given it was pouring with rain."

"Then?" the detective asked, her stylus poised over the tablet. Chief Gladwell stood in the background, watching us all with his arms folded over his chest and his eyes tracking every movement in the room.

"I had the feeling something was going on and I didn't want to intrude, so I turned the lights off on the car and shut the door to stop the rain getting in. Then I went home but . . ." He shook his head. "Something wasn't sitting right. I can see into their kitchen from my home office and I saw Mrs. Barnes at the table and a woman holding a knife to her neck. That's when I called the police."

"And you decided to intervene when there was an armed assailant," the chief finally spoke. "That's incredibly reckless."

"If it wasn't for Jake, we might be dead," Grandma Rose said sharply. "Because Andrea wasn't arrested for the murder and so she was free to break into my house. That's on you."

The chief's jaw tightened. "That doesn't excuse civilians getting involved in police business."

"I'm sorry," Jake said, holding up his hands and clearly wanting to keep the peace. "I acted on instinct, but that's no excuse."

"I'm grateful you came," I said, meeting his eyes across the room. "Thank you."

He nodded, but didn't say anything more. The questions had been coming thick and fast for an hour. When did the threatening call come through? Why did I come home early from yoga? How did I know something was wrong? I answered them all until my throat was raw.

Eventually the chief bid us a goodbye so he could return to the station to question Andrea. One of the uniformed officers escorted him out, but Detective Alvarez stayed behind.

"We've got evidence that Andrea was the one who attacked you in your store," she said, taking a seat on the single sofa chair to my right. She tucked her tablet and stylus away and braced her forearms against her thighs. "CCTV footage captured a woman with dark hair changing out of a black hooded sweatshirt behind one of the shops near yours before getting into a dark vehicle. The plate number matches a car registered to Steve Boyd."

"Then why wasn't she in custody?" Grandma Rose asked.

"We believed Andrea was covering for Steve, or that they were in it together. The plan was to bring her in when we returned to the house, so we could observe her first and gather more evidence." The detective looked down. "At that stage we didn't think she was the one who murdered Brendan."

I wanted to make a snide comment about how much time they wasted looking at my aunt when they could have checked out Andrea's alibi more thoroughly, but I decided to hold my tongue. It was over now, and I didn't want to stir up trouble.

"But this means if you want to press charges against Andrea for your assault, there's evidence to back it up," the detective said. Then she looked at my grandmother. "You too, Mrs. Barnes."

I swallowed. "I don't want to. She murdered Brendan. So long as she goes to jail for that, then what happened to me doesn't really matter."

"Of course it matters," Grandma Rose said, aghast.

"I understand that you might want to, Grandma. And I would support you one-hundred percent. But Andrea is a broken, bullied person who'd gotten to the end of her rope. She needs help, not punishment." I looked at the detective. "Can you recommend that she gets therapy while she's in custody? I know what she did was wrong, but . . . I saw how she was treated for years. If she'd been born into another family, she would never have become a murderer."

A look of respect washed over Detective Alvarez's face. "I can certainly ask."

"Thank you."

Part of me wasn't happy that Andrea was going to jail. This whole thing could have been avoided if someone had stepped in when Brendan was young, before things got out of control. He didn't deserve to be murdered, of course, but nor did Andrea deserve to be pushed to a point where rage was the only way she felt she could have control in her life.

"What's going to happen to Steve?" I asked.

"At the moment he is confessing to the crime," the detective said. "So we can't let him go yet. He's trying to protect her."

"He knew, then. He knew all along it was her."

"It appears so," Detective Alvarez said. "He was the one who broke into Brendan's house and it appears that he disposed of potential evidence."

I remembered the broken photo. I wondered if it was a family shot that had been sitting on the desk, and maybe he tore it up in a rage at the ripple effect of what Brendan's actions had caused.

The room fell silent, the drama of the last few weeks settling like stones on my back. But my grandmother was alive, my aunt was no longer a murder suspect and Jake had proven that a white lie wasn't who he really was.

For now, the people of Azalea Bay could sleep easier at night.

# CHAPTER 26

*Two weeks later . . .*

I walked along my street, breathing in the balmy salt-drenched air and balsamic sweetness of cypress and the tang of lemon from one of the houses that had a cluster of citrus trees in their backyard. The woman who lived there was friendly and kind, and she'd brought a bag of lemons over to us a few days ago because she heard I was a baker. I'd whipped up some simple but sweet lemon loaves with a zesty sugar drizzle and was planning to drop one by her door later this afternoon.

Azalea Bay was officially back to normal.

Talk of the murder had started to slow, even as the shock of Andrea Chalmers's arrest still rocked the town. I wasn't sure how to feel about it all. I understood that her brother had been a great source of pain and anguish over the years, but murder was never the answer. Neither was attacking an elderly woman in her own home.

I'd almost gotten it completely wrong. I'd almost made an error that would shove all the errors I'd made in my life into the background forever. Thank goodness Jake had been around.

"Speaking of people I'm not sure how to feel about . . ." I

said to myself. At the sound of my voice, Antonio looked back over his shoulder, his big brown eyes putting warmth into my heart. "At least I know how to feel about you, bud. It's one hundred percent love all the way."

Satisfied he was the only man in my life, Antonio turned back around and continued trotting along, tail high in the air and ears pointing upward. As I approached our house, I saw a splash of bright color on the doorstep. Flowers.

Pausing at the mailbox, I grabbed the stack of envelopes, and then headed toward the door. Antonio yanked on the lead, eager to stick his face into the flowers.

"I don't think so, little guy." I scooped him up, in case he decided to chomp down on anything. Phillis was right about the dog, he *was* well-mannered . . . unless there was anything edible in reach. And apparently to him, edible also included plants, as my grandmother's basil bush would attest.

Holding Antonio to my chest, I bent to check the card on the flowers. That's when I noticed that there was not one, but *two* boxes. The larger one was filled with an array of flowers in all shades of pink, and the smaller box contained a chili plant. The flowers were for Grandma Rose and the chili plant was for me. They both came from the same flower shop on Shoreline Street.

I opened the front door and put Antonio inside, freeing him from his harness so that he could do his little post-harness shake. The tag on his collar rattled and it made me laugh. I stuck the letters into my purse and picked up one flower box with each hand to carry them inside.

"Oh, what's that?" Grandma Rose came out of the living room. The cut on her face had completely healed and while her wrists had been lightly bruised from being bound, she was now back to her usual vibrant self. "Flowers! I hope they're for me."

"They are, actually."

I carried everything into the kitchen, where I found Aunt Dawn making sandwiches and sneaking Antonio a treat.

"Betty and Lawrence are stopping by for lunch," Grandma Rose informed me.

"That explains why you're wearing your favorite dress," I teased.

"Hush now. Nothing wrong with looking presentable." She came over to inspect the flowers. "These are lovely."

"Open the card." I went to give my aunt a kiss on the cheek and I noticed that she'd finally rid herself of the dark circles under her eyes. I could only imagine how much better she must be sleeping at night, knowing that she was no longer a murder suspect.

"They're from Jake." Grandma Rose made an *aww* sound. "How sweet."

Jake? I plucked the card from the chili plant and opened it up. Sure enough, it was also from Jake.

> *To Chloe,*
> *I know I messed up and I'm sorry. Can you forgive me?*
> *I thought about sending flowers, but a chili plant seemed*
> *more your style. It reminds me of you: strong and fantastic*
> *in the kitchen.*
> *Jake.*

Okay, so the gesture was kind of perfect. I wasn't really a flowers woman, in truth. I liked them, but a chili plant was much more my speed and my mind was already whirring with ideas for how some spice might pair with cannabis. A spicy chocolate tart, for instance? I could chop up fresh chilis and then dry some for a colorful garnish.

"The boy knows how to make a gesture. He even got my favorite color," Grandma Rose said, smiling. "I wonder how he knew?"

"Anyone who looks at you for more than two seconds knows what your favorite color is," I said with a laugh, gesturing to her dress, which was a pale dusty pink with deep pink roses all over it. "You have a strong visual presentation."

"I'll take that as a compliment," she replied with a nod.

"You should." I grinned. "Now, where should we house a chili plant?"

We decided that we would transplant the chili plant outside once lunch was done, so I left it on the kitchen windowsill for the time being, out of Antonio's reach. Then we took Grandma Rose's flowers out of the delivery box, unearthing a beautiful pearly pink vase inside. Jake had clearly gone for the fancy option at the florist.

"Do you think that someone who lies once will always lie?" I asked her.

"I think people do silly things when they're scared of what others will think." She smiled. "Did I ever tell you the story about how I gave your grandfather a fake name the first time he asked me out?"

I gasped. "No, you did not!"

"I thought he was no good for me and I told him my name was Gladys Evernight. Well, he went looking for fake Gladys everywhere and eventually he found me while I was waiting in line at the bank. I thought he would be mad, but he said I was a woman worth a wild-goose chase and then some."

"That does sound like something Gramps would have said." I pressed a hand to my chest. He had been a suave man, still wooing my grandmother until the day he passed. "Did you say yes when he asked you out?"

"Heavens no. He was a bad boy, a real James Dean type." She laughed. "He wrote me letters and sent me flowers and I made him jump through every hoop in the book."

I raised an eyebrow. "Are you saying I should do that?"

"No, dear. I'm saying first impressions are not always correct. At the very least, they're not the complete picture."

That would give me something to think about, for sure. Because I felt like I owed Jake so much. Without his quick thinking and bravery, I might not be standing here with my grandmother.

"I'll go talk to him later," I said. "I should say thank you for the flowers and the chili."

My grandmother patted my arm. "Please pass on my thanks, too."

Aunt Dawn caught my eye and winked, and I shook my head. My family might be a little unconventional, but I wouldn't change it for the world. Grandma Rose disappeared into the dining room with a jug of lemonade and I leaned against the kitchen cabinet, watching my aunt lay paper-thin pieces of prosciutto over a generous bed of arugula and sliced tomato.

"What do you think?" I asked her.

"About Jake or about the fact that my mother forced my father to jump through hoops to date her?" Mischief sparkled in her eyes. "I'd say on the latter that you and I both inherited her independent spirit. On the former . . . that's not a question for me to answer."

"I like him," I admitted. "And on some level I *do* understand why he made up the story about his brother. I guess . . ."

"You're scared of getting duped again."

"Yeah." I nodded. "Finding out about Jules's cheating made me feel really stupid and small. It made me feel totally insignificant, like I must be nothing if he could toss my feelings aside so easily. And I don't want to feel like that ever again."

"There's an easy way to ensure that," she said, closing the sandwiches up and placing them on individual plates.

"There is?"

"Never form a relationship ever again." She laughed when I frowned. "Sorry, Chloe, but the only way to never get hurt is to never put yourself out into the world. It's not fun advice, but it's true. Falling in love is risky, starting a business is risky, living is risky."

"I hate risk."

"No, you don't. You decided to roll with my idea of the weed café even though it was totally outside what you'd planned for yourself."

"That's because I trust you and it was a great idea," I protested.

"I could steer you wrong. You never know."

"You wouldn't do that."

"Not intentionally, but no one is bulletproof. You have to learn that, about yourself and about others."

As I helped her carry everything to the table a question played in my mind.

"You never told me what you were doing in the park that night," I said. When she didn't reply, I asked, "Were you there with Maisey Brent?"

To my surprise, she nodded. "Yes."

Their voices must have been the ones Andrea heard shortly after she murdered her brother. The very voices that caused her to run away without grabbing the knife. But something about the way my aunt answered made me still.

I looked at her closely, noting the tension in her face and the vibrating energy around her. Something important was about to happen, I could feel it. I didn't dare say a word, because my gut told me that my aunt needed time to gather her thoughts and speak from the heart.

"We'd started to become friendly through the canine free-style group that we're both part of on Facebook. When we found out we lived in the same town, we started catching up." Dawn looked over my shoulder, staring into space as though she was watching her memories on a screen. "Never in public, for some reason. She always came to my house or I went to hers."

"Okay." I wasn't sure where this was going.

"She told me that she and her husband weren't happy. Hadn't

been for a long time. And then she . . ." My aunt drew in a big breath. "She told me she wanted to start a relationship with me."

"But she's married." I shook my head in confusion.

My aunt laughed, though the sound had no humor. "Aren't you going to say 'but you're both women' or something like that?"

"Well, no. I mean, I never knew for sure but . . ."

There had always been part of me that suspected my aunt was gay. Not because she was single and didn't want kids—because I knew plenty of straight women who didn't want those things, either. But there had been a few hints over the years, the way she'd looked at and talked about certain friends. Other small inklings.

But I figured she would share it when she felt comfortable. And if she never felt comfortable, then that was that. She didn't owe anyone an explanation or a label, and I would love her regardless.

"It's your business, not mine," I said.

"I thought you hated liars."

I pulled a face. "This is different."

"Is it?"

"Yes," I said fiercely. "You never lied."

"I feel like I've been lying all my life," she admitted. "Everyone thought I was so strong and so rebellious for not getting married and yet I could never say it out loud. I *wanted* to get married one day . . . just not with the kind of person people thought I should marry."

It occurred to me that the day I'd followed Maisey Brent into the secondhand bookshop, she was probably talking to my aunt on the phone. It made me feel even worse for invading the woman's privacy. But hopefully she would understand I was only trying to protect my family.

"You understand why I couldn't tell the detective my reason for being at the park, right? I couldn't do that to Maisey."

"I understand." It made a whole lot of sense now.

"And I couldn't risk telling you, only for you to hand that information over to the chief in order to protect me. Besides . . . I was afraid of what you and your grandma would think."

"Who you want to be with doesn't matter to me, so long as they treat you right."

"I'd never have an affair with a married person. That's just wrong," Aunt Dawn said. "But Maisey told me she received an anonymous letter this week. It said that her husband is stealing from the company and there were some reports and photocopies included. She suspected he was doing something dirty, and now she has proof."

Steve. He must have found the evidence that Brendan was holding over Ross, and sent it to Maisey.

"The letter said that Brendan was trying to blackmail Ross. She'd been trying to get rid of Brendan for a while, but Ross convinced her to give him chance after chance. Now she knows why—her husband was worried that if Brendan was fired, that he'd tell Maisey everything."

"Wow." I shook my head. "Poor Maisey."

"Once she divorces her husband . . . I don't know." She scrubbed a hand over her face. "Maybe . . ."

"I love you no matter what you decide to do." I pulled my aunt in for a big hug and buried my face in her hair, sucking in her signature rose and patchouli perfume. "Just the same as you love me no matter what. We're family. There are no conditions on that."

I felt a wetness at my forehead, and I squeezed her even harder. "You've got a big heart, girlie."

"I learned that from you and Grandma Rose."

I felt another pair of arms wrap around me as Grandma Rose squeezed into the hug. We stood there, three generations of strong women who'd made mistakes and gotten lost along the way, but who were trying their best to keep growing and improving.

"Did you know, Mom?" Aunt Dawn asked.

"Yes, dear. A mother knows their child," she replied. "I echo what Chloe said, I love you no matter what."

I don't know how long we stood there, embracing. It was big news and yet it wasn't. My aunt was still the same person, but I hoped now she would know whoever she chose to bring into her heart, it would be with our full support.

After a while we broke apart. Wiping a tear from my eye, I went to grab my bag and noticed the envelopes sticking out of the top. Bills, probably. I leafed through the stack, until a very official-looking envelope caught my attention. Holding my breath, I tore it open. For a moment the words swam in front of my eyes, almost as if I was trying to read alphabet soup rather than a letter.

*Focus, girl.*

I blinked and righted my vision. An excited squeal leaped from my throat and a bubbling energy raced through me, making my hands quiver. "We've got the license!"

Aunt Dawn and Grandma Rose were at my side in an instant, peering over my shoulders to read the paper trembling in my hands. I was almost frozen with shock as they kissed my cheeks and squeezed my shoulders, Antonio pawing at my legs because he didn't want to be left out of the action.

Baked by Chloe officially had the green light.

"Call Sabrina and tell her to come around after work," Aunt Dawn said, scooping Antonio up and dancing around as if they were partners on a ballroom floor. His tail wagged happily. "We're going to celebrate. I'll pop out and get some champagne."

"And I'll bake," I said, joy filling me up. My life might have taken a turn I didn't see coming, but I was back on both feet with my eyes fixed on the horizon.

The future was different and new, and I couldn't be more ready for it.

# RECIPES

**Cannabis-Infused Butter (aka Cannabutter)**

Infused butter is the backbone of many cannabis baked goods and you can substitute it in a 1:1 ratio for regular butter in any recipe. Beginners can reduce the amount of cannabutter by supplementing regular butter to make up the correct quantity.

*Ingredients*
   1 oz. high-quality cannabis flowers
   2 cups unsalted butter

Note: these ratios are only a guide. How much cannabis you use will depend on the particular strain you're using, how experienced you are with using cannabis and your personal tolerance levels. If unsure, use less.

*Directions*
Begin by decarboxylating your cannabis to make it psychoactive (the process which allows you to experience a high from consuming it):
   1. Preheat your oven to 245 degrees F/120 degrees C with a rack in the middle of the oven. Line a baking sheet with parchment paper.
   2. Break up the cannabis flowers into smaller pieces to allow it to bake evenly.
   3. Now, you have two options. You can either:
      A. arrange them evenly across the baking sheet and create a pouch with the parchment paper; or,
      B. place them into an oven/turkey bag. This option is more effective than option A in helping to avoid making your kitchen smell.

4. Bake for 30 minutes. The cannabis should now be a brownish color.
5. Remove from the oven and allow to cool in the bag or parchment pouch.
6. Store in a cool, dark place if not using immediately. It's recommended to use within three months.

Now it's time to infuse the butter. This recipe uses a slow cooker, but it's just one of *many* ways to infuse butter. Experiment with the different methods to find the one that suits you best!

1. Grind your decarboxylated cannabis flowers to a coarse consistency (think ground coffee). Don't grind it too fine, as it will make it harder to strain your butter later on.
2. Set your slow cooker to low (around 160 degrees F/70 degrees C, but no more than 200 degrees F/90 degrees C).
3. Add butter.
4. When the butter is starting to melt, add your ground cannabis flowers.
5. Cook for a minimum of three hours, up to eight hours. The longer it cooks, the more potent the flavor of the butter.
6. Once you have cooked for your desired amount of time, turn the slow cooker off and allow butter to cool.
7. Using a fine mesh strainer or a piece of cheesecloth set into a funnel, strain the butter to remove all the plant matter, which can then be discarded. Be patient, this process can take some time.
8. Store butter in an airtight container in the refrigerator.

**Special Salted Caramel Brownies**

A classic with a twist! Salted caramel adds a delectable addition to your "special" brownies. These are a favorite in the Barnes household. Use the cannabutter from the previous recipe to give your brownies a higher purpose, or make them with regular butter for a simple and sweet family dessert.
Serves 12

Begin with making your caramel. If you are making your brownies on the same day, also take your eggs out of the refrigerator to allow them to come to room temperature.

*Ingredients for Caramel*
    2 cups of granulated sugar
    1 cup of heavy cream (minimum 36 percent fat)
    170 g / 6oz of unsalted butter
    Half a vanilla pod
    Flaky sea salt to taste

*Directions*
  1. Cut vanilla pod lengthways and scrape out seeds.
  2. Add sugar to a heavy-bottom saucepan and heat over medium-high heat.
  3. As sugar is melting, swirl pan frequently or use a whisk to ensure that nothing is sticking to the bottom. Continue until the sugar is fully melted (no clumps left) and becomes a rich amber color. Do not allow it to become dark, as this indicates burning.
  4. Add butter and whisk to combine until butter is fully melted. Mixture may bubble vigorously at this time, so be careful!
  5. Remove saucepan from heat and slowly add cream and vanilla.

6. Add salt. Salt levels are totally personal, so start with half to one teaspoon and increase from there.
7. Allow caramel to cool in saucepan for 10–15 minutes before transferring to a jar or container. Ensure caramel is completely cooled before putting in the refrigerator.

Note: Caramel can be stored in an airtight container in the refrigerator for up to four weeks or up to three months in the freezer. If freezing, allow to thaw for a few hours at room temperature before use.

While your caramel is cooling you can commence making your brownies.

*Ingredients*
½ cup cannabutter
1 cup white sugar
⅓ cup cocoa powder (if you really want to make these special use Valrhona pure cocoa powder)
⅓ cup coarsely chopped high-quality dark chocolate
Vanilla (you can either use the other half of the pod to finish it up, or 1 teaspoon of extract if you have run out of vanilla pod)
¼ teaspoon salt
2 eggs
¾ cup all-purpose flour

*Directions*
1. Take your eggs out prior to baking to let them come to room temperature, about half an hour before you want to start baking.
2. Preheat your oven to 350 degrees F/180 degrees C and grease your brownie pan, typically 8-by-8 inches.
3. Chop your chocolate into chunks.

4. In a double boiler, melt the cannabutter and chocolate over medium heat. When fully melted, remove from heat and stir in sugar and vanilla until fully combined.
5. Add eggs one at a time, beating until well incorporated.
6. Sift flour and cocoa together to remove any lumps. Then fold into batter mixture until just combined (don't over-mix).
7. Pour batter into pan. Take spoonfuls of caramel and dollop onto batter, pushing them slightly so they sink down. Using a butter knife, cut through caramel to create swirls through the batter.
8. Drizzle a little extra caramel over the top.
9. Place into oven and bake for 25–30 minutes, depending on desired consistency.
10. Allow brownies to cool for at least half an hour before serving.

Tip: consuming products with THC content can encourage munching, so it's a good idea to have some other non-cannabis snacks on hand (or even better, another batch of brownies made with regular butter) to prevent overconsumption.

Always consume responsibly.

## Chloe's CBD Chai Latte

This spicy, warm drink is like a hug in a mug! Calming CBD and crushed spices make this a great way to relax after work or on the weekend. Play around with the spice ratio to get the flavor profile that suits you best. Chloe likes hers with lots of pepper, so feel free to dial that back.
Serves: 1

*Ingredients*
   4 green cardamom pods
   3 whole cloves
   1 star anise
   6 black peppercorns
   Half-inch piece fresh ginger, cut into thin rounds (or grate if you want a stronger ginger kick)
   Half a cinnamon stick
   1 cup water
   1 bag Darjeeling or Assam black tea
   1 cup whole milk (or substitute dairy-free, if required)
   2 teaspoons sugar (substitute high quality maple syrup or honey, if desired)
   Unflavored water-soluble CBD powder. Follow product serving suggestions and adjust to your own needs.

*Directions*
   1. Crush or bruise dry spices using the side of a knife, mallet or mortar and pestle.
   2. Muddle ginger in the bottom of a small saucepan.
   3. Add spices and water, bring to the boil.
   4. Once water is boiling, turn heat to low and add tea. Let it steep for five minutes or until it develops a nice deep color.
   5. Discard teabag and add milk, sugar and CBD powder. Whisk to combine and ensure sugar is fully dissolved.
   6. Strain tea into mug. Enjoy.

# ACKNOWLEDGMENTS

I have wanted to write mysteries from the time I picked up an Agatha Christie book at age eleven. After spending the first eight years of my publishing journey writing an entirely different genre, I finally put fingers to keyboard and dreamed up Chloe, Grandma Rose, Aunt Dawn and the rest of the Azalea Bay world.

It's a dream come true to publish in a genre that's very close to my heart and so I want to say a *huge* thank-you to every reader who took a chance on this story. I hope it provided you with a great puzzle to solve and a cast of characters to love. I hope you visit Azalea Bay again soon!

A huge thank-you to my amazing editor, Elizabeth Trout, for helping me catch all the hanging threads to make sure Chloe's story shined, and for getting as excited about the canine freestyle dancing scenes as much as I did! Massive thanks to the whole Kensington team, for being so excited about this series.

Thank you to my agent, Jill Marsal, for supporting me when I wanted to write something new and for being so enthusiastic about finding me a home in cozy mysteries.

Thank you to my husband, who is always the first person to say "you can do it" when I doubt myself and who's always there to brainstorm when the plot has me stuck. And for bringing me coffee when I'm racing toward a deadline.

Thank you to my family, who have fostered my love of reading since I was a child. To my grandmother, who took my sister and me to the bookstore or the library whenever we asked. I miss you so much. To my mother, who is one of the strongest women I know. Cancer survivor, book visual merchandiser, *and* she makes the best cakes. To my sister, fellow bookworm and all-around excellent human, thanks for always cheering me on. To my father, the most creative person I know, who has always told me I could do anything.

And finally, thank you to Zorro, the littlest Chihuahua with the biggest heart and the inspiration behind Antonio, because he gives the best cuddles.

Visit our website at
**KensingtonBooks.com**
to sign up for our newsletters, read
more from your favorite authors, see
books by series, view reading group
guides, and more!

**BOOK CLUB**
**BETWEEN THE CHAPTERS**

Become a Part of Our
**Between the Chapters Book Club**
Community and Join the Conversation

**Betweenthechapters.net**